By Dean Murray

Burned

Dean Murray

Burned is a work of fiction. Names, characters, places and incidents are the products of the author's imagination or are used fictitiously. Any resemblance to actual events, locales, or persons, living or dead, is entirely coincidental.

Published by Fir'shan Publishing

ISBN 978-1-9393635-5-8

www.FirshanPublishing.com

First Edition

For Blue Redux

You know who you are.

Prologue

Kaleb Graves
Three miles off of the Strip
Las Vegas, Nevada

Kaleb hated Las Vegas—had for decades—and his current surroundings weren't doing anything to put him at ease. The strip club his contact had chosen for the meet was the kind of exclusive place that had a cover charge measured in hundred-dollar bills.

That was good because it meant that there wouldn't be many people around to eavesdrop, but the club was also the perfect metaphor for the city. Needlessly ostentatious, and completely without purpose other than to separate fools from their money.

If it had been up to him, he never would have set foot inside the city boundaries again, but he was depressingly certain that he would end up paying the City of Sin countless additional visits over the next century. Being the leader of one of the two biggest shape shifter packs in North America and the de facto head of the Coun'hij—the ruling body that kept all of the wolves from going their separate ways—meant that he had an incredible amount of power, but he wasn't as free to do whatever he wanted as he would have liked the rest of the world to believe.

When it came to the man he'd flown more than a hundred miles to see, that was even more the case than normal. As evidenced by the fact that Kaleb's contact was late—again.

Kaleb looked at his watch—a six-thousand-dollar Rolex—for the third time in as many minutes and told himself that he would leave if his contact didn't walk through the doors within the next four minutes. There were appearances to maintain, after all. When you got right down to it, an uncomfortable amount of Kaleb's power rested on nothing more than appearances—especially after his son had made off with billions of dollars' worth of liquid assets.

Kaleb still wasn't poor—not even close—but losing that much money had put him in a definite liquidity bind. His people, Donovan especially, were in the process of selling off some of the hard assets that the Graves line had acquired over the centuries, but it was one more symptom of the state of affairs since Alec and his friends had defected.

Kaleb was low on funds, low on able bodies to throw into the war he'd started on the US-Mexican border, and suddenly being hounded by more enemies—both within the Coun'hij and without—than he'd had to deal with in more than a decade.

Less than three seconds before Kaleb was going to stand up and walk out of the club, Puppeteer walked through the door followed by two skinny, malnourished men in their fifties.

"What's the matter, Graves? Is this not your kind of place? I've heard nothing but good things about the performers here..."

"You're late."

There were a lot of other things that Kaleb would have liked to add, but he wasn't fooled by the feeble appearance of Puppeteer's bodyguards. It was standard practice for the members of the Coun'hij to conduct meetings via electronic means, but Puppeteer generally insisted on face-to-face meets. He also ignored the tradition of not bringing guards to the meetings. Kaleb had never bothered airing his dissatisfaction with that particular habit. The rule was in place for a good reason—so that they wouldn't have leaks getting back to the rebellion—but Puppeteer's guards weren't going to leak anything because despite their appearances they weren't men.

Kaleb was aware that some of the members of the Coun'hij were considering bringing bodyguards of their own to these kinds of meets, but not him. It wouldn't have done any good. No two of his people could have possibly come out on top in a fight against the seven-foot-tall towers of bone and muscle that the werewolves would become at a single silent command from Puppeteer.

Brandon Worthingfield probably could have taken one werewolf by himself, but that still would have left the problem of the second werewolf. Besides, Brandon was the last person Kaleb wanted close to the other members of the Coun'hij. Brandon was best kept as far as possible away from the real power in their world.

That wouldn't work indefinitely, but Brandon was still young enough that Kaleb had mostly been able to keep him distracted with the trappings of power. Eventually Brandon would wise up, but that was a problem for another day.

Kaleb spared a moment to once again run through his future plans for Puppeteer. The other man was incredibly slippery when it came to staying off of the grid for a man approaching two hundred. Some of the other members of the inner circle showed up on video feeds throughout the country as often as every week or two, but not Puppeteer.

Each and every time Kaleb met with Puppeteer he risked his own life, but Kaleb was capable of being patient and running risks. Bringing guards—even guards who stayed out of sight—would just result in Puppeteer bringing along more of his enslaved werewolves, or something even worse. No, the answer was to come to each meeting completely vulnerable right up until the day when Kaleb decided it was time to kill Puppeteer. When that day arrived, Kaleb would have Brandon and a dozen other hybrids waiting to ambush Puppeteer.

The resulting fight would be quick, bloody, and solve one of Kaleb's problems at the same time it spawned a dozen more. His life sometimes felt like nothing more than an extended balancing act, one with stakes that most of the rest of the world couldn't even begin to understand.

The series of thoughts running through Kaleb's mind had taken only seconds, but he never broke eye contact with Puppeteer during that time. Dominance was about more than just who could beat the other person to a pulp. It was a lesson that some hybrids never learned, but it was one of the things that had allowed Kaleb to rise to the pinnacle of power inside of the Coun'hij in record time once he finally decided to throw his lot in with them rather than continuing to fight the inevitable.

Puppeteer gamely refused to drop his eyes, but Kaleb could sense that the other man was beginning to grow nervous. Someone like Puppeteer was nearly always the most dangerous person in any given room. He was used to having everyone around him cower in some way or another as they acknowledged that fact. It did more than just make him uneasy when someone refused to back down, it made him worry that he was overlooking something—something important.

Eventually he would decide that Kaleb was bluffing, that Kaleb was one of those rare hybrids who were able to lie with their scent and pulse as well as just with their voice, but Puppeteer apparently wasn't quite to that point yet—not today.

Kaleb saw Puppeteer's eyes go the tiniest bit distant as the other man checked to make sure that both of his bodyguards were still there and still under his control. It was a reflexive action, one that Puppeteer did hundreds of times per day. Given that he'd compelled two of the most dangerous creatures on earth to wait on him hand and foot, it was an understandable habit to develop, but Kaleb wasn't in the mood to be understanding.

Kaleb took a single step forward as though planning on rushing Puppeteer, but then adjusted his course at the last instant to take him out around Puppeteer and his minions. Puppeteer redeployed his bodyguards, tiny old bodies that looked like they were only weeks away from death, so that they were positioned to make sure that Kaleb wouldn't be able to get his hands on Puppeteer. It was exactly the reaction Kaleb had been hoping for.

Puppeteer let him get almost to the door before sending out a flare of power. The energy danced across Kaleb's arms like a thousand tiny insects, demanding that he turn around and address Puppeteer, but as powerful as Puppeteer was, he wasn't powerful enough to compel Kaleb with nothing more than a display of strength. A fact that doubtlessly frustrated Puppeteer to no end.

"Where are you going, Graves?"

"I'm leaving. You are the one who called me here. This meeting was your idea—your demand, really. I have better things to do than stand here and exchange glares with you. The next time you feel like taking in some girls, do me a favor and don't call me to accompany you. I have much better things to be doing."

The entire exchange had taken place in a tone that was only barely into what would be the audible range for humans. The two beasts behind Puppeteer probably heard everything that had been said, but the club employee, a distinguished-looking man in a suit, didn't seem to have heard any of it.

Then again, he didn't have to have heard any of it to know that Kaleb and Puppeteer were only heartbeats away from attacking each other. The body language between the four patrons had been strong enough that nothing else was necessary for someone who made his living at a place like this. The strip club might be a high-class kind of joint, but any time you mixed alcohol and beautiful women of the sort who took their clothes off for a living, you were asking for violence.

"Can I have drinks brought out to you two gentlemen? Amber is just about to start her set—you're not going to want to miss her..."

Kaleb didn't look away from Puppeteer. He'd already taken the measure of the club employee. The man was fit, but he was used to dealing with the club's clientele when they arrived—generally sober and compliant. He wasn't the kind of man to throw himself into a fight—not even a fight where he got the first hit against someone with their back turned to him. He would call in the club's bouncers and then steer clear of the resulting mayhem.

It was still a risk. Even normally mild-mannered men could react unexpectedly if pushed far enough, but Kaleb had run—and would run—much worse risks before reaching his end game. He left his back to the employee and waited for Puppeteer to break.

It took several seconds, but Puppeteer finally took advantage of the distraction and broke eye contact to address the human.

"A drink would be good, but there's no need to have it brought out—we'll go on inside to the main area. I have news to share with my friend here."

Kaleb didn't have any desire to go inside to the flashing lights and loud music, but he nodded. "As long as you're actually ready to talk."

Less than a minute later the two of them were seated at a table with the two werewolves seated a short distance away. Under other circumstances Kaleb probably would have faced the stage just so as not to stand out, but not this time. There was no need, not with how out of place the two werewolves looked—even in human form. They never looked at the stage once, instead looking at Puppeteer and Kaleb with unsettling, unblinking eyes. Besides, Kaleb was willing to occasionally turn his back to unarmed humans, but he wasn't in the habit of doing the same kind of thing to werewolves.

"Don't you want to take in the show? Given how much money you must have lost when young Alec ran off, it can't have been easy to pay the cover charge to get in here. You might as well get your money's worth."

Kaleb forced his face not to respond to the jab. That part was easy. Controlling his body temperature, blood flow, and heartbeat was quite a bit more difficult. He didn't manage it as well as he normally did, but for once their surroundings proved to be an advantage. Even shape shifter hearing struggled to pick out the sound of a single heartbeat when surrounded by the thumping base washing over them.

The truth was that Puppeteer didn't have any idea how much money Alec had made off with. Given that Kaleb's son had managed to escape capture for so long, it wasn't a huge leap to assume that he'd gotten away with *something*, but Puppeteer was fishing. He wanted some sign of just how weakened Kaleb was at that moment.

"If you have something to say, then say it. I have a number of other things that I should be spending my time on right now."

"You never have been any fun, Graves. I keep inviting you here to the city that never sleeps in the hope that you'll loosen up, but you always manage to disappoint me."

"I don't have time to loosen up, and you know it. Neither of us do—not given the stakes that we are playing for. Now, what do you want?"

It was a not-so-subtle reminder of the purpose that bound them together. Puppeteer looked for a moment like he wanted to argue the point, but the truth was that they couldn't afford anything other than constant vigilance, not with the list of enemies currently gunning for both of them.

"After our most recent series of losses, you're pack is far and away the largest single pool of manpower in our organization. I'm going to need you to loan me some people."

"Absolutely not. You know our deal. You control the less savory of our assets and I have carte blanche when it comes to when and where my people are used. I'm not going to let you waste members of my pack the way you've wasted others of our kind over the years."

"You can monitor them—you can be a full partner as far as the operation goes, even. There will be plenty of glory to go around after this one."

The offer was unusual enough to make Kaleb pause. "What do you have in the works?"

"You remember that failed rescue attempt that your son led against the group we had escorting Agony north?"

"Of course I do. We lost almost two dozen people in that operation, an operation you and your agent assured us we couldn't lose."

"There's only so much I can anticipate, Graves. It was your people who were supposed be our insurance policy. You were the one who told us that Brandon was more than capable of defeating any three hybrids."

It was all that Kaleb could do not to flinch at the reminder. Those had been his exact words, which was embarrassing because it had indeed been a group of three hybrids that had stopped Brandon.

"I stand by my words. Brandon went up against two hybrids armed with swords from the time of the monarchy, and Agony of all people. Despite that, he managed to kill Agony single-handedly. It would have only been a matter of time before the other two would have joined that traitor in death if not for the presence of a fourth combatant who shot Brandon several times before he managed to get away."

The two of them stared at each other for several seconds before both breaking away at the same time. There had been plenty of dishonor to go around when it came to that particular operation.

Kaleb let the silence stretch back out for a while, but when it became apparent that Puppeteer wasn't going to say anything else without being prompted, he took the bait.

"How does your operation tie back to the business with Agony?"

"I'm going to use the same resource. The pieces are already all lined up; we just need the right push to knock them over. I can't make that happen with just my resources though—not without risking the other side being able to track me down—and that would be foolish at this juncture, even for a prize like bringing your son down."

"Yes, heaven forbid you run the same risks that the rest of us run on a daily basis."

"It's not the same and you know it. You're a target, but everyone knows that you dying would only slow down our plans slightly. I, on the other hand, am the last member of our little group that any member of the rebellion would gladly sign their life away to kill."

Kaleb leaned back in his chair. "I need more details before I can commit."

"No, not here, not now. Our last operation went too far off of the rails not to have been compromised on your end."

"I told you already. Leaking the information to Samantha was the only way to be sure that Alec would show up and hit the convoy where we wanted it to be hit."

"Maybe, but it appears that your beloved wife has much deeper ties with the rebellion than any of us have been led to believe. She needs to be put down."

Kaleb's knuckles had gone white, but for once he didn't have to worry about hiding his true feelings. "If you ever even consider acting on that little suggestion of yours, I'll see you dead. Samantha serves a necessary purpose inside of my pack—a purpose that is all the more vital now that Alec isn't serving as a counter balance to Brandon. Samantha is a lightning rod for all of the discontent inside of the pack—if she were dead it wouldn't make the whispers go away, they would just go underground where I couldn't monitor them anymore."

"So you say. I'm beginning to doubt our little arrangement, Graves. So far I haven't said anything to our...employer to indicate that things with your son are as serious as they actually are, but being the one to come clean about that little problem would go a long way toward cleaning the ledger where my past transgressions are concerned."

Kaleb felt himself go completely still. It was a lack of reaction that in its own way was nearly as bad as jumping up and down on the table in front of them, but he couldn't help it. Everyone had fears—everyone. Kaleb was no exception to that rule. He was fortunate in that most of his fears revolved around *things* rather than *people*, but there was one person he didn't even begin to pretend—at least not to himself—that he wasn't scared of. Puppeteer had just referenced that person, a person Kaleb was working very hard to keep in the dark regarding a large number of things.

"I think that you're overestimating just how much leeway a revelation like that would buy you. Your past indiscretion is a very serious matter, a matter that I've faithfully kept secret for more than a decade now."

"You're not leaving me much of a choice, Kaleb. I know how hard it is to sign the death warrant of someone you helped bring into this world."

"This isn't about that—this is solely about the fact that I can't afford to lose anyone else right now. Participation by the unaligned packs is at an all-time low. It's obvious to me that Alec found out about some of the measures we've been taking to keep a steady flow of new recruits headed down to the border."

"You think that he told someone before he left?"

"I'm nearly certain of it. My money would have been on Juan, but he died within hours of the operation that I think Alec stumbled onto. I don't think there was time for Juan to have communicated anything to his contacts—Juan wasn't the kind to act on something until he'd had a chance to confirm it for himself."

"If not Juan, then who? I thought we had a good line on all of the communications flowing back and forth between the independent packs."

"We do, but nothing in our business is ever guaranteed. Either Alec has gotten the word out since he left home, or Juan had some kind of failsafe in place that was activated by his death."

"This could be a very big deal, Kaleb."

"I know, but there isn't anything more I can do about it until accusations start to surface. I've already taken all of the precautions I can—it's just a matter of waiting now, but that's all the more reason to conserve what people I have left."

"I've been unwilling to do this up until now because I didn't want to let myself get into range of one of those trackers, but if you have a particularly difficult mission that needs to be carried out, I might be willing to go down and use my...assets...to make sure it's taken care of."

Kaleb pursed his lips. That was a definite departure from Puppeteer's past stance, and they both knew what that signified.

"That's a very generous offer—one that I might very well take you up on if the circumstances warrant it—but if we're wrong about the reason that the independents have stopped coming south, that will destroy all possibility of getting the flow started back up.

The independents view this as something separate from the Coun'hij in many ways. You joining in will just make them feel like there isn't any need for them to help out."

"That would make our…sponsor…very unhappy."

"Indeed. That little war has been the wedge I've used to get through a number of my initiatives that he would otherwise never have agreed to."

"Yeah. The only thing that can compete with the idea of us killing our cousins and being killed in turn would be the idea of us killing the parasites."

"Exactly, except we tried that and we had to use your werewolves to make it happen, and it wasn't bloodless where your assets are concerned. I ran the numbers back then—even before *he* came back ready to tear me to pieces—and it's not a favorable rate of exchange. Are you sure there isn't something you can do to change the equation there?"

"No, unlike the werewolves, my other assets are oddly unwilling to get involved in those kinds of fights. I can force them to do it, but they are never very effective when compelled like that. The only way to get any kind of real benefit out of them is to manufacture a situation where their interests and mine coincide. We will just have to continue on as we've been up until now."

Kaleb reached up and rubbed his eyes, and it was only partly an act. He was tired and getting more that way with every passing year. Sleep didn't do anything to cure this kind of exhaustion. It was a fatigue of the soul—assuming he still had one—more than anything else.

"Can't you give me anything else to go on? It isn't that I'm unwilling to help you, but I'm not going to send my people in blind—there's a limit to how many plates I can keep spinning at one time, and this isn't just about you and me. Some of the junior partners are starting to eye me. I can tell that they are considering the idea that a good push at the right time might be sufficient to eliminate me and claim my spot as their own."

Puppeteer looked away for several seconds, and Kaleb wondered if the other man was accessing some distant asset. It was possible—it happened much less frequently with that particular strain, and when it did happen it rarely happened when Kaleb was around to see it.

"Okay, here's what I can do. I want you to have a group in the area awaiting my word. As soon as I have confirmation I'll call you up and you can assume control of that side of the operation. It's got to be a priority for you though, Kaleb. You can't just put this on the back burner like you have with so many of our operations in the past."

"I have appearances to maintain. I can't just disappear at the drop of a hat. More importantly, you still haven't given me any details about how this is going down. Schedule it in advance and tell me what you've got up your sleeve and we can make this work. Otherwise we'll just have to both make our separate cases to *him* and hope for the best."

"I hated you back before you were brought on as a member, Kaleb, and nothing has changed over the years. How did we ever end up on the same team?"

"I'm not sure. I lived through it, and I'm still not sure how *he* managed it."

Kaleb slowed his breathing down a little further and steepled his fingers so that he could look at Puppeteer over top of them. Puppeteer stared back for nearly a minute before finally responding.

"It's just like I said. I have very limited information about your son and his allies. That's not something that my asset is particularly interested in, but it's very clear that they are trying to build a fortress on top of a foundation of cards. It's only going to take a small push at the right time to split them up and it won't be pretty when things start falling apart.

"You know the breed we're dealing with, Kaleb. They have a kind of sixth sense when it comes to this kind of thing. Based on what I'm getting this time around, the results are going to be spectacular. Some of them will welcome death by the time Brandon and the rest of your people show up and execute them."

Kaleb could tell that Puppeteer was watching him—looking for any sign that he wasn't as committed as he needed to be. That was one thing that Kaleb knew Puppeteer wasn't going to see—not today, and if their joint plan went the way that Puppeteer seemed to think it would, then not ever.

"You can't tell me anything else about what's going on with that cell of the rebellion? I'm nervous about getting blindsided again. Neither of us anticipated that Dream Stealer would be able to put together a second force of that size to interfere with the Agony movement. Heck, I even told you that Alec had taken my sword, and we still didn't expect him to use it, let alone find some swordmaster from a school that was supposed to be long dead to train him in its use. If we're wrong about who their allies are and how much help they've managed to drum up, I could lose everything."

Kaleb had been suspecting that Puppeteer was holding out on him, but the look in the other man's eyes confirmed it. Puppeteer was very good at everything he did, but he spent too much time off by himself with no other companionship but his thralls. It made him rusty when it came to dissembling in person.

"The only other thing I know is that both your son and Dream Stealer have run into problems with vampires over the last little while. They managed to win in both instances, but they lost people—a lot of people. It doesn't speak very highly for their abilities, which frankly is a big part of why I haven't been more inclined to bring it to the attention of our…patron. For them to lose more than a dozen people in fights with a bunch of piss ant parasites indicates that they've had a healthy dose of luck in getting this far without being torn apart by our people."

Kaleb didn't respond, just continued to stare at Puppeteer, and eventually the other man shifted uncomfortably in his seat. "That's it, that's all I know. My asset hasn't told me anything else—in fact it's been all I could do to pry that much information out of him. Beyond that, both groups have completely disappeared. It's like they're a bunch of ghosts—you know that as well as I do."

Kaleb finally nodded. "Okay, I'm in. Get your asset to start the pieces into motion and I'll come up with some kind of pretext for dropping out of sight along with Brandon and a group of my best fighters. It will have to be something that won't make it back to the other packs or the cats either one, so it won't be easy, but I'll find a way."

Puppeteer smiled, but it was a cold expression, the kind of thing you'd expect from someone who'd just buried their nemesis. Kaleb told himself that the expression had everything to do with the impending defeat of Alec and Dream Stealer, and nothing to do with Puppeteer having managed to back Kaleb into a corner.

It didn't help.

Chapter 1

Alec Graves
Club Inferno
Chicago, Illinois

Under other circumstances I wouldn't have felt comfortable interacting with Shawn—not without a full retinue of guards at least. The last time we'd seen each other rogue elements inside of his pack had tried to kill him. The fact that they hadn't been there specifically to kill me hadn't been a lot of comfort once blood had started flowing.

This time I wasn't just dropping in unannounced though, which meant that Shawn was presumably taking extra precautions when it came to his security. Especially with regards to forces inside of the Chicago pack who wanted Shawn's father, Ulrich, to side with the Coun'hij in the coming war.

That was great in theory, but it didn't particularly reassure me—not when there was a decent possibility that the real threat to my safety was *Shawn*. Our mission to save Agony just a few weeks earlier had every sign of having been compromised by someone in the know.

Whoever was running things for the Coun'hij had been smart about it. They'd made it look like Brandon and his people had just been a general security precaution, but I wasn't buying it, and neither was Taggart. That meant that feelings were running hot in both of the groups that had nearly been killed when Brandon had parachuted out of the sky and then proceeded to tear through our people until Agony, Carson and I had managed to stand him off for long enough that everyone else had been able to escape.

If it had been up to some of my people, I wouldn't have been meeting with Shawn at all—not without enough bodies to make sure that I could put him down as a warning to Ulrich for what happened to people who double-crossed the rebellion. They had a valid point about the risk inherent in meeting with him, but they were behind the times when it came to just how much protection I needed.

In fairness, that wasn't entirely their fault. I'd been working very hard to keep the full extent of my abilities a secret from everyone but James, Jasmin, Jess and Carson. So far I seemed to have been successful, which was especially heartening because it meant that the first time I used my ability on a group of our enemies they were in for a fatal surprise.

We were still exploring the full extent of my capabilities—a hard task given that I could only practice on the four of them, but the early results were more than just promising. I'd used my ability to bring groups of vampires to their knees on three different occasions now, but it had taken a lot out of me each time.

An ability that neutralized everyone around you wasn't hugely helpful if it meant that you also passed out—especially not given that my attack was only somewhat targetable. I could manipulate the size of the absorption field my ability created, and I could pick a center point for the attack, but I couldn't pick between targets inside of the area of effect.

That meant that things got tricky once the fight was joined—whoever was on my side probably wasn't going to appreciate being drained dry of energy at the same time I was rendering the bad guys immobile—but as luck would have it, the problems I'd experienced early on with my ability seemed to have been more the result of the strength of the vampires we'd been fighting in both instances rather than an inherent limitation of my powers.

I'd managed to drop all four of my friends at the same time, forcing them to collapse bonelessly to the ground as the strength was sucked out of their limbs, for as long as ten minutes at a time before the exertion caught up to me and I joined them on the ground. When it was just one person I seemed to be able to hold the absorption field in place almost indefinitely, which was cool, but the real kicker was the fact that *I* could move around inside of my absorption field without being affected.

That meant that I could casually kill anyone I'd rendered defenseless, and the only way for anyone to get at me would be for them to use some kind of distance attack that allowed them to hurt me from outside of my absorption field, or to rush me with enough bodies that they overwhelmed my ability.

Carson had cautioned me repeatedly against starting to think of myself as being invulnerable, but it was hard not to get at least a little caught up in the sheer potential of my ability. I'd taken down a group of vampires that would have made mincemeat out of just about any other single hybrid I could think of, and that had been before I'd even had any real idea what it was that I could do.

I'd noticed a few other things along the way as well. It was a lot easier to neutralize Jess than it was to bring down Jasmin. James was a bit harder to take down than Jasmin was, but he was much less of a strain on my gift than Carson was. All I could figure was that there was a limit to how much energy I could absorb at any one time, and there were significant power differences between each of my friends.

I'd always known that Jasmin was exceptional for a wolf—even a royal wolf—but I'd never appreciated just how close she'd come to making whatever metaphysical cut was required to manifest a hybrid form. It really wasn't fair. Jasmin had busted her butt for years trying to be the most dangerous, capable fighter she could be. If she'd been a hybrid she would have been one of the pack's best fighters.

James had worked hard to get where he was too, but it wasn't quite the same obsession for him that it was for Jasmin. No matter how hard she'd worked, she hadn't been able to compensate for the tiny bit of extra power that allowed James to manifest his hybrid form. It sucked, but there was a lot about our existence that sucked.

All of which brought me back to the fact that I'd agreed to meet with Shawn by myself despite all of Jack's protests. I'd considered bringing Carson along—his ability to influence people's emotions would have been invaluable if he'd been willing to use it on Shawn—but I was pretty sure that Carson wouldn't agree to do anything of the kind.

Carson was perfectly happy to use his gift to its full extent in life-or-death situations, but he'd sworn an oath not to use it to influence people in certain ways, and Carson was nothing if not honorable. If it came to fighting I would be able to drop Shawn and whomever he brought for at least a few seconds, which would be plenty of time for me to dispatch them.

Most importantly though, by going to the meet by myself, I was sending a powerful message. I was telling Shawn that I wasn't scared of him—or his father. I was announcing that I was more than ready to deal with whatever rogue elements that might show up from his pack, and I might even lull him into showing his hand earlier than he'd planned.

I wasn't particularly looking forward to Shawn attacking me if that was what he was planning, but I'd rather him betray me in a situation where I could take real, unavoidable vengeance in response. That was the kind of thing that I could deal with much more easily than having him send us into another ambush—if that was what he'd done the last time around—while he was hundreds of miles away.

It was long past time for me to figure out once and for all which side Shawn was on.

The meet was taking place in another club, which shouldn't have surprised me—Shawn was big on clubs. The part that did surprise me when I did my due diligence about the club was that Shawn apparently owned this one.

I gave the alias Shawn had provided me to the bouncer at the door and bypassed the line entirely, which was nice. Unlike last time I'd slipped into a club to meet up with Shawn, I was wearing a black leather jacket. I'd picked it out because it was the kind of thing that I usually didn't wear, and because I wanted to see just how much fuss the bouncer would put up at the door.

Guns were redundant in most situations we shape shifters found ourselves in—and knives were even more useless—but if Shawn was trying to set me up then the odds were very good that some of his intent had communicated itself to his employees. If I got a lot of flak from the bouncer that would be a pretty good indication that Shawn was particularly concerned about making sure that I wasn't carrying a wire or any kind of weapon.

Interestingly enough, the bouncer called for someone else to man the door and then took me inside—walking me around the metal detector without even a second glance. Either Shawn was willing to trust me not to double-cross him, or he'd brought such overwhelming backup that he wasn't concerned about anything I might be bringing to the party.

Too bad I hadn't brought my sword. It would have been an even more interesting test of what the bouncers were willing to let me get away with. I would have brought it in the special bag that Carson had commissioned for it, but that still wasn't the kind of thing any club owner would want inside his establishment. I dismissed the idea as the passing fancy it was as I followed the bouncer to the edge of the dance floor.

It was late enough that the party was in full swing. The local celebrities were probably only minutes away from starting their appearances and people had imbibed enough alcohol to have abandoned most of their inhibitions, but not so much that they were falling down drunk yet.

I was led past a velvet rope guarded by two bouncers in expensive suits who looked like they'd seen serious action at some point in their lives. I reached down to my beast and coaxed him close enough to the surface to send out a flare of energy. It was an unmistakable show of dominance, but neither of the bouncers at the rope responded to the challenge.

Interesting—I'd been expecting Shawn to have augmented his normal security with members of his pack. Either he was working extra hard to keep me from suspecting this was a trap, or he had an incredible amount of faith in the humans who staffed his normal security force.

My escort led me to the bar in the more exclusive area of the club and then nodded at a door in the back wall. He leaned close even though it wasn't necessary given how keen my hearing was.

"That's the entrance to the owner's suite. There is going to be a distraction four minutes from the time you entered this area. Grab a drink so that you blend in and then work your way back to that wall. When the distraction happens go inside—the door is unlocked."

I nodded my understanding and turned to the bartender and slid him a fifty-dollar bill. "Your best vodka—I don't care what it is."

I followed my instructions—drink in hand—and was less than five feet away from the door, casually leaning against the wall, when the lights went out. My beast had been oddly docile lately, but neither of us had been expecting complete darkness and he sent out a surge of power that made the hair on the back of my neck stand up.

Some people would have dismissed it as useless dominance posturing, but I was in tune enough with my beast to know that there was a definite purpose behind the flare of energy. He wanted to know if there was anyone dangerous around us. Shape shifters—even in human form—have great low-light vision, but that's not quite the same thing as being able to see without any light at all.

An odd hissing sound had started a couple of seconds before the lights had died and I picked up a new scent as my beast roared to the surface. For a split second I worried that Shawn knew about my ability, that he'd chosen to poison an entire club full of people to get to me, but I was familiar with most of the commonly-used poisons and this wasn't one of them. It didn't burn my nose, and it wasn't leaving me feeling sluggish or sleepy.

Several surges of power crashed into me as I started moving toward the door to Shawn's suite, but they were all weaker than I would have expected from someone willing to take issue with my show of dominance. That meant they were all a ways away from me.

I'd been moving with the enhanced speed so natural to a shape shifter, so all of that happened while everyone else was still fumbling for their phones. As my hand found the doorknob, the first of the lights from the phones started to appear, but they were oddly muted, as though being seen through a thick film of smoke.

The hissing had been fog machines kicking on full bore. They probably hadn't been cool for at least a decade, but they'd served their purpose. It was still too dark for anyone to see me and I slipped inside the door as the DJ cut the music and started yelling for everyone to stay calm and hold still.

"It's just a temporary outage—we'll have the lights back on momentarily. Please hold still so that nobody gets hurt."

The door closed with a click that was much too loud. I heard an electronically-controlled deadbolt slam home a fraction of a second later, and my muscles tensed up.

Carson had been right—I'd been too caught up in the raw power of my ability. I hadn't spent enough time thinking about how I would have circumvented it if I'd been going up with someone with the same ability. I'd never even considered the fact that Shawn could poison the air inside the club.

He hadn't, but that didn't necessarily mean that I was safe. I was alone in darkness as complete as anything I'd ever experienced before. I stepped to one side, silently shifting position so that I wasn't standing exactly where they would expect me to be if they had something nasty in store.

I scanned through the darkness, trying to pierce the veil in front of me, but it was all to no avail. In wolf or hybrid form I would have been able to pick out the light from living things from quite a ways off, but in human form I'd have to practically be on top of someone to know they were there unless they were an extremely powerful hybrid.

I couldn't move forward—not without knowing what was waiting for me—and I couldn't go backwards unless I was prepared to try to batter down the door behind me. Based on the way it had moved, it was reinforced steel.

Chills of unease worked their way up and down my spine. It had been too long. I didn't want to shift prematurely and appear jumpy, but if this was all just part of an over-complicated scheme to get me into the owner's suite without being seen then Shawn would have been here—by himself—waiting for me.

I shrugged out of my jacket—the only thing strong enough to give me problems during a transformation—and let my beast out of the cage where I usually kept it confined. I shifted forms to the sound of ripping cloth and then moved forward and to the other side, trying to make it hard for anyone who might be tracking me by the sound of my transformation.

I was now only a few inches off of seven feet tall, and I was more than a hundred pounds heavier than I'd been—all of it preternaturally strong muscle and dense bone. Hybrids weren't the very top of the supernatural food chain, but they were close. In this form I was a lot harder to kill, and my razor-sharp semi-retractable claws, foot talons and fangs meant that I was capable of bringing down any natural predator in seconds.

I was still scanning the darkness, looking for the cool, golden light of living organisms, but there wasn't so much as a cockroach wandering around out there. I started forward, crouched with my claws up to protect my head and torso, but before I could take my third step the sound of a door opening pulled me up short.

"Alec, it's me. We're having a problem getting the lights back on—somebody threw the wrong switch upstairs. Just stay there for a second until we can get the lights in the club back on—I don't want you to fall down the stairs."

His voice sounded like it was coming from ahead and below me, but that was the only evidence I had that he was telling me the truth.

"This isn't what we agreed to, Shawn. If I pulled something like this on you I'd never hear the end of it, and I'm not the one who backed out of a rescue operation that then went to crap under suspicious circumstances. I didn't even bring a phone because you were worried it might be tracked. Tell me why I should think that this is anything other than a trap? I have half a mind to rip your expensive door off its hinges and take my chances in your club."

"There are something like a hundred and eighty people out there, Alec. If you are in your hybrid form when the lights come on there's going to be no way to keep this quiet. The Coun'hij will send in teams to clean up the mess, but even Oblivion won't be able to wipe away all of the evidence."

"I'm already out of favor with the powers that be, Shawn. I'm not sure why I should care about creating more work for Oblivion or any of the rest of them."

"Then don't do it for them, do it for the innocent people you'll be forcing them to kill. If we have a breach of that magnitude they'll take drastic measures."

I wanted to shrug off his concerns—they were exactly what he would have said if this was all just so he could get me off by myself where it would be easy to kill me—but there was something in his voice that made me think he was telling the truth.

It was enough to stop me from really turning the screws, but not enough to make me back down completely.

"I'm still waiting for a reason, Shawn. You've got exactly five seconds before I rip your door off of its hinges."

"The Coun'hij is fully capable of manufacturing a crisis to bury something like this, Alec. If you do this they'll set off a dirty bomb in downtown Chicago, or stage a massive train crash, or one of a dozen other things that will result in tens of thousands of deaths. They will do anything to bury your headline so far down nobody will even remember seeing a hybrid stroll through my club."

"Maybe, or maybe they won't do anything to anyone but you. You've gone to a lot of trouble to make sure that nobody else knew I was here. If I'm seen leaving your suite, you and your dad are going to have to answer some tough questions—questions that you might not survive answering."

I cocked my arm back, ready to slam my claws home into the reinforced steel of the door, and for the first time Shawn sounded desperate.

"Alec! Stop! You can't do this. Of course I'm worried about the Coun'hij finding out that you were here. Hell, I'm almost as worried about my dad finding out I invited you here. That's all true, but that doesn't change the fact that I didn't lure you here so that I could ambush you."

"Prove it. Turn on the damn lights or we're done here."

"I can't—they're out in the entire club. I've been on the phone with my people trying to walk them through getting them turned back on—that's the reason I didn't come out to talk to you before now."

"Then get your phone out here and use it as a flashlight."

Even as I spoke, I raked my claws across the metal of the door, testing the thickness of the steel by cutting deep furrows in it. Shawn swore again, and I heard him fumbling in his pocket, and then right as I started my hand forward a dim light peeled back the darkness.

"Sorry. I should have thought of that before now. I was worried about anyone seeing light under my door and knowing that you'd just come down here."

I took careful stock of my surroundings. I was standing at the top of a long stairwell that doubled back halfway down. The light was enough for me to be able to see the steps, but not enough for me to be sure that there wasn't some kind of tripwire or other nasty surprise waiting for me partway down.

"I want more light. You've got people there with you—some of them have phones. Get them."

Apparently I'd just given Shawn one order too many. I felt a flare of power slam into me, but my beast was long past being docile today. My answering flare of power was a bare-knuckled assault on Shawn and everyone else down there with him.

There had been a time where I'd tried to hide the full extent of the energy crackling around inside of my beast, but that time was past. I had a bigger secret to keep now, so anything that made Shawn back down before I had to uncork the miniature black hole inside of me, was a good thing.

Someone down there gasped in astonishment at the sheer power I'd just unleashed, but it wasn't Shawn and that meant it didn't matter. When Shawn spoke again I could hear his beast straining against his control.

"I know I was the one to reach out to you this time, Alec. I also know how things must look to you right now, but you don't get to come into my house and tell me what to do. Calm down or I'll have my people calm you down."

"No, Shawn, you won't. If you don't get me some additional light I'm going to go through this door regardless of how much trouble it might get you and your dad in with Kaleb and the rest. Then I'm going to watch the resulting fireworks, and when everything settles down I'm going to pay you a visit and rip your heart out of your chest, and nothing you—or your people—can do will stop me."

It was my beast talking. This was why most of the communication between packs took place via phone or video conference. It was entirely possible that Shawn and I really did want the same thing right now, but things had escalated and now neither of us could back down without losing face.

Under other circumstances I would never have even dreamed of issuing an ultimatum like that to someone with Shawn's level of power and influence, but that didn't stop me from meaning it in that moment. I heard a growl from somewhere below me, but contrary to what I'd expected, the growl didn't come from Shawn.

He should have been tearing up the stairs in his effort to get to me and settle the question of who was dominant to whom once and for all. I'd actually viewed that as a benefit because it would mean that I'd have proof that the stairs were safe.

His lack of response sent chills up my spine. He was either acting completely out of character, or he was refusing to rise to my challenge because he knew that the stairs were a death sentence. Before I could spin back around and rip the door in half, Shawn spoke back up.

"Say that again, Alec."

"Now who's the one giving orders?"

"Please, say it again. The promise you just made—can you repeat it?"

"Word for word? Probably not, but it basically boiled down to the fact that if you don't stop jerking me around I'm going to come back here and rip your heart out of your chest."

Shawn cursed again—too softly for a human to hear. "Vicki, get your phone out—we need to create enough light for Alec to feel safe traversing the stairs."

Her subvocalized response was too quiet even for me to make out, but a second later another point source was added to the light coming up the stairwell. I was debating as to whether or not that was enough light to make the journey safe, when a third phone was added to the mix.

I moved to the railing and confirmed that Shawn was standing down there by himself—still in human form. The stairs looked safe, but I suddenly had an idea of how to bypass them completely.

"You might want to back up a little, Shawn."

He obeyed without question, and I hopped over the railing and fell straight down for more than forty feet. It was far enough to shatter bones for humans. Even we shape shifters couldn't guarantee that we'd come out unscathed from that kind of drop in human form, but my massive hybrid legs absorbed the impact without any sign that they'd been stressed despite the crash as my feet hit the concrete.

"I guess that means we're good?"

"I don't know—it will depend on what you brought me here to say. I haven't forgotten about the fact that you and your dad hung me out to dry just a few weeks ago."

Shawn winced. "I know that I deserve that, but please hear me out anyway."

I nodded and followed him through the door. Despite everything else that had happened, part of me still half expected to find his bodyguards waiting on either side of the door to put me down. What I saw instead was completely at odds with anything I'd expected.

Shawn's bodyguards were clear on the other side of the room, and neither of them looked happy about it. He was standing less than five feet away from me—still in human form, and his best hope of beating me if things got physical were much too far away to get to him in time if I decided I wanted him dead.

"Does your dad know that you don't always let your minders do their jobs?"

Shawn's grin was remarkably similar to the one on the face of the bigger of his two bodyguards—the guy. The girl on the other hand looked anything but amused. I recognized Vicki from the last time I'd been in Chicago; she hadn't been any more welcoming then—even after I'd helped save Shawn's life. Apparently she didn't like being called a glorified babysitter.

"Dad stopped being surprised by anything I do a long time ago. He knows that I make life hard on Vicki and Dax. He doesn't like it, but he also knows that I have to be somewhat...flexible...in order to carry out my function."

The lights came on with a flicker, but I didn't let that distract me.

"And what exactly is your function?"

"I keep the Coun'hij guessing as to where our true loyalties lie."

I pulled his words in and rolled them around inside of my mind, sucking all of the meaning out of them before I responded.

"Ulrich's loyalties have always rested squarely with Ulrich and only Ulrich. The fact that you're lumping the two of you together doesn't inspire any confidence in me—exactly the opposite, in fact. I came here primarily because you've been so publically against your dad's policy of strict neutrality."

"I know that—believe it or not, that's a huge part of why we've chosen to play things this way. The Bishops have been monarchists for a lot longer than anyone suspects, but we've always been very careful not to give off any hint of favoritism to either side in this conflict."

"That's a lovely story, but if that's the truth why did the two of you decide to break with tradition where you are concerned? Having you constantly yelling about coming out openly against the Coun'hij has to have made things difficult for your dad. Even if it helps in the short term, it's going to lock you into something other than neutrality once the pack is yours."

"We changed things up because the Coun'hij has been ramping up the pressure on my dad since even before I was born. We've looked back through the archives and there aren't any signs that it's ever been this bad before. It was bad even before your dad jumped into bed with Puppeteer and the rest, and it's only gotten worse since he got on board. We needed an insurance policy for my dad."

"Because they know if anything happens to Ulrich it will mean the Chicago pack will come out against them before his body is even cold."

"Yeah. For the first time in centuries, the Coun'hij is doing everything it can to keep the head of the Bishop line in power rather than trying to arrange for an accident in the hopes that his replacement will prove more malleable."

"Okay, I buy that—in theory at least. I can even see most of the advantages. The Coun'hij protects your dad, and he makes sure they know he'll turn on them in a heartbeat if anything happens to you. I get the feeling there's more to it though..."

"Yeah, it's like I said before. In the time of my dad and his dad, we had to actually be neutral or else risk our secret getting out. Dad doesn't think that we can make it another three hundred years under the current system. One way or another, our society is headed to a massive rebellion. By framing me as the rebel of the family, it gives us some latitude to make contact with 'divisive' elements without worrying about leaks getting back to the Coun'hij."

"Because when the leaks happen it's just you who's implicated rather than your dad."

"Yeah. That's the thing, Alec. We've been watching for the right chance to throw our weight behind the rebellion, but haven't seen anyone come along who had a snowflake's chance of succeeding—until you. When I promised to come help you, I wasn't promising as Shawn the no-account rebel. That operation had my dad's full approval. I was going to bring the cream of our fighting strength down there to help bust Agony out—everyone who we thought was trustworthy."

"Everyone who was trustworthy, or everyone he figured he could disavow if things went badly?"

"Both. Dad has been quietly shuffling things around inside of the pack since I manifested my hybrid form. He's got a lot of the paper tigers still reporting to him, but most of the best, most dependable hybrids—the ones who have an ax to grind with the Coun'hij—all report to me in some form or fashion."

"You ever wonder if your dad is just setting you up, Shawn? After all, it wouldn't be the first time that an alpha decided to eliminate his competition via external means."

"No, Alec, the thought never even crosses my mind. My dad is many things, and he can be a real bastard when the circumstances call for it, but I've never doubted his loyalty to the crown or his love for me. This is the real thing."

A spark of anger started growing inside of me. Everything Shawn said was seductive. It was powerfully convincing precisely because it was exactly what I wanted to hear. Two years ago it would have worked on me just like Shawn and Ulrich had planned, but I'd been through too much—seen too many terrible things—since then.

I thought I had the spark under control, but then my beast got behind the emotion and pushed. The spark exploded into a bonfire and my claws punched into the wall next to Shawn's head.

"Stop lying to me, Shawn. If any of what you've just told me were true, you wouldn't have left me hanging in the wind down in New Mexico. Agony died because you weren't there to back my play."

I'd been watching Dax and Vicki out of the corner of my eye. I'd expected them to shift forms and come crashing toward me. When you really got down to it, I'd been expecting Shawn to shift forms and do his best to rip my throat out, but nobody was behaving like they should have.

Dax started forward, but Vicki grabbed his arm before he could take more than a step. She didn't look happy about it, but she also hadn't attacked me. Out of anyone there, she was the last one I'd been expecting to pour oil on troubled waters.

Even odder, Shawn hadn't shifted. He wasn't even looking at me. He was looking at Vicki like she was his personal totem.

"You had a leak, Alec. I don't know who it is, or why they sold you out, but the Coun'hij knew that an operation was going down. You kept things compartmentalized, so we didn't know that you had a second group down there to help you. We thought our pulling back would be enough to convince you to call off the rescue. If we'd known that you had an entire other force in reserve, we would have shown up and helped out."

"I didn't have another force in reserve. That was all Dream Stealer—I didn't even know that he was going to be there. We went forward because we had access to a hybrid with an ability we figured would let us carry the day. We were right—at least until Brandon showed up. I wasn't compartmentalizing, I just didn't know what was going on. That's our biggest problem, we aren't a unified force. We're nothing more than a bunch of little fiefdoms who can't even agree to work together half the time."

Shawn ran his hand through his hair. "Yeah. I wish you'd told me about this hybrid with the game-changing ability. Maybe that would have been enough. You're right though. If we had one key leader who called all of the shots then we'd stand a heck of a lot better chance of winning this war."

I gave him a sardonic grin. "Are you and your dad ready to subordinate yourselves to someone else?"

"No—at least not yet—which means that we're part of the problem."

I looked around the room we were standing in, noting the thick carpet and expensive leather upholstery. I'd seen more luxury in a few rooms back at the estate, but not many. In some ways Shawn and I were practically the same person, and in others we were as different as night and day.

We'd both grown up groomed for leadership, both grown up with silver spoons in our mouths and a knowledge that money was never going to be in short supply. We both apparently wanted the Coun'hij overthrown, but that was where the similarities ended.

Shawn had a good relationship with his father, and had been trusted enough that Ulrich had given him the cash necessary to buy one of the hottest clubs in Chicago and outfit it in whatever style he wanted.

I'd had to steal my billions, and if my father and I ever saw each other again, one of us wouldn't walk away from the encounter. I took a deep breath and realized that there was one more similarity.

"Neither am I. I guess that means I'm part of the problem too."

Shawn looked like he wasn't sure whether or not it was okay for him to agree with me. He settled for just shrugging.

"What you said earlier about coming back here and ripping my heart out if I was trying to screw you over. That wasn't just an idle threat, was it? You really thought that you had a chance of making good on your promise."

The sudden change of topics caught me off guard. I nodded before I'd had a chance to think through my response.

"Yeah, I wasn't just talking to hear the sound of my voice. Why?"

It was a risk. I hadn't come right out and told him that I'd manifested an ability, but the implication was there.

"I...I can't tell you why I'm asking, Alec. All I can say is that the answer is important."

He was...not lying exactly, but definitely holding something important back. Any thought I'd had about trusting him with my secret evaporated.

"Let's just say that I now have access to...assets who you aren't prepared to deal with. Assets who are willing to accept me as the leader of the rebellion."

It was a lie and we both knew it, but that was the point. I'd just sent exactly the message I'd wanted to send to him. I'd told him that I had *someone* who made me a player, and I'd lied, so he knew that there was *something* else going on, something that I wasn't willing to share with him.

Shawn met my gaze for several seconds and then nodded. "If that's really the case, then maybe it's time I talk to my dad about changing our tune. If you have the ability to get to me then maybe you really are the best man for the job."

I kept the smile I was feeling off of my face, but it was hard.

"You didn't invite me here for a bunch of posturing, Shawn. You're either a better liar than I think you are, or you're telling the truth. What do you want?"

"It's the Tucson pack, Alec. Jaclyn Annikov and all of her people aren't going to last the week unless someone does something."

Chapter 2

Adriana Paige
Rest Easy Hotel
Arcadia, Florida

I'd spent too much time in bed over the last few days, but I couldn't seem to bring myself to care—not even enough to get out of bed when I heard a knock at my door. I didn't particularly care who was out there waiting for me, but the fact that the door opened a second later told me everything I needed to know about my visitor.

Nellie had been with Isaac's group for months now. She'd been one of the wolves who'd been working their way around the perimeter of the building while I'd been in the center...while my parents had been killed.

She'd spent days stuck inside the bunker in Wyoming with all of the rest of us, but I hadn't gotten to know her very well until after the big...fight...in Minnesota. Taggart, Cindi, Tristan and I had split off from Isaac and his people within twenty-four hours of defeating the vampires.

It had been a necessity—keeping that many people hidden from the Coun'hij while they were gathered together in one spot was the next best thing to impossible—but it had been more than that. I hadn't wanted to see anyone I didn't have to. Isaac, Heath, even Dominic, they had all been reminders of the fact that we'd failed my mom and dad. I'd brought all of my closest friends and we'd come loaded for bear, but in the end it hadn't been enough.

We'd killed the vampires—Alec had killed the vampires—but it hadn't been enough to save the two people I owed everything to. If there'd been a way to go off completely by myself—without Taggart, Cindi and Tristan—I would have. Unfortunately there wasn't. Taggart was the one who had all of the cash, and I'd already had a very brutal crash course on just how dangerous the world actually was.

He was right to refuse when I told him I wanted a hundred thousand dollars and time by myself, but it didn't make it any easier to hear. Once I knew I wasn't going to lose Taggart, I couldn't really refuse Cindi. She'd lost just as much as I had.

Tristan just never gave me a chance to tell him no. He'd just always been there with his bags packed every time I was ready to leave. That was a pretty big accomplishment for someone who was barely to the point of getting around without a wheelchair, but it was more than that.

Tristan had given up a lot to be there for Cindi and me. He was probably wanted by the police back home, and it was a virtual certainty that his parents had disowned him by now. He'd given up a billion-dollar inheritance and a promising career in football because he knew that we needed his help. He'd done it all without being asked.

I couldn't turn him down—not even knowing that he was eventually going to break Cindi's heart. From what little I'd seen, he'd been great to her ever since Alec had rescued her from the vampires. He was attentive and sensitive—perfect in every way but one.

He liked Cindi, but he liked me a lot more. He was going to cause her problems down the road, but I couldn't deal with the future right now. It was all I could do to deal with the present. If Tristan could help Cindi pull herself back together before he did something stupid that ruined everything between them then I was on board. Call me short-sighted, but it felt like the least of several evils.

Somehow in all of the craziness of our departure from Minnesota, Nellie had managed to attach herself to our group. Isaac ran a much more democratic organization than most shape shifter alphas. He probably could have gotten away with ordering Nellie to leave us alone, but he wouldn't—not unless he was sure she was stepping over some kind of boundary.

I would have said she was violating my privacy, but nobody asked me and Taggart was overjoyed to have someone else around who could help ride herd on his three human charges. Nellie was just a wolf—and therefore only a half-step up from a cocker spaniel in the preternatural pecking order—but she was still faster, stronger and more deadly than any human. Her presence meant that Taggart could feel safe closing his eyes when he needed to sleep. She might not be able to fight off all of the big bads out there, but she could at least hold them off for the few seconds it would take for Taggart to wake up and get into the fight.

It was almost humorous to think of Taggart—the fearsome Dream Stealer—babysitting three damaged humans and a submissive wolf. He'd gone his own way for centuries, considered too violent to fit into any conventional pack, but somehow that had all changed over the last few months. He was the best protector anyone could have asked for.

I knew that I was breaking his heart, that he was more and more concerned about how despondent I'd gotten, but I just couldn't bring myself to care. I slept fitfully when I slept at all—scared to death of going back into someone else's dreams—but I rarely got out of bed.

Nellie was the only person who seemed to be able to cut through the storm clouds. She cared about me, but not so much that she wasn't willing to kick my butt a little when she felt like it was necessary. She was the one who made me eat when I wanted nothing more than to just starve to death. For a few days I'd almost thought she was going to get me back outside walking around and pretending that I was a normal human being.

It was odd. I knew that Taggart cared about me, but his company never seemed to do anything to dull my anguish. Nellie on the other hand seemed to be able to buffer the worst of my pain simply by sitting next to me and holding my hand. Just having her around put a layer of gauze between me and my emotions.

That had all changed somehow when we arrived in Florida. Days before that I'd become so sleep-deprived that I'd started having waking dreams—hallucinations really. They had always been disturbing, but in Florida I'd started seeing Alec in my dreams.

That was the last straw for me. Intellectually I knew that Alec couldn't have known that the vampire leader had twenty tons of machinery suspended over my parents' heads when he'd come crashing into the center of the building and sucked away all of her energy. He'd been doing the best he could, and he'd saved the lives of Taggart, Isaac, Dom, and Heath. He'd even saved Cindi. He'd saved the lives of *almost* everyone I cared about, but all I could think about was the fact that he'd failed.

He'd been the one who'd sent the machinery crashing down that had killed my parents.

I tried to tell myself that it wasn't Alec I was seeing, but it didn't work. It was Alec and I knew it. He was older looking, and sterner, with unforgiving eyes, but it was him.

I'd started out ignoring him—and the shadowy presences just outside my field of vision—but it didn't work. He didn't go away, didn't disappear to be replaced by some other hallucination. I was reaching the end of my rope.

Ignoring the fake Alec hadn't worked, and at some point I was going to start yelling and screaming at him. Once that happened, Taggart was going to have no alternative but to sedate me. I could see it all bearing down on me, an unstoppable freight train, and I just couldn't bring myself to care enough to get off of the tracks.

As it always did, Nellie's presence took away the smallest part of my anguish, but the effect never lasted for very long. It went away sooner than normal when I saw that she wasn't alone.

There was a reason that I'd given her a key to my room, but not given one to Taggart. Our shared ritual of hot coco in the evenings had fallen by the wayside. Underneath all of the concern, Taggart's eyes had become too judgmental for me to spend time around him.

"We have news, Adri. Alec has heard rumors that the Coun'hij is preparing to take out the Tucson pack."

Taggart obviously wanted some kind of response from me, but I didn't give him one. He sighed and then continued.

"I know you don't know anything about the Tucson pack, Adri, and I know that you don't want to be reminded about Alec right now, but those are real people out there. They have people who love them, and they're in terrible danger. If Alec's intel is right, the Coun'hij has decided to start purging dissident packs. They're starting with Tucson because they are small enough that Kaleb figures they can be eliminated in one fell swoop, but big—and strong—enough that it will send the right kind of message to anyone who's been thinking about declaring openly for the rebellion."

"You're right, I don't know anything about the Tucson pack, and I don't want to. If you want to save them, then go ahead. Take Nellie, call up Isaac and Heath, and go meet up with Alec. You don't need me and I'll be better off without you."

Taggart turned to Nellie. "Leave us."

To her credit, Nellie looked like she wanted to argue with him. She cared about me every bit as much as he did, and she could see what was coming as well as I could. She wanted to tell him this was a bad idea, but arguing with a dominant—especially a dominant as strong as Taggart, one who was obviously just looking for a reason to let his anger off its leash—was a bad idea.

Taggart waited until she was gone and then pulled a handgun out from the back of his waistband. It wasn't just any gun, it was my gun. It was the gun that I'd used to drive Brandon off, the gun I'd used to shoot vampires after...after Mom and Dad had been killed.

That gun had been a promise of power, of never being defenseless again. It had been my own personal talisman, and it had all been a big lie. It had failed me. I'd stood there powerless, unable to move while my parents had been executed.

He tossed my weapon on the bed. "Pick it up."

"Go away."

"This isn't you, Adri. The girl I knew wouldn't have let herself spend twenty-three hours of every day in bed. The Adri I knew was a fighter. She was willing to go head to head with the most dangerous things out there in the darkness rather than just roll over and die."

"That Adri was nothing more than an illusion, Taggart. I'm sorry that you had to find out this way, but it's better for you to find out now rather than later."

"If that Adri wasn't real, then pick up that gun and end it. If you're not willing to fight then you're betraying your father—the man that I watched face death looking his killer in the eyes.

More than that, you're betraying Isaac, Heath, Dominic and me. We all put our lives on the line for you—not your parents, you. We went up against something that still gives me nightmares because we cared about you and thought you were worth saving."

I opened my mouth to tell him that I hadn't asked any of them to risk their lives, but I couldn't remember if that was true. It was all a big hazy mess of repressed memories. Everything from immediately before and immediately after my parent's death was too blurry to pick out anything useful from it.

I could remember the instant when my parents had been crushed in perfect, painful detail, but everything else had faded away into nothing.

The flare of anger I'd felt at Taggart's words was new. It wasn't one of the emotions that had taken me over since the fight. It wasn't safe. I looked at the gun lying on the bedspread, scant inches away from my fingers, and felt an overpowering urge to pick it up.

Taggart wasn't done talking though. "Do you want to know the worst part? You've betrayed Alec, and that is a transgression I never thought I'd see you commit."

"How dare you! How dare you mention his name to me. You of all people. You spent weeks telling me that he couldn't be trusted. First it was because of who his father was and then it was because he'd addicted Brindi to his touch. You had a hundred reasons why he was wrong for me."

"Yes, and all of them were wrong. He—"

"They were right! He killed my parents, Taggart. Don't you tell me to pick up that gun. If I pick it up I won't use it on myself. I'll hunt Alec down and use it on him."

Somewhere along the line I'd jumped out of bed and thrown myself at Taggart, but he caught me and easily immobilized me so that I couldn't hurt him.

"It's okay to be mad at him, Adri. It's natural to want someone to blame, but it's not his fault. You need to allow yourself to grieve so that you can work past this. You can't stay mad at him forever."

"No, you were right all along. He's no good. He's a glory hound who only cares about making sure that he's seen as the hero who saved the best hope of the rebellion."

"He went in after Cindi expecting to die, Adri. He didn't want you to have to pick between her and your parents, so he came up with a plan that was believable enough that you wouldn't question it. His power wasn't working when he set out to 'rescue' Cindi. You know this—or if you don't you should.

"Alec isn't the villain here, he's the one who saved Cindi. He was ready to sacrifice his life for nothing more than the hope that you would be happy. The real question is how many people would be willing to do that for you, Adri."

"You just finished telling me the answer to that question. You, Isaac, Dom, Heath, and more than a dozen others."

"No. Being willing to risk one's life isn't the same thing as going into a fight knowing you will die, Adri. You should know that better than anyone. You were ready to do exactly that for your family. Would you do that for Dom? For Isaac? For me?

"Alec is going to try to help the Tucson pack simply because it's the right thing to do. The only question is if you're going to let him go into battle by himself. He needs us—needs you. You don't have to be past what happened to your parents, but you need to acknowledge that it wasn't Alec's fault."

I was shaking, sobs wracking my body, and somewhere along the way Taggart's restraining hold turned to an embrace. As the sobs finally started to die down, I looked down and realized that I had my gun dangling from my right hand.

Taggart saw my questioning look and wiped away my tears. "You have one of the strongest survival instincts of anyone I know. I didn't know any other way to get through to you."

"That's a hell of a risk for you to be taking—for both of us."

"It wasn't loaded, but even if it had been, it would have been a risk I would have been willing to take—for you."

Chapter 3

Alec Graves
The Comfort Motel
Minneapolis Minnesota

I knew I was dreaming because Brindi wasn't anywhere to be seen. I'd spent years trying to train myself to be aware of my dreams enough to detect when Dream Stealer—Taggart—paid me a visit, and it had all been useless, but a lack of Brindi's presence instantly alerted me that this couldn't be reality.

Even as I thought it, I knew that wasn't fair. Kaleb—my father—had warned me that it had taken him more than a decade to learn to instantly recognize his dreams, so it wasn't as though I was surprised at not having mastered that particular discipline yet.

It was funny really. There had been a period of time where I'd held out hope that Kaleb's training was secretly because he didn't want Dream Stealer to find out that he was working against the Coun'hij. It was by far the less-likely explanation, but somehow my young mind had fixated on that idea rather than just understanding that Kaleb was every bit as bad as my mother had been telling me he was.

Of course she turned out not to be so amazing herself.

As far as Brindi went, that wasn't quite fair either. She was around on a nearly constant basis—she'd been waiting for me back at our hotel when I'd finished up with Shawn—but she was genuinely making an effort to work on the skin addiction.

It wasn't uncommon for her to go eight hours at a time without any physical contact with me, but I'd realized somewhere along the way that whenever she was out of my sight I could feel an invisible timer ticking away in the back of my mind. It counted down the seconds until she needed to see me again.

It wasn't exactly that I was looking forward to seeing her—although it was nice to have one person in my life who was always glad to see me—it was more like an acknowledgment of the fact that she depended on me. If the clock got too close to zero without her making it back, then I knew I needed to track her down before the shakes settled in and she lost the ability to make it back to me.

That was actually one of the reasons that I knew Brindi was making an honest effort to distance herself from me. The old Brindi would have never let herself get more than a dozen yards away from me for more than an hour. The new Brindi actually pushed the envelope more than she should have. There had been a couple of times already where she'd stayed out so long that James or one of the girls had been forced to go retrieve her.

It was frustrating. She was trying so hard now, but the withdrawal symptoms had gotten even worse. Carson didn't have any more experience with the Ja'tell bond than I did, but he agreed that this was unlike anything he'd ever seen before. He'd even floated the theory that the strength of Brindi's addiction had something to do with my being from the royal line.

I'd been racking my mind ever since in an attempt to remember exactly how bad things had gotten with my mother, but she'd mostly retreated back into her rooms when her symptoms had gotten the worst. Rachel was of the opinion that Mom's addiction hadn't been as bad, but that had just confirmed what I'd already been suspecting. The simple fact was that Brindi hadn't been this bad before I'd manifested my ability.

Somehow *I* was doing this to Brindi. I suspected that Brindi had come to the same conclusion, and that was part of why she was trying so hard to get some distance from me, but I hadn't had the courage to ask her yet.

Not hearing that timer ticking away had been all I needed to know that what I was experiencing couldn't be real. Some part of my subconscious mind knew that Brindi was sleeping on the second bed in my room, that she was safe.

I looked around at my surroundings and realized that I was back in the gardens that surrounded the estate in Sanctuary. It was just as breathtaking as always, but then again I'd reconstructed this from my memories of home, so it only made sense that it would meet my expectations in every way.

I inhaled a lungful of the scented air, and briefly considered switching forms. The gardens were an aromatic banquet that could only be appreciated in wolf form, but doing that would mean that the amazing colors of all of the vegetation would be washed out in the cool light that all living organisms gave off in that form.

It was a familiar conundrum. In the end, I chose to remain in my dominant form and enjoy the gardens on two legs. I ended up being glad of my choice a few seconds later when I heard a whisper of movement behind me and whirled around to find someone who looked like Taggart less than a dozen feet away from me.

"Hello, Alec."

"Hello. How do I know if you're really who you appear to be? Our usual encounters don't start out—or end—this amiably."

That earned me a smile. "I'd tell you that it's very unlikely you'll run into anyone but Adri or me inside the privacy of your dreams, but the truth is that we ran into someone a little while ago who seemed to be able to do at least some of what we could do."

The thought sent chills skittering up and down my spine. "For centuries you were the only one who could dream walk, and now suddenly there are three of you. That can't be coincidence."

Taggart—or at least the man who looked like Taggart—shrugged. "I don't know. I would have said the same thing, but at this point I'm hoping very strongly that it is coincidence. The alternative is that Kaleb and the rest have figured out a way to trigger specific abilities in people. If that's the case, we're all screwed anyway."

I rubbed my eyes. This was a dream, I shouldn't have felt tired, but I did. Then again, it wasn't a physical exhaustion, it was all mental. I was so tired of trying to keep a hundred balls in the air at once. Worrying about what Kaleb and the rest of the Coun'hij were doing was beyond a full-time job.

Taggart didn't try to get closer, he just stood there with an expression of understanding on his face. It suddenly struck me that the two of us were much more alike than we'd ever given ourselves credit for being.

He'd carried the weight of his sins across his shoulders for centuries as he'd dedicated himself to trying to atone for the help he'd provided the Coun'hij back when their evil had been less apparent. That had made him treat the war as though it was him against the world.

I carried fewer sins along with me, but that was just because my hand had been forced at an earlier point than his had been. I was alone simply because nobody else could do what I could. Even Jaclyn and Heath were in some ways less powerful than I was. That, combined with the fact that I was the heir to the monarchy, meant that most of my burdens couldn't be carried by anyone else.

Taggart understood me in ways that nobody else could, which told me exactly the question I should be asking to establish he was really who he said he was.

"I haven't been able to stop thinking about one thing, Taggart. Tell me about the state of your forces. We're going to need them if we're going to have any shot at winning this war."

Taggart looked at me for several seconds and then shook his head. "You haven't been thinking non-stop about our forces, and you aren't dying to ask me about Isaac and the rest, you've been wondering about Adri."

I closed my eyes and nodded. "Apparently you really are who you say you are. How is she doing?"

"Not good. She's retreated inside of herself in ways that I didn't expect. I knew that it would be hard for her to cope with the loss of her parents, but I didn't foresee this. I...I've wanted to call you a hundred times over the last few weeks."

"I would have come if you had. I would have dropped everything and driven straight there."

"I know you would have. I told myself that I wasn't calling because what you were doing was important. The intelligence that is being gathered needs to be analyzed, and you are the only one who has a chance of uniting all of the disparate pieces of the rebellion, but the truth was that I was worried seeing you would break her.

"I finally forced the issue when I heard that something was going down in Arizona. I knew that you would need both of us at full strength in order to figure out what Kaleb has planned."

"Was that smart?"

Taggart shook his head. "Probably not, but I was at my wits' end. I think that she's going to be okay though. She agreed to come here tonight with me, so that's a huge step forward."

My heart skipped a beat. "She's here now?"

"No, not yet. She may not even manage to connect with your dreams. She's tried several times in the past without success, but the fact that she was willing is promising."

I opened my mouth to ask him for more details and then I felt something I'd never felt before. My ability was coming more and more under my conscious control, but it still sometimes operated at a low level without me realizing it.

It was happening again, but I wouldn't have even noticed it if not for the fact that I could feel odd pinpricks of heat as my ability absorbed energy from somewhere. It probably wasn't the smartest thing to suppress my ability while experiencing something that very well could be some kind of unusual attack, but that never even entered into my mind.

If there was a chance that I was going to see Adri then I needed to take advantage of the opportunity—regardless of the possible risk. I shut down my ability completely.

It was like making a fist with an invisible hand that I'd only discovered I had a short time earlier. It seemed like I was getting better and better at locking down the absorption field that I naturally generated, but even now it wasn't something that I could sustain on a constant basis. Eventually my mental fist got tired and relaxed. Usually it wasn't enough to make a difference, but apparently whatever Adri was doing involved such small amounts of energy it was having a hard time surviving even the most minimal drain from my ability.

BURNED

As soon as my ability stopped sucking in the ambient energy from my surroundings, I felt something snag on a point about an inch below my bellybutton and half an inch below the surface of the skin. I suddenly felt like a very big fish that had just been hooked by an expert fisherman. I felt a tug on my insides, and the urge to take a step forward was almost overpowering, but I refused to be moved. I dug my heels in as the line between us continued to strengthen, and then suddenly I got an impression of movement. It was as if the fisherman had started reeling in the line, but rather than pulling me towards her she was pulling herself toward me.

The line between us vibrated more quickly the closer she got—it felt like a guitar string that had been improperly tuned, that was under so much tension it was going to snap at any moment. I turned my head to ask Taggart if this was normal, and almost missed Adri's arrival.

For the briefest of instants she seemed to exist in three places simultaneously. She was standing in an open field under a purple sky, she was floating in an ocean of pure white light, and she was motionless only inches away from me.

It happened so quickly that my natural tendency was to dismiss it as nothing more than my brain's attempt to deal with something completely outside my normal frame of reference, but it didn't feel like something I'd never experienced before. That sea of light felt somehow familiar. It felt like a home that I'd only lived in during dreams, a home that somehow surrounded my normal existence.

Adri went from immobile to falling as time resumed moving again, and I reached up and grabbed her by the shoulders.

"Are you okay?"

Even as I asked the question I knew how it sounded. There were layers of meaning behind those words that I wasn't sure I wanted answered. Did she still blame me for the death of her parents?

"I…yeah, I'll be fine. It's just the transition from one state to another. It's always a little tricky. I handled it worse than normal this time, but I usually manage not to fall all the way to the ground before catching myself."

She looked down at my hands and I realized for the first time that I hadn't let go of her. I released her shoulders with a pang of loss. There was so much that I wanted to say to her, but none of it was appropriate so soon after her parents' death—especially not with Taggart standing less than a dozen feet away.

I looked into her eyes hoping for some sign that things would eventually be okay, but there was a guardedness to her that hadn't been there any of the times we'd talked before this.

"Adri—I'm sorry. I never—"

"You don't have to say anything, Alec. You saved Cindi, which is so much more than would have happened without you. If you hadn't arrived when you did, everyone who went to Minnesota to help me would have died. Let's just put all of that behind us. Taggart said you have information about some kind of Coun'hij operation that we need to deal with. You and he don't have an unlimited amount of time here—let's get to brass tacks."

I looked over at Taggart and saw a flicker of something that was gone too quickly for me to be sure, but which looked like disappointment. I just wished that I knew whether he was disappointed in her reaction or disappointed that I hadn't managed to break through her guard.

"Right. There's not a ton I can tell you yet. One of my contacts told me that the Coun'hij wants to make an example of Jaclyn Annikov. Her pack is small enough that you can pretty much guarantee they will all be somewhere between Tucson and the border at any given moment. That means that they are easy to contain, which is a big plus for Kaleb and the rest. At the same time, Jaclyn is powerful enough that killing her makes a powerful statement."

Taggart nodded as though contemplating what I'd just said, but I knew he'd already considered all of the angles.

"It's a risky move. The Coun'hij has tried for the last couple of centuries to maintain an aura of legitimacy. They are brutal when it comes to eliminating enemies, but only after they find a violation of the laws they've created. Jaclyn has proven surprisingly good at not actually doing anything worthy of death despite all of her complaints.

"Destroying her pack might scare all of the smaller unaligned packs into the Coun'hij's shadow, but it could just as easily force them all into open rebellion. This isn't the kind of move I would have expected out of Kaleb."

I shrugged. "You're not wrong. He's usually more subtle than this, but it's possible that they don't feel like they have any other option. We didn't manage to save Agony, but we did soundly trounce a fairly large group of enforcers before being chased off. The Coun'hij may not know everything that happened before Brandon arrived, but they must have realized by now that we brought someone with an ability that they didn't expect."

"I suppose you're right. It's easy to get caught up with worries over the fact that Grayson isn't a resource we can count on to help us in the future, but the Coun'hij is probably concerned about the fact that Carson's people—and Heath—represent a completely unanticipated threat."

"Right, and then when you throw in the fact that they haven't been able to track us down since then, they're probably feeling the heat. They don't know that we lost a ton of people in LA. My efforts at diplomacy haven't been bearing any real fruit, but I've been focused on the packs that are already only half a step away from joining the rebellion. Maybe I should have been focused on the independents. If Kaleb and the rest are getting signals that the smaller packs are already considering jumping ship, the Coun'hij may not feel like they have any other choice."

I'd been very careful not to reference Minnesota again, but Adri flinched slightly when I talked about our losses in LA. It was, after all, only a small jump from losing people to super vampires in one place to losing them to super-vampires in another place.

For a moment I thought she was going to crack under the memory of her parents being killed, but she pulled herself together with visible effort.

"Okay, so what next? I take it we can't just call Jaclyn up and tell her to pack her bags?"

Taggart smiled. "No, I'm afraid things are rarely that simple. It is difficult to stay off of the Coun'hij's radar, but it's even harder falling off in the first place. You and I were never really on it, and Alec had the advantage of leaving while most of his father's assets were focused on the more visible threats, but Jaclyn doesn't have either of those advantages."

Adri was putting on a brave front, but I could see her legs starting to tremble ever so slightly. I forced an ornate black wrought-iron bench into existence behind her and then gestured for her to take advantage of it.

"Yeah. Jaclyn's pack is one of the most heavily watched. My bet is that the Coun'hij knows where every penny of the pack's money is headed before it even leaves the bank. They'll have satellites watching the area, and assets close enough to head her off if she just grabs her people and jumps in vehicles to make a run for it.

"The only way they have a chance of getting out is if someone sets up extraction routes for them and then comes in and wipes out the quick response force that's been assigned to make sure she doesn't try anything.

"Once we know for sure how many people we're dealing with, Jack can probably set up extraction plans that will suffice to help everyone drop off of the radar, but that's all for naught if we can't deal with the enforcers down there."

Adri shrugged. "So go down there and deal with them. Based on what you did in Minnesota, you can wipe out the entire group of enforcers all by yourself."

I wasn't sure whether to be happy that she'd managed to reference the battle where her parents had died without crying or sad that she'd put on such a callous front.

"That was my first thought as well, but what little information I'm getting out of that area indicates that there are more werewolves active down in that area than there should be."

"Puppeteer."

Taggart said the name like it was the worst kind of curse, but I couldn't blame him. Puppeteer was a big part of why nobody felt safe expressing their dissatisfaction with the current regime too loudly.

"There is an uncomfortable amount of similarity between my power and what the werewolves do. It's not a hundred-percent match, obviously, but I've seen werewolves absorb an insane amount of power. Jaclyn Annikov's power doesn't even faze them…"

"You're worried that your power won't work on them."

"Correct. I'm eager to find out—preferably in a fairly controlled setting—but until I know that I can drop them as easily as vampires, it's a bad idea to depend on my ability to bail us out. We need a big enough force down there to handle whatever Puppeteer can throw at us."

Taggart sighed, and I saw the same exhaustion in him that I'd been feeling before Adri arrived. "It's not going to be easy to keep that many people hidden for very long."

"I know. I wouldn't ask this of you if the stakes were any lower, but if we can safely extract the Tucson pack—right out from under the Coun'hij's noses—it will change everything. Even if it doesn't result in a tidal wave of support from the smaller packs, it's still worth it if we can stop the Coun'hij from intimidating everyone into going the other direction."

He still didn't look convinced, but I wasn't done playing my cards. He was still thinking of things the way they'd been before I'd manifested my ability, before we'd pulled together such a strong coalition.

"I know what you're thinking, Taggart. If we're all in one spot for that long we'll be giving Kaleb and the rest the opportunity they've been hoping for since before I was born. The difference is that they no longer have the ability to wipe us out all at once—they just don't know it yet.

"It doesn't matter who they bring, I can neutralize them. At this point I'm praying to run into Brandon because I'll finally be able to put him down once and for all. Nobody the Coun'hij has is a match for me, not when I can immobilize them for the few seconds it will take me to kill them. The only thing we have to be afraid of right now is Puppeteer's werewolves, and there has to be some kind of limit on the number of them he can control at one time."

"You're saying that now we are more vulnerable apart—in hiding—than we are together."

"That's exactly what I'm saying."

I could see the gears turning inside of his mind. He wanted to believe I was right. What I was describing was the thing that he'd been fighting for since he'd first turned against the Coun'hij decades ago.

"I'm sure you're right that Puppeteer has limits—all powers do—but he could do the same thing he did when he broke the vampire strongholds in St Louis. Stage shipments of werewolves a short distance away from wherever we are staying, and then run them into us a dozen at a time, wearing us down until we finally break."

"It's a risk, but the potential benefits are huge. Puppeteer seems to have a fairly small range. If he's close enough to attack us with his minions it will mean that he's close enough for us to get our hands on him.

"I've already talked to Jack. His contacts say that they can guarantee us a satellite over the area for at least five days. We'll put analysts on the video coming off of the bird and we'll look for any vehicles that are motionless during the time of the attacks. If we can identify him we can send Heath in with a hand-picked squad. Puppeteer will never see them coming."

"It's risky."

"Sure, but it's also the chance we've been waiting for. If Puppeteer was out of the picture, the whole dynamics of the situation would change completely. All of a sudden the packs would only have to worry about the enforcers. Don't get me wrong, the enforcers are bad news, but there are only so many of them. Kaleb and the rest have been relying on the threat of the werewolves to keep everyone in line—there are too many demands on their manpower to do otherwise.

"We won't go looking for a fight. We'll keep a low profile and try to get Jaclyn's people out quietly, but if it comes to fighting we have a very good chance of coming out on top. I've asked Carson to reach out to Grayson again. Carson can't guarantee he'll be there, but I'm willing to promise just about anything to get Grayson down in Arizona with us. He has to have a price, and thanks to the money I stole from Kaleb, I'm in a position to meet it."

"It sounds like you've got everything planned out. You, Heath, Grayson, Taggart and me. You've basically put together the dream team of hybrid superheroes."

Adri's voice turned something that otherwise should have been a compliment into a bitter recrimination, but I told myself that she was still hurting, that I couldn't take it personally. It helped a little. What she said next just about sent me over the edge.

"Instead of messing around down in Arizona, why don't you just take a quick trip up to Sanctuary and wipe out Kaleb, Brandon and the rest of your old pack? If you really want to change the power dynamic you should start taking out the Coun'hij's most loyal supporters. You probably wouldn't have to take out more than three or four packs before the Coun'hij would start suffering from a massive round of defections."

I realized I was gritting my teeth, and forced my jaw to unclench. "I lived in Sanctuary for seventeen years, but contrary to what you may believe, that isn't the reason that I'm not heading up there and laying waste to every living thing within twenty miles of the estate.

"I lived there—here, actually—for long enough to know that not every member of this pack deserves to die. That's going to be true of any of the packs in the Coun'hij's court. Every pack is full of both good and bad people, but more than that, every pack has people in it who are part of the problem just because they are too scared to stand up for what they know is right.

"I'll come back here at some point—when the time is right—and I'll kill Kaleb and Brandon. Honestly, I'd be happy to kill them sooner, but I'm not going to do anything that will result in a bunch of non-combatants being caught in the crossfire. When I start taking out the key figures who are supporting the status quo, I'll do it in a way that doesn't get a bunch of children killed."

Adri looked for a second like she was going to respond hotly, but Taggart put a hand on her shoulder, and that seemed to bring her back to herself.

"Fine, we'll do it your way. Unless you need something else I should probably get back to my body—if we're about to embark on some kind of extended campaign I suspect I'll need all of the energy I can suck down each day. There's no need to waste it with small talk here."

"You guys came to me—I'm glad you did, but it's not like I'm begging you to stay."

"Right, you're probably just anxious to get back to whoever is keeping your bed warm right now."

Now it was my turn to nearly say something that I would have later regretted, but Taggart stepped between the two of us.

"That was beneath you, Adri. I'm sure that the two of you have already talked about the situation with Brindi. If you had an understanding about her back before the...accident...then now isn't the time to be attacking Alec over something he didn't ask to have happen."

I half expected her to attack him with her bare hands, but she just stood there shaking for a couple of seconds, and then whirled and ran away. She disappeared as she took her second step, and then it was just Taggart and I.

My anger evaporated as quickly as it had appeared. My beast had never really calmed back down after my visit with Shawn. I wanted to blame my fury on the metaphysical hitchhiker that rode around inside my head, but I knew that wasn't the complete truth.

If my beast had been the cause for my feelings then I wouldn't have been able to master my anger instantly like that. My anger had evaporated because I'd seen her face as she'd turned to go. For a split second there her mask had dropped. She *was* angry, but mostly she was just hurting and using rage to cover up the hole inside of her—the one that she was afraid would never go away, the one that she felt guilty about resenting because wanting to get better felt like a betrayal of her parents.

"I'm sorry about that, Alec. I'd hoped that seeing you would help remind her of the connection the two of you share. I fear that I've made a mistake and pushed her too far, too fast."

"No, that was my fault. I should have reacted better. I know what she's going through right now, it was my job tonight to make sure that I didn't let her bait me—a job at which I failed miserably."

Taggart patted me on the shoulder, and I was surprised to find that I was comfortable enough around him to not have my beast freaking out at having him so close.

"You were working at a disadvantage, Alec. Adri has mastered the art of keeping her feelings secret while she's inside of the dream. Here she doesn't have a scent unless she wants to, and it isn't strictly necessary for her to breathe or for her heart to beat. Most people do all of those things out of sheer habit, but she's come a long ways despite having not practiced for quite some time."

I was astonished that I hadn't noticed her lack of involuntary responses, but Taggart didn't give me any time to really consider that bit of information.

"You're in a tough spot, Alec. You feel guilt over what happened even though you acted in the only way you could at the time. That is compounded by the fact that part of you knows Adri should be treating you like a hero. Without you, Cindi would have died, and everyone else we took into that building would have joined her. It's natural to resent Adri for treating you so poorly despite everything you've done for her. Just try to remember that she's not herself right now—not really. In time she'll go back to being the girl we both care so much about. Try to be patient."

"I think that you're giving me too much credit."

"Be that as it may, the credit is mine to give out as I see fit."

He drew a smile out of me despite myself. "Was there anything else you wanted to discuss? I don't want to keep you—I know how valuable your dream time is."

"Two things. The first is easier than the second." Taggart passed me a card with a phone number on it. I memorized it in less than a second and passed it back to him. "That is my current phone number. We'll need to talk if we're to coordinate the operation you've got planned."

"Okay, I'll send you a text tomorrow so you've got my number. What was the second thing?"

Taggart was silent for several seconds, as though he was having second thoughts about what he'd been planning on saying.

"I respect your desire not to pull innocents into this war, Alec. What if there was another way to wage it?"

"I don't know. It would depend on what you had in mind. I want the Coun'hij gone as much as anyone."

"It would mean working together with Adri again, which I know isn't ideal for either of you right now, but it's possible that we could bring the Coun'hij down without ever having to face any of them in the real world."

I felt as though I'd just been struck. If he was suggesting what I thought he was suggesting, then I felt like a fool for not thinking of it myself. The possibilities were endless.

"I thought you weren't able to kill someone inside of their own dreams."

Taggart nodded. "That's right, I can't. It's been pretty conclusively proved though that Adri's gift works in a different way than mine does. She's killed inside of her own dreams once before. The jury's still out on whether she can do it inside of someone else's dreams, which is one of many reasons that I've kept that aspect of her power quiet up until now, but there is a possibility that between the three of us we could take down each member of the Coun'hij one at a time while they are sleeping."

"How would it go down?"

"Adri's getting better and better inside of the dream with every passing month, but she's still no match for someone like Kaleb on her own. When you get right down to it, I'm not even always a match for your father. What I would propose is that Adri and I come here to your dream again like we did tonight. Then she will pull our first target in—that's another trick she has that I can't do.

"Once we have them here inside of your dream, you can use your ability on them while Adri pins them here so they can't avoid death by escaping back to their own dreams."

I closed my eyes, not wanting to admit to myself where this was headed, but I nodded despite my unexpected reluctance.

"That makes sense. We'll have to test my ability and make sure that it still works inside of my dreams—it's good that you'll be here to serve as backup to the two of us—but if it does work, then we can finish off this war without ever having to lose another of our people."

Taggart nodded. "The only price for that miracle will be turning Adri into an assassin—not just once, but dozens, possibly hundreds of times as we work our way through the Coun'hij and then move on to eliminating the known enforcers. It's funny, there was a time when I was desperate to get her to do exactly this, but now the time has arrived and I'm strangely reluctant to take this step."

"I think I understand at least part of what you're feeling, Taggart. Even after having her basically rip my head off tonight, I still don't want to see her turned into the kind of cold, inhuman tool that the Coun'hij uses to do its dirty work, but you're right to have brought it up. If we have a chance to end this without enduring a long, bloody civil war, then we need to take it."

I looked him in the eyes and said what needed to be said—whether he knew it or not. "We need to start with Kaleb."

"No, Alec, I wouldn't ask that of you. We'll start with someone else. Puppeteer or Oblivion would both be better test cases. Puppeteer will be all but defenseless inside of a dream. Once he's been separated from his werewolves, he's no more dangerous than any other hybrid and less probably than most. Killing him will do much more for the war effort than killing your father—you said so yourself just minutes ago."

I shook my head. "You've never seen Puppeteer, and neither has Adri, but she told me the first time we met that she'd watched Kaleb inside of one of her first dream walks. That makes it easier, right? We need to start with someone we know we can pull into my dreams, and there is every reason to go after the single most important person we can manage.

"You can't guarantee that Adri will be able to connect with Puppeteer, and Oblivion is much more dangerous than Kaleb will ever be in a one-on-one situation. If my powers work inside of a dream, then there's a chance that Oblivion's will too.

"Besides, I've met Oblivion before and I'm not sure that he has to be our enemy. It's too soon to tell, but if there's a way to salvage him we should. Regardless of who wins this rebellion we've committed ourselves to, we're still going to have to do damage control where it comes to keeping the humans in the dark about our existence. Nobody is better at that than Oblivion.

"It has to be Kaleb, he has to be first or he'll see it coming and start changing up his sleep schedule in order to make it harder for us to trap him here."

I could see that Taggart agreed with the logic behind my words, but he either wanted to spare me from having to kill my father, or he didn't trust that I would actually go through with it. I hoped it was the former.

"It doesn't have to be like that, Alec. I've already considered the fact that our enemies will eventually start changing up their sleeping schedules. Once we've confirmed that your power works inside of dreams, you and Adri won't need me there as backup. I'll be able to instead spend my sleeping time tracking down and identifying targets for the two of you."

"No, Taggart, it does have to be like that. We can't risk Kaleb being alerted to what's coming or everything will get much tougher. What is it they say? The best way to kill a snake is by cutting off the head. The Coun'hij is more like a hydra than a snake, but the principle is the same. If you want my help then you're going to have to help me kill Kaleb first of all."

We stood there in silence, neither willing to back down for several seconds before Taggart shrugged. "This is a pointless discussion until we know if your ability will be effective under these circumstances. Let's test it out."

I opened up the black hole that I now carried around inside of me at all times. I focused it on Taggart, and opened my imaginary fist up wider and wider. It took longer than it should have—either Taggart was even more powerful than I'd expected, or my ability wasn't as effective here as it was in the real world—but as I hit my maximum rate of absorption he dropped to his knees and I knew the matter was settled.

My gift worked here and we were going to kill Kaleb before we went after anyone else.

Chapter 4

Alec Graves
Highway 12
Western Montana

The drive from our hotel to the rendezvous spot in Montana only took a few hours. Brindi and I usually passed our drive time in companionable silence, but this time it was even quieter than normal because I'd decided we needed to make an extra early start.

It was only possible because I needed so much less sleep than humans did. I'd been pushing things on the first leg of the drive back from Chicago, which meant that Brindi had fallen asleep in the car before we'd made it to the hotel. I'd helped her stumble from the car to the hotel room where she collapsed onto the bed and fell asleep even before I got her tucked in under the covers.

I wasn't really surprised that she was still sleeping when I finished showering a few minutes after five a.m. I carried our bags back out to the SUV, and then once it was warmed up enough to be comfortable, I carried Brindi outside and buckled her into the vehicle.

I'd been expecting the journey through the cold morning air to wake her up despite all of my precautions, but she just burrowed down deeper into my arms without ever opening her eyes. A few minutes later we were checked out and on the road.

Brindi stayed asleep for so long I was actually starting to wonder if she was okay by the time we hit the outskirts of Helena. I pulled my eyes away from the road for just long enough to check her over, and found to my surprise that her eyes were open and she was watching me drive.

"I never even heard your breathing change. How long have you been awake?"

"I don't know—it's possible that I'm still dreaming."

"Not unless you make a habit of dreaming with your eyes open."

Brindi stretched and then rearranged the blanket that I'd draped over her. "In that case, I've probably been awake for twenty minutes or so. I couldn't say for sure though because I never really felt like I woke up. I just kind of transitioned from my dream to the real world. I guess my mind just added in details from the real world while I was dreaming because you were driving just like that in my dream too."

I thought she was done talking, and started to reach for the radio, but she reached over and took my hand, eyes closed as she reveled in the feeling of my skin against hers.

"Honestly, I've stopped worrying so much about which parts of my life are dreams and which parts are reality. Things have become so surreal since I met you that it's hard sometimes to believe that this hasn't all just been one epically-long dream that started in that club in Chicago. You're not like anyone else I've ever met, Alec. You turn reality upside down just by existing."

I shrugged uncomfortably. "I'm sorry to drag you away from everyone else again. You've been making good progress lately, and it hasn't gone unnoticed—and not just by me either. Jess, Jasmin, Rachel—they've all mentioned how hard you've been working at limiting your contact with me. The last thing you needed right now was to be thrown back into such close quarters with me. That can't have made things any easier for you."

"Careful, Alec, if you keep this up I'm going to feel like you support my efforts to drain your bank account down to zero. I haven't been doing anything unusual for a girl faced with a hunky guy with money to burn who wanted them out of the way for as much of the day as possible. What girl doesn't like shopping?"

She released my hand, with a visible exercise of will, and leaned back against her door. She seemed happy to leave it at that, but it turned out that I wasn't. Somewhere along the way she'd gone from being an unwanted burden to being a friend.

I still wanted to reconcile with Adri, but I was more and more sorry about the position that Brindi had been put in, and I'd noticed lately that I felt a pang of loss each time she broke off physical contact with me.

"You talk a good game, Brindi, but I've noticed that your shopping trips are remarkably frugal for someone who claims to be trying to deplete my fortune. You'd have to start spending several times as much per day as you currently do if you wanted to actually make a dent in the interest off of the main operating account."

"Yeah, well, shopping is fun and all, but it's not like we can really afford for me to add an extra suitcase full of clothes to my possessions every day."

"Some girls wouldn't let that stop them—there are plenty of places where you could spend two thousand dollars on a sweater if you really wanted to."

For the first time since she'd woken up, Brindi looked away from me. "Some girls, but not me. I've never run in the kind of circles where people would even be able to tell that I'd spent that much money on an article of clothing. I don't need designer—I'm already living like a queen as it is. Besides, it doesn't seem like a very good repayment for everything that you've done for me."

"You mean like addicting you to my touch and then dragging you all across the country from one dangerous situation to another?"

"No, like getting me out of a very dangerous situation by paying off the people I owed a ridiculous amount of money to."

I'd actually forgotten all about that. In my mind things were long past square between us just based on the fact that she'd saved my life in Chicago just minutes after we met. The silence had suddenly become uncomfortable, but luckily we were turning onto the road where we were supposed to be meeting the rest of our group.

I pointed at a pair of forty-foot-long RV's that were parked side by side at a run-down truck stop less than a hundred yards from the interstate. "I think that's us."

"Good—I've needed to pee for the last twenty minutes, but I didn't really want to stop at a gas station. Those RV's look like exactly the solution to my problem. Not all of us have preternaturally-strong bladders."

I rolled my eyes at her and then turned into the truck stop. Brindi disappeared into the closest RV, as James led me over to the other one.

"You have any problems?"

I shook my head. "No—I'll bring you up to speed in a minute, but let's wait until we've got all of the key people in one spot so that I don't have to tell everyone multiple times."

"You're in luck—everyone but Alison's mom is already here."

He wasn't kidding; the RV was standing room only. I looked over all of the people who'd been waiting for Brindi and me to arrive and felt a surge of relief crash through me as I saw that none of them had been killed during the time that we'd been separated.

James, Jack, Alison, Jess, Jasmin, Carson, Rachel—they were all there, and they were the most welcome sight I'd ever seen.

Alison pointed back at the second RV. "I can bring my mom up to speed later if you want—unless you need Brindi to be here for this."

"No, that's fine. Before I get started though I'd like to hear how things in LA ended."

There was a moment as everyone looked around at each other. I'd gone to great lengths in order to stop everyone from getting carried away with the question of who was dominant to whom. It was working because I was so clearly dominant to everyone else, but it did occasionally have some downsides.

"Jack, you were the one taking point on that operation—why don't you go ahead and report on it?"

"Not much to tell. Losing James, Jasmin, Jess and Carson put a real crimp in our operations, but we managed to keep a lid on everything until they could get back. We killed another four vampires and just shy of two dozen gang members who were in deep enough that they'd picked up that odd, almost vampire scent that Addison noticed while she was there."

"So you would say that the problem has been contained?"

He shrugged. "It's hard to say for sure. I think that the gang is in tatters. The fact that we could sniff them out meant that we killed all of the members who were very committed. We destroyed about a million dollars' worth of drugs, and seized another hundred thousand in hard currency. They aren't going to be rebuilding the gang into a force in that area any time soon—at least not without outside help.

"I don't think that we need to worry about the humans finding out about us—not this late in the game—but there isn't any way of knowing for sure if the vampires got a message out to whomever they report to before we wiped out the group that was holding Addison."

I nodded. Out of everything that had happened, I was most worried about whoever was at the top of the organization that was fielding super-vamps in such great numbers. We'd run into two of them in LA, and then killed three more in Minnesota. I'd managed to kill all of the ones that we'd tangled with so far, but it was far from guaranteed that I was going to continue to be able to do so.

I could only be in one place at a time, which was bad enough, but I was even more worried about the sheer level of power that would be required to unite such a powerful group of vampires together. It had been all that I could do to bring down the more powerful of the vampires we'd encountered—what would happen if I faced off against the head vampire and it turned out that he was too powerful for me to use my ability on him?

Not only that, every shape shifter we killed over the course of this war was one less soldier who could be thrown into the fight if the vampires decided to start expanding their operations over onto our shores. It was very possible that I was weakening our race at the precise time we could least afford it.

Someone like Puppeteer could be an invaluable weapon if we suddenly found ourselves awash in ridiculously powerful vampires, but only if he could be counted on not to turn against us at the first sign of weakness. No, we were going to have to eliminate the Coun'hij just as Taggart and I had discussed. Hopefully once all the smoke cleared there would still be enough of us—with powers or otherwise—remaining to stem the tide of the invasion I knew in my bones was headed our way.

I pulled myself back to the present conversation. "Good work all around. Go ahead and split up the money according to the number of days that everyone was involved in containing the problem in LA. A double share goes to Jack as the person running point, but there should still be plenty of money to go around."

It was a small gesture, but it was important to let them see some kind of benefit from all of the fighting and killing they'd just been through.

"Thank you for that report, Jack, everyone is to be commended. I know we didn't fundamentally change the state of things in LA—a lot of innocent people are still going to die there every year—but at least now they are going to be killed by other humans rather than sucked dry by a gang of vampires.

"The long and the short of my most recent trip is that I've found out there's an operation going down outside of Tucson. The Coun'hij is targeting Jaclyn Annikov's pack. My contact thinks that the Coun'hij wants to make an example out of them."

"Thereby scaring all of the smaller packs into lining up behind them."

Jack's words were bitter beyond anything I'd expected out of him. I'd known that he was struggling with having lost so many people in LA, but I'd been hoping that sitting out the Minnesota operation—combined with helping take down what was left of the gang that had kidnapped James' mom—would be enough to help him start to put the loss behind him.

"Yeah, that's the general idea."

"Does your contact have a name?"

The belligerence in Jack's voice was only getting worse. I'd missed something in my response to his report, but I wasn't sure what.

"Yes, my contact has a name, but that information is strictly need-to-know, and none of you need to know."

"I could figure it out, and we both know it, Alec. Brindi probably knows—if not, she at least knows where you went. It wouldn't take much to get that information out of her."

I stood as straight as I could, reaching for every inch of height I could muster. At the same time, I relaxed my grip on the greedy rift at the center of my being. It wasn't enough to actually bring Jack to his knees, but between one second and the next I manifested a tiny, insubstantial black hole just above his navel.

I'd never tried something so tiny before now, but my ability had precisely the effect I'd been hoping for. Jack was suddenly faced by someone nearly as big as him at the same time that a wave of weakness and exhaustion rolled over him.

"I'm sure you could make Brindi talk, Jack, but doing that would be a very big mistake. I'm prepared to admit that I may have gone too far in stopping everyone from establishing a clear dominance hierarchy inside of our group. If you all want to beat the tar out of each other so that you can figure out who is the most deadly, I'm fine with that. I will not, however, stand by while members of my pack are intimidated or tortured. If you want to know something you come and ask me. If I tell you no, then that's the end of it. No bullying Brindi, no pulling mileage readings off of the SUV, none of that."

"I didn't sign up to be part of your pack, Alec. I signed up as an equal partner, not as some kind of subordinate."

"I know, Jack, and I'm sorry if you feel like you've gotten a raw deal out of this, but half of the rebellion's problem is our inability to work together under a central authority. I would give just about anything to bring back your people, but I can't. All I can do is deal with reality as it stands right now."

"Reality."

Jack practically spat the word out, but he hadn't shifted and thrown himself at me yet, so that was better than I'd expected.

"Yes, reality. The reality of our situation is that for the last several weeks you've been eating and sleeping on my dime and giving orders to my people. That isn't a complaint—I'm more than happy to cover your expenses while you're helping me out—but it's past time we stopped pretending that this is some kind of alliance of equals. We moved beyond that when I finally manifested my ability.

"I don't plan on abusing my power, but as long as I'm the one who has to deal with the ultimate consequences of our actions, I should also be the one to be making the decisions."

Everything hung in teetering, shifting balance for several seconds as Jack tried to settle on a course of action. I considered cranking up the strength of the absorption field nested inside of Jack, but dismissed the idea. Reminding Jack exactly why I should be the leader of our little group was reasonable, but beating him down with my power would be a step too far.

I felt odd surges of power flickering across my absorption field. It reminded me a little bit of what I'd experienced the night before when Adri had been trying to find me so that she could pull herself into my dream. It was definitely similar, but there were differences. With Adri, all of the surges had felt like tiny points of heat. This time it was more like the tendrils were coming across from multiple directions. It was like having a mass of cotton candy pressed down on me, cotton candy that melted away as soon as it touched Jack.

Just before Jack made his decision, I realized what was happening. It was Carson. He was trying to influence Jack's emotions, trying to calm him down enough to defuse the tension. It was tempting, but I couldn't let Carson break his oath like that. It would only mask Jack's actual feelings. Besides, there was no guarantee that Carson's ability would take effect quickly enough to offset the surge of energy Jack would feel as I shut my ability down.

I looked Jack in the eye and refused to blink. It was enough—barely.

"Fine, this is your show, Alec. If you want to send us all into some kind of massive trap again and get us killed, I guess that's your prerogative as the alpha."

"You don't have to stay here if you don't want to, Jack. I want you here—I value your knowledge and experience—but I'm not going to force anyone to stay with me who doesn't believe in what we're trying to do. If you stay things aren't going to get any easier. We should start having additional recruits showing up over the next little while, and I want to put you in charge of the wolves.

"You've got a ton of expertise when it comes to taking a group of submissives with no common ties and turning them into an effective force. Just as important, you know how the world works. In addition to training them, you'll be in charge of making sure that none of them are sleeper agents of one kind or another."

I turned to Carson. "I'd like you to take responsibility for the hybrid recruits, Carson. Your ability makes you uniquely suited to keeping a group of dominants from killing each other. I know that you have a certain code of behavior when it comes to using your powers, but it's possible we can think of a solution that will let you help out without violating your personal code."

It was a low blow considering that he'd just finished trying to influence Jack like that, but there was a chance that he didn't know that I knew. If he did realize that I'd short-circuited his attempt to put a finger on the scale, he didn't show it.

"What did you have in mind, Alec?"

"I would propose that we tell the new recruits that you'll be manipulating their emotions. As long as they know at the outset what they are getting into, you won't be doing anything to be ashamed of."

I looked back and forth between the two of them. "What do you think, gentlemen?"

Jack nodded. "Okay, I'm in. Working with younger wolves has always been the part of my job that I enjoyed the most. I suspect some of our recruits are going to be older than I am, but that's okay—most of them will just sail through any training course I could come up with."

Carson was much slower responding, which was a bad sign. Of the two jobs, the one I was trying to hand him was the more difficult proposition. Jack was a hybrid, which meant that he was automatically going to have a leg up on any of his recruits. Sure, he might get some particularly aggressive wolves—someone more like Jasmin than Jess—but by and large they weren't going to cause him a ton of problems.

That wasn't going to be the case for Carson. He was good—maybe the single best fighter I'd ever seen—but his gift didn't necessarily make him a more lethal fighter. He was going to have to stay on top of his charges or he could end up in some kind of dominance challenge.

"I wouldn't hand you any special cases, Carson. I'll deal with anyone who has a combat-oriented ability myself."

That brought a ghost of a smile to Carson's face. "That's actually not what I was thinking about."

"What were you thinking about then—if I may ask?"

I was beginning to think that I'd made a mistake asking him in public like this. I wanted him to say yes, but it was starting to look like this wasn't going to be as open-and-shut a decision as I'd expected it to be. If we couldn't sit down and talk his concerns over because of all of the listening ears then I might not get the response I'd been counting on.

"I was considering whether it is a good idea to trust me with such an important task. My history of carrying out critical missions is not a particularly good one. I—"

I stopped him with a gesture before he could disclose anything that he would later end up regretting.

"I don't care about what happened before we met, Carson. I care about what's happened during the time I've known you. Since we started working together you've been one of the pillars of our success. You were the one who brought Grayson down to our attempted rescue of Agony. Without Grayson, none of us would have survived long enough for Dream Stealer's people to arrive to our aid.

"I was the one who killed the mentalist and the pyromancer in LA, but that would have been all for naught if you hadn't used your ability to lure the rest of the gang into an ambush when they returned to the warehouse. You've taught me how to use the sword I stole from my father, and you provided support and assistance in Minnesota that was critical to our victory there. I need your skills, your experience, and your contacts."

"All three of those things are yours, Alec. They are yours regardless of whether or not I'm in charge of training the hybrids who join your cause. Perhaps it would be best to use me as nothing more than an instructor. Let someone else be in charge."

I shook my head. "I appreciate your willingness to help in a less...glorious fashion, but there isn't anyone else, Carson. We have some good fighters, but anyone I put there will face nothing but a constant stream of challengers. You are the only one I can trust to do this."

Carson sighed. "A long time ago someone much more like you than you would ever have believed said almost the exact same thing to me. I failed that man, Alec. I loved him like a father, and I failed him. If you demand this of me I will do it, but know that I accept with a heavy heart, sure that despite my best efforts I will end up failing you too."

"It's settled then. You'll accept and do your best. It will be enough because that is the kind of man that *you* are, but if it isn't enough then I will make up the difference because that is my job."

I turned and looked at the rest of the people gathered inside of the RV. "Up until now I've been dancing around the question of who was really in charge because I didn't feel qualified to lead all of you. I realized while I was gone that I don't have any other choice. Our culture—our very nature—requires that the best killer among us step up and lead. To do otherwise creates confusion when things get difficult and lives are on the line.

"I've known most of you for years, and I owe all of you a debt that goes beyond money. I hope that you will stay, but if you decide to leave I respect that and you can go without any fear of future reprisals."

I looked around, but all of them met my eyes without any trace of doubt in their countenance. For better or worse, they were now mine. I was going to have to lead and protect them to the best of my ability and just hope that it was enough to keep us alive.

It wasn't the beginning I would have wanted, but it was a beginning—one that I hadn't actually ever expected to see. I spared a moment to wonder where we would eventually end up.

We'd declared war on the Coun'hij, but just tearing the old structure down wasn't going to be enough. We were going to have to replace it with a new form of government, and it was only logical that whoever led the rebellion to its final victory would end up heading the new government.

I knew all of the other major figures in the rebellion. None of them were my equal in power. Some of them had more experience, but if I stood aside for them it would create exactly the kind of problem that I'd been worried about Carson creating if he refused my assignment.

No, that wasn't the answer. I was going to have to unite the entire rebellion under my leadership and just hope that I would be smart enough to keep us all from being outmaneuvered.

None of the earliest records of the monarchy had survived, but in that moment I wondered if this was how Jaldul had felt when he'd begun his bid to create the first monarchy.

Any sense of pride I might have felt was swept away as I met Rachel's eyes and remembered what I still needed to tell her.

"Please split up between the various vehicles. We need to get moving south now in order to ensure we arrive in Arizona in time to make sure nothing happens to the Tucson pack. I'll provide more information about my plan at our next fuel stop, but right now I need to talk to my sister."

Chapter 5

Alec Graves
I-15
Southern Montana

Brindi made it into our RV just before the vehicles started forward. She didn't try to come touch me—she'd had her fix in the SUV earlier—but I felt a weight lift off of my chest at the knowledge that she was close enough to get to me if her withdrawal symptoms suddenly took a turn for the worse.

Rachel followed me into the bedroom at the back of the RV without saying anything. I wasn't sure what I was expecting. Rachel was normally like a puppy that had been given a double dose of lovability. Despite everything that had happened, despite the betrayal of both of our parents, she still rarely had any expression other than a smile on her face.

I'd been dreading having to wipe that joyful look off of her face, but seeing her like this—somber and serious—was almost worse. It took a lot to bring Rachel that low—it didn't seem fair to add to her sorrows.

"Are you okay, Rach? Nobody has been giving you any grief, have they? James and Carson both told me that they would keep an eye on you while I was gone."

"No, nobody has bullied me. I'm just trying to prepare myself for the fact that you called me in here to send me away again."

"What? No, that's not what I wanted to talk to you about at all. Why would you think that?"

"The right question is why *wouldn't* I think that? You kept me at arm's length for weeks while you traveled all over the western hemisphere. First the Cayman islands, then New Mexico, then LA and Minnesota. I thought maybe things were going to be better when you let me help out with the mission to rescue Agony, but that was just a temporary blip. I don't know why I thought things were going to be better when you let me rejoin everyone after Minnesota. You've barely spent any time here at all since I arrived, and now you are here trying to figure out a way to break the bad news to me again.

"Don't try to tell me otherwise, Alec. You may have the rest of the world fooled, but I've known you for my entire life. You get a particular look when you feel like you have to disappoint someone for their own good. You have that look right now."

I shook my head. "I'm not sending you away, Rachel. I mean I probably would be, but now that I've finally manifested my ability this is actually the safest place for you. Before I was trying to keep you away because I knew I couldn't protect you. I'm still not positive that I can deal with everything headed our way, but I think you have a better chance of surviving the next few months *with* me than *without* me.

Rachel gave me a confused look. "I don't understand—if you're not getting ready to ditch me again, what are you so worried about?"

"It's kind of complicated. You know what Dream Stealer and Adri do, right?"

"Yeah. Dream Stealer has been the pack's boogeyman for as long as I can remember. It's honestly been kind of hard to remember that we're all on the same side now. You said that Adri is like Dream Stealer—she can visit people in their dreams too."

"That's right—only with one key difference. Dream Stealer has never been able to do anything more than torture people inside of their dreams. Adri can do more than that, she can actually hold people inside of her dreams—hold them there until they are dead."

"I don't understand what this has to do with me, Alec."

Rachel's expression and scent both gave lie to her words. She knew where I was going, she just didn't want to believe that her suspicions were correct.

"For a long time now Adri hasn't been willing to target people, but that all changed a little while before she lost her parents. When you combine that with the fact that my power makes me the next best thing to unbeatable, we now have a chance to start eliminating the worst of the Coun'hij without having to cut our way through all of the enforcers and half of the loyalist packs in order to get to them."

"You're talking about murder, Alec."

"Are we? Maybe you're right, but I'm having a hard time seeing the difference between killing them in their sleep or hunting them down in the real world. Any human court in the world would have condemned most of the enforcers and all of the Coun'hij to death for even half of what's happened in the last fifteen years. Killing them is going to make the world a better, safer place."

She turned away from me. "You're going to go after Dad first, aren't you?"

"Yes. He's a key member of the Coun'hij and his death will throw them into a state of confusion. We can't even identify half of the members of the Coun'hij. Anyone who's really high up has kept their identity a secret, but there is one person who we know has met every single member of the

Coun'hij. Dad is the key to all of this. We can break him—force him to tell us everything he knows—and then we can kill him and make sure that the Sanctuary pack is too busy trying to work out a new dominance chain to bother us. With a little bit of luck we can remove half of the Coun'hij leadership before the month is out."

"This is a bad idea, Alec. You should start with someone else."

"Why is it a bad idea, Rach? Kaleb tried to sell you to Vincent as a way of securing Brandon's loyalty for another few months. There isn't any good in him—maybe there was at one time, but not anymore—not for years. I don't understand why you keep defending him. Every once in a while it seems like you're going to finally see the truth, but somehow you always end up right back here trying to give him the benefit of the doubt."

She whirled on me and hit me in the arm. It was like being assaulted by a hamster. "You're right, you don't get it. It's true, there isn't any objective reason that I should believe Dad is anything other than evil, but that doesn't change the way I feel. I think there is still something else going on that none of us understand, but this isn't even just about that.

"This is about you, Alec. Killing Dad isn't going to be something that you can just blow off after it happens. It's going to change you, and that scares me more than anything else."

"I've killed before, Rachel. Vampires, werewolves, jaguars, even other wolves and hybrids. This isn't going to be anything new."

"That's where you're wrong, big brother. Before this you've always fought because your back was against the wall. You killed because you had no other choice. This is going to be the first time you go after someone when you don't have to. This is going to be murder and you know it."

Chapter 6

Adriana Paige
The Verdant Canopy Motel
Beaumont, Texas

Things between Taggart and I were back to being strained. He'd been right to yank me up short when I'd torn into Alec, but that didn't make it any easier to deal with. I knew that he was just trying to keep me from saying anything I would end up regretting later, but the truth was that for months now I'd thought that Taggart had my back no matter what.

Finding out that he was as concerned about Alec as he was about me was a slap to the face, one that I hadn't been ready for. It was enough to send me to Nellie in tears, but at least I managed not to break down in front of Taggart.

I was all about small victories these days—they seemed to be the only kind of victories I could manage as of late.

His request that I help him with the attack he and Alec were going to carry out against Kaleb was another bitter pill. It shouldn't have been—I was the one who'd told him I was ready to do whatever was necessary to bring down the Coun'hij—but it was. After spending so long telling me that he didn't want to turn me into a weapon for other people to use, he'd jumped on my first moment of weakness to do exactly that.

I knew that there was a good reason to do what we were going to do—lots of people were going to die if we didn't stop the Coun'hij—but I was still having a hard time with how fast everything was moving.

We'd spent the entire day driving to meet up with Isaac and the rest, which meant that I'd been cooped up in a small space with Cindi and Nellie for hours. Nellie wasn't so bad—she seemed content to let me work things out on my own—but Cindi kept asking me if something was wrong. I was just glad that Taggart had finally agreed to buy a second vehicle. Things would have been really horrific if we'd been all crammed into one vehicle—especially one as small as the ones that Taggart seemed to favor.

I ended up putting in my earbuds and pretending to sleep. I didn't actually sleep though. Either my training had decided to kick in so that I wouldn't get off of my normal sleep schedule, or I was just still freaked out about what I would see if I closed my eyes. I hadn't seen the older, more judgmental version of Alec the night before after I'd left his dream, but it was too soon to be chalking those dreams up to a phase that was dead and gone.

Still, even without sleeping I managed to zone out enough that I lost track of a few hours in there somewhere. I opened my eyes as the car slowed down and I realized that it was getting dark outside.

"What's going on?"

Nellie looked back at me. "I'm getting tired, and we're basically out of gas. Taggart took the last exit and seems to be headed into town looking for a place to spend the night. I'm guessing he's got some kind of dream meetup that he doesn't want to miss out on."

I grimaced, but didn't say anything. I would have told Nellie exactly what we were planning on doing once we fell asleep—talking to her would have helped me work through my feelings—but Taggart had knocked on my door only moments after I woke up and made me promise not to talk about our plans with anyone.

He was probably just being paranoid, but he did have a point about the fact that he and I were going to move to the very top of the Coun'hij's list of enemies once they realized that we were helping Alec take them out one by one in their sleep. It was unlikely that they would be able to track us down—Taggart was very good at staying off the grid—but there was no reason to move forward the time when they figured out that their fellow despots weren't just dying in their sleep from natural causes.

Nellie wasn't a traitor, but if we told her then Cindi and Tristan would know too, and one of them was almost guaranteed to let our secret drop by accident once we got back together with Isaac and the rest. Hopefully Alec was being just as cagey about what was going on with his people.

Nellie yawned and I shook my head at her, but I didn't say anything. Shape shifters didn't generally need as much sleep as us humans, but there were exceptions to every rule, and Nellie seemed to be one of those exceptions. I'd thought about asking her exactly how much sleep she needed every night, but with my luck her need for extra sleep was tied to the fact that she was weaker than most other wolves, and then I'd have offended her over something that didn't matter.

Taggart had agreed to have her along because he'd wanted help defending Tristan, Cindi and me, but Nellie had become way more than just a bodyguard in the last couple of weeks. It wouldn't have mattered to me if she'd been the weakest wolf in the world, she was still the one person other than Taggart that I wasn't sure I could have lived without.

It took us less than an hour to find a hotel and get ourselves situated in our rooms. Taggart and Tristan shared a room—Taggart was too cheap to pay for any more rooms than we absolutely had to have—but Tristan had taken to spending the first few hours in Cindi and Nellie's room. Usually by the time he went to bed, Taggart was already done sleeping for the night.

Nellie supposedly shared a room with Cindi because Cindi knew even less about defending herself than I did, but we all knew it had more to do with the fact that I was a freak who was only half a step away from falling apart at any given minute. We were an odd number, so it wasn't likely that we'd cram down to just two bedrooms anytime soon, but maybe now that I was supposed to be pulling myself together Taggart would suggest different sleeping arrangements.

Cindi would love that idea. She was desperate to share a room with Tristan, but Taggart was pretty old-fashioned when it came to stuff like that. My bet was that Cindi would end up with her own room and Nellie would bunk with me because even a weak wolf was better protection than no wolf at all.

For now though, I was still sleeping by myself because Taggart didn't want to risk anything getting in the way of our mission. I showered in the hopes that it would help me unwind and then pulled on shorts and a tank top before double-checking the lock on the door and setting my pistol on the nightstand next to me.

In the long weeks since my parents had been killed I'd completely stopped wearing it. Maybe that was because I'd associated it with the violence that had killed them, or maybe I'd just been trying to deny the world I now lived in.

I wasn't ready to wear it again—not really—but there wasn't any other choice. The world I shared with Taggart and the rest of the shape shifters was simply too dangerous for me to be walking around unarmed. Like it or not, that gun was a part of my new existence.

I dropped down onto the bed, and was asleep within seconds, and dreaming sooner than I would have liked. The plan was to remain in my normal dreams for a few minutes and then hunt down Alec's dreams so that I could join him there.

It was a valid plan—Alec's dreams were the place where he would have the most control and be most likely able to use his power to immobilize Kaleb—but I suddenly decided that I wasn't going to follow it.

I didn't want to be in Alec's power, I wanted to be here where I had the most control. Without thinking twice, I sat down on the ground and visualized Alec at the same time that I remembered how he made me feel.

Gone were the feelings of security and the kind of breathless crush that rarely survived spending real time with someone. The second part had probably been inevitable ever since the first time we'd met, but I was sad about the change in the first emotion. I liked feeling safe, and the conflicted, guilty dislike that had replaced my feelings of security was a definite change for the worse.

Despite my lack of practice recently, the seeking filaments—threads of pure energy that were spun out of the center of my body—shot out with an ease and speed that were nothing short of remarkable. I would have been worried about how quickly my strength was pouring out of me, but after only a second or two I felt the first of the threads find what it was looking for.

The thread snapped as Alec's ability sheared through it, but I reabsorbed what was left of it, and other threads headed that direction. I lost a few more, and then suddenly one of them hooked onto him and it was time to absorb all of the rest of my filaments.

I poured strength into the line that connected the two of us, and then anchored myself as I pulled on the thread—now a cable—that would guide him directly to me. I expected it to be hard—pulling someone into my dreams was always hard—but this was different.

I'd never pulled Alec to me before this. The one time that we'd shared our dreams had been inside of his world, but I'd expected it to be much the same as pulling anyone else to me.

It wasn't. Alec felt...heavier...than anyone else I'd ever pulled to me. It was like uprooting the Empire State Building. It should have been just as impossible, but here in this place, what I believed was more important than anything else.

I believed—no, I knew—that I was capable of forcing Alec to come to me, and I poured my strength out to make that belief a reality.

By the time Alec hit the invisible wall between our realities, he was moving impossibly fast. Each time I pulled someone into that barrier it felt like I was tearing a hole in reality, but this time I half expected the universe to shatter in protest at what I was trying to do.

It was like trying to shove an elephant one molecule at a time through the world's smallest keyhole, but the momentum that he'd built up before he hit the wall was enough. I once again got the feeling that for one impossibly brief instant—too short even for a shape shifter to register—he was in some kind of in-between place, a place that was nothing more than a sea of light and warm energy.

It happened too quickly for me to get more than a sliver of an impression, and then Alec was sliding into my reality and everything went terribly wrong.

At the very end of him colliding with the wall, I'd felt something that I'd never experienced before. Alec wasn't just an inanimate object being hauled from one place to another, he'd reached out to me and added his strength to mine. I would have welcomed the help but for the fact that I could feel him somehow sliding up against my soul as he came into my reality.

It was hard to explain. I hadn't been really convinced that humans—or shape shifters—had anything you could term a soul until that instant, but there was no arguing with what I felt. I wasn't reading Alec's mind—I didn't get anything as formed as thoughts out of the experience.

I got something though. It was like I was experiencing Alec on a much deeper level than even he realized existed. He felt like a warm, shiny sphere of light. The beauty of him in that form was even more incredible than how he looked in the flesh, but that wasn't what stayed with me the most.

Alec felt good in the way that very few things had ever felt to me before. Touching him reminded me of the love of my dad, my mom when she actually slowed down long enough to remember she was a mother in addition to being a photographer, Cindi when she wasn't too immersed in sibling rivalry, and Taggart.

Nearly everyone was capable of that kind of selfless concern for others, but usually it was restricted to only those closest to them. With Alec I was getting that same feeling, but I couldn't tell if that was because he cared about me or if it was something else entirely.

Part of me was curious about that feeling, about just how selfless Alec was capable of being, but mostly I just wanted distance between us. People were never meant to be that close to each other, to have so many of their most precious illusions stripped away. I knew that I should be excited about the chance to get a look at the real Alec, but I was too busy being worried that he might be getting the same kind of up-close, no-holds-barred look at me.

I finished hauling him into my dream with an expenditure of brute force, and then distanced myself emotionally and mentally as quickly as possible.

"I thought that was you, Adri. What happened? You and Taggart were supposed to come to my dream."

"Change of plans. Had Taggart arrived there at your dream already before I pulled you here?"

Alec shook his head, and for a moment I was nearly overcome by just how amazing he looked. Already my mind was retreating from the memory of the pulsing silver light I'd just experienced—it was like I needed to dive into the physical masterpiece in front of me as a way of forgetting what I'd just experienced.

Alec was taller—something over six feet—and his shoulders if anything had gotten broader since I'd first seen him in his dream so many weeks ago. He'd been big and muscly before, but the rigors of fighting for his life so frequently since then had hardened those muscles in a way that no gym ever could have hoped to.

He was wearing nothing but his ha'bit—the loose stretchy pants that were designed to survive the transition from human to hybrid and back again—which meant that I didn't have to imagine the chiseled abs or the biceps that were as big around as my thigh. His body was nothing less than amazing, but it was his eyes that I couldn't seem to look away from.

I'd always liked blue eyes, but his were stunning—especially against his dark hair. It was like looking into two clear pools that went on forever. I felt a quiver building inside of me as tears started trying to work their way to the surface.

I wanted to throw myself at him again, but unlike the last time we'd seen each other, I wanted to bury my face against his chest and hope that he would wrap his arms around me. Part of me wanted things to be like they were before, but the rest of my emotions were too much of a tangled mess to act on the urge.

Alec would probably do exactly what I was hoping, but it wouldn't be fair to him. Right now I wanted to hug him, but in a few moments I might want to shoot him. The anger and guilt was just too much of a swirling mess, and for once Alec's innate goodness was a liability.

If he'd been the terrible person I kept wanting him to be, then I would be free to hate him and start moving on. Eventually I probably would have even gotten to the point where I realized that what happened with my parents wasn't his fault.

That couldn't happen though because part of me knew that he was one of the best guys I'd ever met. I kept wanting to hate him, but I knew it wasn't fair, which meant that the only person I could hate was me.

My feelings were all screwed up, but I couldn't just cast them aside. I'd tried, but they were with me for better or worse. Until I figured out a way to work through them I was going to have to accept that there wasn't some kind of easy answer that would allow me to just flip a switch and go back to feeling nothing but love for Alec.

"Why did the plan change?"

Alec's question brought me back to the present, and I responded without thinking. "Because I don't want to be alone with you inside of your dreams. If I have to be with you I want it to be here where I have the most control."

He recoiled like I'd slapped him. It was more than just a mistake, it was deliberately hurtful. Alec had never done anything to intentionally harm me. He didn't deserve the venom in my voice, but the fact was that he had hurt me whether he'd meant to or not.

His face went distant and cold. Even Alec wouldn't accept an unending stream of abuse. He was a shape shifter—his beast's anger at how he was being treated would eventually bleed over into all of our interactions and once that happened there wouldn't be any going back.

Maybe that was what I wanted. Maybe I would feel better if he was hurting as badly as I was.

There was no way of knowing what would have happened next if Taggart hadn't shown up right then. He looked back and forth between the two of us, and I could tell that he sensed the tension. I checked my scent, respiration and pulse, but they were all non-existent. Either he was being cued in by something else I was doing or Alec wasn't doing as good a job hiding his unhappiness.

"I guess Adri changed the plan. Are you ready to go, Alec?"

Alec nodded. "Let's get this over with. You still want to try to get the names of the rest of the Coun'hij before we kill him, right?"

"Yes, but only if it doesn't threaten our ability to end his life. That is the most important thing. Killing him will eventually force the others out into the light. Without him to interact with the packs, the Coun'hij won't have any choice but to appoint another of their members to be a spokesperson for them."

"Okay, let's get him here so we can get started."

"Don't you want to double-check that you're still able to use your ability here inside of Adri's dream?"

Alec looked over at me and a wave of weakness suddenly crashed through me. A second later my knees hit the featureless off-white ground of the plain we were standing on.

"It looks like it still works. Let's get started."

I knew I probably deserved that after everything I'd said in the last few minutes, but that didn't stop me from being mad. I bit back half a dozen nasty comebacks, and just closed my eyes to focus on finding Kaleb.

"Are you sure you can do this, Adri? You must have used a lot of energy bringing Alec here..."

"I'll be fine—assuming that the two of you can be quiet for more than twenty seconds at a time."

Taggart probably should have taken me over his knee like the spoiled brat I was acting like, but he just went quiet and a few seconds later I didn't have any other excuses to delay what I knew was going to be an exhausting undertaking.

I took a couple of deep breaths and then focused on the anger I always felt these days when I thought of Alec's dad. To hear Taggart tell it, Kaleb had been the rebellion's greatest hope for several decades. He'd been too cagey to do anything that the Coun'hij could use as an excuse for execution, but all of the smart money had been convinced that he was quietly building a coalition that had a chance of giving the powers that be a run for their money.

He could have created an entirely different world, one where the Coun'hij was overthrown before I entered kindergarten, one where vampires like Jackson were executed by roving bands of wolves, one where the entire continent had been freed of the bloodsucking scourge that cost so many lives each year.

He'd gone against everything good and right in order to expand his personal power. Even with my feelings for Alec being so muddled, it was still easy to grab onto the white-hot anger that I'd used the last time I'd needed to stalk Kaleb inside of his own dreams. He was just that evil.

My seeking tendrils went out and found him without any problems. They drained my strength to the point where it was difficult for me to maintain the initial connection, but I managed to hold onto it until I was able to start reabsorbing the energy from the other tendrils.

Part of me wanted to call the whole thing off. The smart thing would be to tell Taggart and Alec that I'd made a mistake, that we would have to wait until tomorrow, but I was too stubborn for that. I grabbed hold of the invisible link between Kaleb and me, and started pulling on it with everything I had.

It was worse than pulling myself to someone else, worse even than when I'd pulled Taggart into my dreams, but it wasn't as bad as what I'd just experienced with Alec. I got Kaleb up to an unimaginable speed and then just as I felt like I couldn't pull any harder he slammed into the wall between our two realities.

The immovable object and the irresistible force had met yet again, and somehow I managed to find the energy to give one last tug on the cable between us. The universe quivered from the strain of resisting Kaleb's transition, and then the barrier tore and I felt Kaleb go through the in-between space. Unlike Alec, there wasn't any sensation of tugging there with Kaleb. He sailed through the in-between and popped into existence ten feet in front of me.

He was fast. He'd never been pulled into someone else's dream before—it wasn't something that Taggart was capable of—but you wouldn't have been able to tell that based on his response. He spun around and threw himself at me, in a ruthless bid to eliminate the one person capable of keeping him in the dream.

If I'd been nothing more than the human girl I appeared to be I would have died right then. Luckily I now thought and reacted with the suddenness of a shape shifter. Even better, here inside of my own dreams, I could move with the same speed as well.

I threw myself to one side, fighting to get far enough away that he wouldn't be able to reach me with his claws, and then two things happened at once.

Taggart stepped in front of me, placing his body between me and the threat that Kaleb posed, and Alec cut loose with his ability. Neither effort would have been enough to save me without the other. Taggart hardened his skin to something that looked like obsidian, and that turned Kaleb's initial attack, but I saw Kaleb's claws shimmer before my eyes and somehow knew that he'd just done something to make them capable of piercing Taggart's reinforced exterior.

He never got a chance to use them though, because a second later both he and Taggart went down in a boneless heap. I wasn't sure what to expect next, but Alec simply waved me back as he strode forward and grabbed Kaleb's massive hybrid arm with one of his human hands.

No shape shifter could have casually moved so much weight inside of the real world while in human form, but Alec apparently was capable of simultaneously using his power and altering his strength inside of my dream. He hauled Kaleb back several feet, far enough that Taggart was no longer inside the sphere of Alec's power.

"I'll bet you didn't expect that, did you, Dad?"

I could count the number of times where I'd heard Alec refer to Kaleb as his father on one hand with fingers left over. This wasn't like him, but even more unusual was the sheer amount of venom in his tone.

I was still trying to process the abrupt change in Alec's manner when he dropped Kaleb to the ground, shifted forms, and hamstrung him. The brutal savagery took me by surprise—especially since it wasn't going to slow Kaleb down for long. He healed at incredible speeds even in the normal world. Here in the dream he was nearly unkillable.

"Alec! What are you doing?"

I didn't realize it was me who had yelled the words until Alec looked up at me. "I'm testing the limits of his ability here. Taggart indicated that his power is magnified inside of the dream world, but that's based on you guys being inside of his dream rather than him being inside of yours."

As Alec spoke he casually slammed his hand into the right side of his father's chest, collapsing a lung.

"Taggart, anything you can do to counteract his efforts to heal more quickly would be appreciated—I'd do it myself, but I won't be able to maintain my ability, concentrate on that, and torture him all at the same time."

Kaleb laughed—a mocking sound that told me that his lung had already reinflated itself. "I didn't think you had it in you, son."

"You'd be surprised what I have in me, Dad. I should probably be thanking you for that. I spent my entire life scared of you, Brandon, Mallory and a dozen other bullies. It wasn't until you pushed me over the edge that I finally realized I was capable of doing what needed to be done to protect Rachel and stop people like you."

Taggart stepped forward, obviously wanting to edge Alec out of the way, but equally aware that he didn't dare get close enough for Alec's ability to start draining him too.

"Alec, let me do this. You step back and focus just on keeping your ability up and impeding your father's healing. I have more experience at this than you do."

Alec didn't look away from Kaleb, shaking his head as he slammed his claws back into his father's chest again.

"I don't think so—not this time, Dream Stealer. You may have more experience, but I'm never going to have as good an opportunity to learn as I will today. I can do just about anything to Daddy dearest without killing him. Besides, certain things should be kept in the family."

Taggart must have started exerting his will to stop Kaleb's healing because when the other man spoke again I could hear the terrible whistling of a punctured lung.

"It's good to see that you've found your natural home with the world's most dedicated terrorist. I don't suppose that this is his real hybrid form, but who knows—I'll be sure to enter it into our database when I get back to the real world. Who's the lovely specimen over there? She's new."

Alec grabbed his father's arm and slammed his fist against the back of Kaleb's elbow, shattering the joint.

"You don't get to ask the questions here. I want names and descriptions of the rest of the Coun'hij. Let's start with Puppeteer."

Undeterred by the pain he had to have been in, Kaleb flipped himself onto his back and shook his head at Alec.

"You can't honestly imagine that this is going to work. You know that we don't feel pain the same way in this form. I'm not going to tell you anything."

Alec smiled again, and this time the expression made me want to cry. "That's the thing about this place. Your reality here is whatever we want it to be. Make him feel it—make him feel it all."

Without even waiting for any kind of acknowledgment from Taggart, Alec slashed his father across the stomach, and this time Kaleb screamed. Alec didn't even flinch.

"I'll bet that you thought you'd be able to combat that particular change to your nervous system, but I've spent most of the last twenty-four hours thinking about how this needs to go down. Those injuries you're suffering from aren't just designed to hamper your ability to fight, they are also designed to start bleeding away your strength.

"You might be Taggart's equal inside of your own dream, but here I rather suspect that you're not even in the same league. Between the damage your dream body has already sustained and the constant, unrelenting drain of my ability, you're even less of a match for him than you would normally be."

Alec stabbed his father again, and the rage that I'd been conjuring up in an effort to keep Alec at arm's length flickered away—replaced by a growing horror at what he was doing. I wanted to be sick. I'd only *thought* I was ready to watch someone be tortured. The actual experience was so much worse than I'd expected it to be. Even Kaleb didn't deserve this.

Between the collapsed lung and the screams, Kaleb was gasping for air now, but that didn't stop him from spitting at Alec.

"You're still a child. You talk about me not being Dream Stealer's equal, but it's you who's trying to play far outside of your league. With every action and word you betray information that you should never have betrayed. I don't need the girl's name—not when I can return home and have her likeness sketched. I'll have her inside of our facial recognition software before the sun rises.

"You've signed her death warrant, and you've revealed the fact that you've finally manifested your power. I have to say that you're a disappointment in that just like you've been a disappointment in every other way. You have no idea what you're up against—no idea of the stakes we're playing for."

Alec leaned in and raked his claws up his father's left side, razor-sharp edges snicking across ribs. "That's where you're wrong. Maybe this operation didn't have the days of planning behind it that you would have gone in with, but we aren't fools. There is only one reason that we would have allowed you to see any of our faces, only one reason that I would allow you to know that I've manifested an ability. You'll never be leaving here."

Alec must have opened his ability up all of the way—it was the only explanation for what happened next. Between one heartbeat and the next, Kaleb's massive hybrid body expanded outward and then contracted back into his human form.

For the first time I saw fear in Kaleb's eyes. He'd thought Alec's ability was much more limited than it was, but even more importantly, he'd just realized why Alec and Taggart had included me in this operation. I wasn't here just because I could pull him into my dream where he would be fighting at a disadvantage, I was here because the three of us thought that we could eliminate him permanently.

"You're not giving me any incentive to cooperate with you, Alec. If you're really capable of what you're implying, then you're going to kill me no matter what I do or say."

"Of course. The only question is just how much you're going to suffer before I finally allow you to die."

Kaleb smiled through all of the pain, and I instantly realized what he was about to do. His heart stopped beating a split second later.

I considered and discarded the idea of trying to amp up his healing ability—it was too late for that, too late for trying to get information out of him.

"Hold him, Taggart!"

Even as the words left my throat I reached out, pushing him against the ground with an intangible wall of force that I hoped would be enough to keep him from leaving the dream. Taggart joined in, creating a metaphysical wind that quickly ratcheted up to gale force.

"What just happened?"

Alec was the only one of us who didn't understand. Kaleb had stopped fighting Taggart, stopped trying to strengthen his natural regenerative abilities. He'd thrown his efforts the other way, suppressing his body's systems to the point where his organs had all shut down at exactly the same time.

It was inconceivable, the kind of thing that even the most disciplined of minds couldn't have hoped to accomplish by themselves, but Kaleb hadn't been working by himself. He'd had all of Taggart's considerable strength pushing against his inherent desire to live, and Alec's ability had been there to provide whatever other impetus had been needed.

I pushed against Kaleb with my mind, anchoring him to the ground in a desperate effort to keep my identity a secret, but I could feel my strength burning away at a rate that was more than just scary. I'd been so foolish.

I'd allowed my anger to goad me into pulling Alec to me rather than sticking to the plan. That had burned up precious reserves, but then I'd compounded my mistake by not thinking to change my appearance before pulling Kaleb to me. I'd put all of us in danger and now I was too short of strength to rectify my mistake.

I watched the light start to go out of Kaleb's eyes, but it was dying at a slower rate than my energy was being expended. I clawed desperately for the will to remain there in the dream and see to Kaleb's execution.

I'd never wanted anything so bad. Before this there had always been a tiny part of me that had been convinced that if I wanted something badly enough that I could obtain it. This time it didn't matter how much I wanted it. I'd expended too much of my strength—there wasn't anything left with which to fight.

Exhaustion ripped me away from my dream and blackness claimed me.

Chapter 7

Alec Graves
The Caravan RV Park
Tucson, Arizona

Losing our grip on Kaleb had thrown me for more of a loop than I'd expected it to. Even now, two days later, I was having a hard time keeping focused on the task before me.

Really the entire night had been a bust. I'd wanted to reconcile with Adri. I'd actually felt a burst of excitement when she'd first pulled me into her dream and I'd realized that it was just the two of us. I'd thought it was going to be an opportunity to start to work things out. I couldn't have been more wrong.

My anger with her had goaded me into one impulsive action after another. Taggart had been right; I should have allowed him to work Kaleb over for information. I had no experience with that kind of thing, and I'd gone too far. In the real world it wouldn't have been an issue—not up against someone like Kaleb—but we hadn't been operating in the real world.

I'd let too much of our plan drop in an effort to rattle Kaleb, and it had produced exactly the opposite reaction. Despite being in tremendous pain, he'd outthought all three of us and successfully latched onto the one option that gave him a chance of escaping.

If it had been up to me I would have gone after him again the very next day, but Taggart had overruled me. We both understood the danger of letting Kaleb communicate his findings to the rest of the Coun'hij, but in all likelihood he'd done that as soon as he'd awoken the next morning.

Killing Kaleb now wouldn't put that cat back in the bag, and apparently Adri had pushed way too hard in her effort to keep him inside of her dream for long enough to actually kill him. To hear Taggart tell it, Adri would have gladly gone back after Kaleb, but her physical reserves were simply too low.

Denied any form of meaningful action, I'd been left with two recurring thoughts that only grew more disturbing with each passing hour. Kaleb had been right. I'd been in over my head when it had come to our plan to kill him. It hadn't just been the fact that he'd outthought me, either. I'd known that Adri pulling me into her dream was a less optimal course of action and I'd let the mission proceed anyway.

That mistake had cost us our best chance at taking him unawares and getting the information we needed out of him, and it might very well cost dozens or even hundreds of lives before all was said and done. It wasn't the kind of thing any leader could get away with doing on a regular basis. I'd been in over my head inside the dream where we'd had all of the cards. Was I just as outclassed here in the real world?

That thought all by itself would have been enough to keep me up at night, but I was also having a hard time coming to grips with my actions during the dream. We'd needed to get the identities of the rest of the Coun'hij out of Kaleb, and torture had been the only way to accomplish that, but I'd gone to a much darker place than I'd intended on going.

I wanted to build a better world, but if I replaced Kaleb and turned out to be just as bad then I wouldn't be doing my people any service.

Carson, James and the girls had all arrived with me in Arizona more than twenty-four hours earlier, but there wasn't much we could do all by ourselves. I'd detached Jack so that he could begin setting up extraction routes for everyone. He'd taken more than a million dollars in unmarked bills, and his last surviving people with him.

I'd considered sending Alison and her mother out to set up an alternate set of contingency plans, but she just wasn't as good at it as Jack was. Maybe in a few months she'd be up to it, but right now there was too much chance that she would get caught on camera somewhere and end up squarely in the Coun'hij's crosshairs.

Taggart and his group had met up with Isaac's people about the time we'd arrived in Arizona and had finally made it here to Tucson less than an hour ago. We'd already planned out our next course of action using a series of coded texts, so there wasn't any reason for me to linger around our base of operations hoping for a chance to see Adri.

Instead, Carson and I had set out within minutes of Taggart's arrival. We weren't leaving unaccompanied though—Heath was coming along with us. I'd met Heath briefly in Minnesota and been very impressed by the sheer power of his ability. Invisibility was a huge force equalizer, and it was useful in a much broader set of circumstances than Grayson's power.

Unlike Grayson, who was only marginally useful in one-on-one situations, Heath was more than capable of taking out most other hybrids without them even realizing what had hit them. The jury was out on who was the most deadly in a bigger engagement. Heath was limited by the number of people he could keep in his field of view at any one time, and he couldn't do anything about the sound of them moving around or even the sound of their hearts beating, but Grayson was likewise limited with regards to just how many people he could immobilize at one time.

If I'd had to choose between them though, I would have picked Heath. Grayson had proven oddly undependable for someone with the potential to be so lethal. Heath on the other hand was very nearly the perfect second-in-command. He was honest, dependable, and seemed to have no real desire for the top spot.

Even better where I was concerned, I was pretty sure that my absorption field would nullify his ability, which meant that even a change of heart down the road wouldn't be enough to allow him to best me in single combat. Isaac had been incredibly lucky to find Heath. I was eventually going to have to take control of that group—the only question was whether that was going to cause hard feelings on Isaac's part.

It was becoming apparent to me that I was going to need Isaac's counsel if I was going to have any hope of defeating the Coun'hij without getting all of my people killed. I was going to need all the help I could get.

I shoved the latest round of worries to the back of my mind and focused on the task at hand. The three of us were in wolf form, covering ground on four legs at a prodigious rate with Heath at the back of the formation so that he could keep all three of us hidden from observation—satellite or otherwise.

It was a unique experience. Carson and I had to be careful not to make any sudden changes in direction that would result in Heath losing track of us, but after a few problems early on where one of us suddenly materialized back into view, we figured it out and quickly crossed the ten miles between our base of operations and the Annikov estate.

I was more than a little nervous as we approached the house—not that we wouldn't be able to fight our way out if it came to that, but that in doing so we'd ruin the entire operation and end up forced to exercise the extraction protocols that Jack was still trying to get into place. If that happened some of us probably weren't going to be able to fall off of the Coun'hij's radar, but I couldn't continue to wait—not when the Coun'hij might be attacking the Tucson pack at any time.

I probably would have screwed up the infiltration into the house, but luckily Carson stepped up and took point, effortlessly leading us around all of the security. I spared a moment to wonder if his ability extended to more than just manipulating emotions. If he was actually capable of sensing emotions from a distance, then he had an even bigger advantage over most hybrids than I'd realized.

We found an empty room and shifted back to human form, momentarily flickering back into existence as Heath lost his concentration, and then it was time to go invisible again and resume looking for Jaclyn. We found her in a windowless study at the very center of the house. She was talking to a blonde girl who looked like she was in her early twenties.

Jaclyn looked up as we entered the room and then lunged to her feet. I reacted without thinking and opened up the rift inside of me wide enough to drop both of them to the ground as Carson stepped back and closed the door.

I gave Heath a nod, and then we were fully visible. I looked down at Jaclyn and realized that she wasn't just on the ground, she was panting for breath. I'd been so concerned about her response that I'd used almost the full strength of my ability on just the two of them.

"I'm sorry about the circumstances, Jaclyn, but we had to talk to you in a way that wouldn't leave any evidence behind. I'm going to release you now, but if you call out things will go very badly for all of us."

Jaclyn didn't respond until I bottled my ability back up, and even then she pulled herself back to her feet before saying anything.

"Are you really coming here to my territory—my house—and threatening my people? You're no better than your father."

"I don't have to come here and threaten you, Jaclyn. Kaleb and the rest of the Coun'hij already do that just by existing. Will we fight, and even kill, if it comes to it in order to leave here when we're done talking to you? Yes, absolutely, but

I'm not the real threat. The Coun'hij is organizing an operation to wipe your pack off of the face of the map. We're here to *help* you."

She stepped toward me and I held up a hand. "That's close enough. I'm not going to let you close enough to use your ability on me. You can talk from where you are, or you can talk to me from the floor. Your choice."

She shot me a look so full of venom that I half expected her to throw herself at me, but she stopped.

"Fine, let's talk. You're right, you don't have to verbalize any threats because just your presence is enough to bring Kaleb and his murderers down on my people and me. Do you have any idea how hard I've worked over the last hundred and fifty years to stop that from happening? Coming here was beyond reckless, it was an act of war."

She lashed out with surges of energy, flailing me with a hot, prickly wind as her beast punctuated each word with a tangible manifestation of its anger. I wanted to respond in kind, wanted to slam a hurricane of power into her, but that would just result in things continuing to escalate.

Carson had agreed to use his power to get us out of the house without having to kill anyone if it came to that, but he'd steadfastly refused to interfere with the actual negotiations—they were strictly up to me. I had to find a way not to lose my cool.

"Listen to yourself, Jaclyn. You and I believe the same things—we want the same things. We shouldn't be a hairsbreadth away from killing each other, we should be working together to stop Kaleb and the rest. You're one of the single most deadly hybrids in the entire world, but you're forced to bow your head to a bunch of ruthless thugs. We can change that."

She looked me over as the other girl—presumably her daughter Natasha—stepped to her side. "I've never felt anything like that, Mother, he—"

Jaclyn stopped her daughter with a gesture. "He didn't just mistakenly use his ability on us, Tasha. That was a demonstration—something he planned on doing. That is why he's here."

I shook my head. "I didn't mean for things to happen like that. I was hoping to find you by yourself and then just talk to you."

She laughed, a mocking, bitter sound. "You're either stupid or a liar. If you didn't want to come here and make a pointed demonstration of just how powerful your ability is then you would have used other channels to communicate with me. You're here because you want to try to establish the fact that you are dominant to me."

My beast didn't like her tone, and I was losing my grip on him. The power level inside of the room spiked for a moment before I could rein him back in.

"I came here because your pack is under an order of execution. We have only a matter of days—maybe even just hours—before the Coun'hij descends on your territory with a force that you can't hope to match."

"That's a likely story, except that I've heard nothing about any buildup of forces. Let's be honest, once you manifested your power it was only a matter of time before you were going to come here under whatever pretext you could manage. That's how petty dictators always work. Sooner or later you are going to work your way through every pack in North America just so that you can make sure that everyone knows not to cross you."

I shook my head. "Maybe you're right about the necessity of visiting every single pack, but if so it's only because there wouldn't be any other way to actually *talk* to the other alphas. I know exactly how conversations via the normal channels go. They take forever and nothing gets said because neither side is willing to cross any lines that will get them killed if the other person takes the conversation to the Coun'hij."

Jaclyn looked deep into my eyes, almost as though trying to see into my soul. Despite all of the advantages we had when it came to hearing heartbeats and a myriad of other tells, there was still no guarantee that you weren't working with a particularly skilled liar.

"Are you trying to tell me that you aren't planning on setting yourself up as the undisputed leader of the rebellion, Alec? Do you really expect me to believe that you aren't setting yourself up as the next king?"

There it was—the same issue I'd just finished resolving with Jack, the same issue that I was going to have to settle with every single alpha of any pack I wanted to bring over to my forces.

"None of us like to give up our power voluntarily, Jaclyn. For the best of us that's because we're honestly concerned about protecting our people. For the worst of us it's because we enjoy having the power of life and death over our pack. I'm no different than you, I have people who depend on me, people who've risked everything to support me. I'm not going to hand responsibility for them over to someone else lightly."

I could see her response coming, but got the rest of my words out before she managed to interrupt.

"If I meet someone else who's better able to protect my people, someone whose beliefs I respect and who has the integrity to live those beliefs, then I will turn the leadership of my pack over to them, but otherwise I will do everything in my power—every moral thing—to maintain my position, to protect my people, and grow my pack to the point where we don't have to worry about any conceivable external threat."

"That's an easy promise to make for someone who's apparently manifested an unbeatable power."

I gave her a wry smile. "Nothing is unbeatable—as I'm sure you know. I'm very aware of the fact that you're busily brainstorming ways to get around my ability. Your point stands though. I'm unlikely to have to turn over my position any time soon."

"I guess that leaves us at an impasse then, Alec. You're not willing to hand the reins of power over to me, and I'm not willing to turn the lives of my daughter and the rest of my pack over to you...unless you came here to force me to bend my knee to you."

My beast's response would have been a tsunami of power, an unmistakable, resounding yes, but I was more than just the beast that was angrily pacing back and forth inside my mind. It would be so easy to unleash my power once again, to force her back onto the ground, but that wouldn't buy me her allegiance. It wouldn't even buy me control over her pack. It might grant me a temporary illusion of control, but I needed more than that.

"I'm not going to force you, Jaclyn, but it was only weeks ago that I looked you in the eye and told you that I wasn't my father, that I wasn't a monster. You gave me a time and a place and sent me off to a situation that could have gotten me killed. I trusted you enough to go there, and that decision has shaped everything that has happened since in my life. I trusted you, why can't you do the same for me?"

"I'll admit that you surprised me, Alec. I never expected you to go there, and even if I had, it would have been too much to hope that it would cause you to break with your father. Your actions the last time you were down here have bought you some leniency. I'll let you leave here—the way you came—and not report your presence to the Coun'hij, but that's all I can do for you."

"That's worth nothing!"

Tasha grabbed at her mom's arm—a dangerous thing to do considering the energy I could feel humming off of the other woman—but Jaclyn refused to acknowledge her daughter.

"Be careful, Alec, or I'll revoke that indulgence and you'll find out just how much it's actually worth. You went to Naco as a boy with nothing to lose but your own life. Very little has changed. You're still just a boy—now with a shiny new toy—a boy who has nothing to lose. I have everything at stake. Be glad that I'm not willing to turn you over to your father in the hopes of buying myself a few more months of safety."

I stepped towards her, putting myself in range of her claws if she chose to transform, and I cracked open the rift inside of me, bleeding off some of the electricity dancing in the air between us.

"That's where you're wrong. I have everything to lose. My sister, friends who have been my family since even before I first transformed, new friends who have stood beside me in the fires of hell, they are all at stake here. I came down here to offer you a way out, a way to save your people. I suggest you think about that. You've got a limited amount of time before that offer expires."

Chapter 8

Adriana Paige
The Crazy Cactus Motel
Tucson, Arizona

I'd put on nearly five pounds since our failed attempt at assassinating Kaleb. That was really good for less than three days' time, but Taggart still probably wasn't going to let me back in to take another shot at Kaleb tonight. Doing better than expected with regards to adding weight back on didn't do anything to nullify the fact that I'd lost far too much weight in the last attempt. I was starting from almost zero.

It just went to prove once again that I was an idiot. I'd stayed out of the dream world for days, days in which I could have been adding bodyweight like crazy, but instead I'd basically stopped eating. I'd let myself forget about everything else while I was...grieving...and now I—and everyone else in the rebellion—was paying the price.

I was so screwed up that I barely knew whether I was coming or going, and I wasn't sure how to fix myself. It was more than just about my feelings for Alec, but they seemed to be at the very center of the knot that I was having so much trouble unraveling.

The fact that I'd stayed out of sight once we'd arrived was just another example of that. I wasn't a kid—okay, I was a kid, but I was a kid who'd fought vampires and managed to survive. I should have long since been past the point where I needed to hide away from the guy I was supposed to like.

I told myself that again and again, but it didn't seem to be making any kind of difference. I was still hiding out in the room that Taggart had rented for me at the motel that bordered the RV park where Alec's command vehicle was parked. It had been hours since Alec, Carson and Heath had left, but the only time I'd left had been to bolt down some food.

The knock at my door just as it started to get dark shouldn't have come as a surprise, but it still made me jump. I went over and unlocked it expecting to see Nellie, but instead found Tristan waiting for me.

"Hey."

"Hey, can I come in?"

I closed my eyes for a second, trying to come up with a way to avoid what I could sense coming, but my mind had frozen. The silence grew to the point of being awkward, and then I finally stepped back out of the way so that he could enter my room.

"Tristan, I—"

"You don't have to say it, Adri. I already know what you're going to say, but I need you to listen to me anyway. After the…accident I knew you were hurting. I asked you what I could do to help and you told me that you wanted me to be there for Cindi. I've done that. I left you alone just like you wanted, and I've held Cindi's hand every step of the way."

"I know, Tristan, and I'm really grateful to you."

He waited for a second to see if I was going to say anything else, but I couldn't think of anything that wasn't going to make things worse.

"Cindi's getting better, Adri. She still has bad days, but she's well on the way—she's not struggling like you are. She doesn't need me—not like you do."

"No, Tristan, you can't do this right now. You're right, Cindi seems like she's getting better, but that will all evaporate in an instant if you tell her that you're not interested, that you want…"

"She knows, Adri. Every step of the way I've been honest with her. I've been there for her, but I haven't done anything that would make her think we were going to get together. She's great—she has the potential to be really nice, and she's smart and pretty, but she's not you. You don't need anyone else to help bring the good out in you—it's just there, all the time. It's who you are, and that's the most amazing thing anyone could ask for in a girlfriend."

Tears were starting to pool in the corner of my eyes, but I couldn't have said whether it was frustration over having to deal with Tristan, or unhappiness that I'd done so much to prove him wrong over the last few days. I wasn't good or nice, I was a vindictive witch.

"Tristan, you obviously don't understand girls. It doesn't matter how many times you tell her that you only think of her as a friend, or that you want things to always stay just the way they are. She's heard all of that, but she's got her hopes pinned to the idea that someday your feelings are going to change. If you tell her you want to start dating me, she's going to lose it. You'll ruin everything."

Tristan looked like he wanted to get angry, but he just shrugged. "So just like that the matter is closed? Maybe you're right, maybe I don't understand much about girls, but you've got a pretty sizable blind spot yourself, Adri. You refusing to date me isn't going to make me fall madly in love with Cindi. I've stayed here because I wanted another chance with you. If that's never going to happen—if you're never going to give me the time of day—then just tell me now. It will be better for us all."

"I...I don't know what to think anymore, Tristan. For the longest time I thought you were a complete jerk. This isn't the first time that you've led Cindi on, but I guess it's the first time that you've done it at my request. If I still thought that you were that same guy who was playing with her emotions as a way to get at me then I'd be able to tell you that there is no way we could ever be together."

"I'm not that guy, Adri. I never was—not really. Maybe I did some stupid stuff and listened to the wrong advice, but I never wanted Cindi to get hurt—not any more than she deserved. You don't know how hard it was for me to just stand back and watch her scheme against you."

I nodded choppily. "I can imagine. You're right, that wasn't her finest hour, and maybe this is the price that she has to pay for giving into all of the petty jealousy that was so much a part of the cheer squad. You're also right that you aren't that guy. You've done stuff I never would have believed possible for that guy. You fought a vampire for me and then you helped me kidnap a police officer and came with me to rescue my family. I owe you a lot, Tristan—more than I can ever repay."

"I don't want you to repay anything, Adri. You either feel something for me or you don't. It's that simple."

"I...I just don't know. I think I want to. You've turned out to be pretty amazing and if things were different I think we could be good together. If I'd been born without this crazy power maybe we could have made a life together, but I just can't see any way for that to be the case now."

Tristan looked away from me and sighed. "It's Alec, isn't it? I was starting to think that maybe you were ready to move on from him and let someone else into your life."

I shrugged, lips trembling from the effort of trying not to just break down in sobs. "I guess it is Alec. I want to be ready to move on, Tristan. I can't look at him without being thrown back into that building. I don't remember very much of what happened. All I get are bits of memory, the machinery falling, shooting vampires, the complete sense of powerlessness, but it's still too much. I can't deal with him, but I can't seem to just cut ties completely. I've done and said such terrible things lately. I'm not sure that he's ever going to want me back."

"If you're still feeling like that, then you need to go talk to him, Adri. Maybe you're right. Maybe there isn't going to be any coming back from what's happened—for either of you—but maybe it's not too late. All you can do is go talk to him. Tell him how you feel."

"I don't see the point. It's not like he can change the past or magically make my feelings disappear."

"The point is starting the dialogue. I want you and me to be together, Adri, but there's no point in even trying for that right now—not when you're still so caught up in your issues with him."

"I don't mean to string you along, Tristan. If you need to go, then you should go. I'll get Taggart to give you some money. It's not going to be enough to replace what you probably lost when your parents disowned you, but it will give you a start. It's not going to solve any of our problems, but maybe you're right that it's time for Cindi to try going forward without you. It will be a lot easier for her if you just leave than if you end up with me."

"I don't want to hurt Cindi, but I'm not going to sacrifice my happiness for hers, Adri, not if there's still a chance for us. I won't leave—not yet—but I'm not going to stay around forever. Go talk to Alec and figure out if there's even a chance for the two of you. When you're done talking to him, you and I can talk."

Chapter 9

Alec Graves
The Caravan RV Park
Tucson, Arizona

I arrived back at the location where we'd set up in a bad mood, but at least the run back had let me work off the worst of my anger. It gave me time to think, time to decide on a course of action. By the time we got back, I knew what I was going to do.

I clasped Heath on the shoulder, thanking him for helping us get in and out of Jaclyn's house, and then released him to go back to his people. Carson followed me into the command RV.

"What are you going to do, Alec? I can see by the set of your jaw that you have a plan."

"How are your negotiations with Grayson coming along?"

Carson shook his head. "I'm not sure. He's being evasive. I'm not sure if he's ashamed of his failure when Brandon's people arrived during the rescue attempt, or if he feels that his debt to me has been satisfied. Either way, he's been slow to commit."

I wanted to slam my hand into the countertop next to the sink, but I knew I'd probably crack it if I did. I needed to control myself if I was going to control the situation we were in.

"I need him, Carson. Heath is good, but he's not our guy. I need someone else other than me who has the ability to incapacitate large groups of hybrids if that's what Kaleb and the rest send down to take out the Tucson pack."

Carson refused to meet my gaze for several seconds, but I'd learned to just wait him out. Carson wasn't capable of avoiding the truth for very long. It was part of what made him so valuable.

"I no longer have confidence that I can bring him over to our cause in the time we have left, but there is another option. If you call him directly it may be enough to bring him here."

"I don't understand. I've met him only once, and even that was just a passing encounter—I maybe said all of ten words to him before the rescue operation commenced, and once everything fell apart there wasn't time for proper goodbyes. If you—who've known him for years—can't convince him, then how am I supposed to do it?"

Carson sighed. "I'm sorry, Alec. I wish I could tell you more, but I can't. Even saying this much comes perilously close to breaking an oath I swore years ago. All I can say is that he may listen to you—Grayson is...old-fashioned."

"Fine, text him so he knows I'm calling, and then give me his number and I'll call him right now."

Less than a minute later I was dialing his number from my burner phone.

"Hello."

Grayson's voice sounded different than I remembered, but I couldn't put my finger on what it was.

"Hello. Our mutual acquaintance told you who I am?"

He'd answered the phone without any distortion to his voice, but I didn't have that option. My phone was running a voice-scrambling program that Jack had provided me. I was too much of a known entity. We didn't think that the Coun'hij had managed widespread penetration of the cell companies, but there was no way to be sure, and if they had, then they would be running voice recognition software on all of the calls they could get their digital hands on.

"Yes, he warned me you would be calling."

I wanted to take a deep breath, but I forced myself not to. I needed to sound like I was in control.

"If you know who I am, then you know what I want. Our friend has been asking for your help, but you've been slow to respond. Now I'm the one who's asking."

"What makes you think that my response to you is going to be any different than my response to him?"

There was an edge to his voice now, but I was almost certain that he was testing me, trying to figure out what Carson had told me, trying to figure out if Carson had violated his oath.

"You answered my phone call—that's a good start. Honestly, I don't have any reason to think that you're going to agree to help me. I don't know very much about you at all, but what I do know tells me that I need you here at my side. I know that you can do things, things that nobody else can do. I know that without your help we never would have made it through the first wave back in New Mexico. We might have won still, but when our enemies dropped out of the sky there wouldn't have been enough of us left to put up an effective resistance.

"Some of my people are probably angry that you didn't stop the second batch. Some of them probably thought that you failed. I'm not them. I'm smart enough to know that not every tool can be used in every situation, and that you can't push anyone past their limits. You did what we needed—what *I* needed—you to do. If you'd been able to deal with the second group that would have been great, but it was my failure that put you in a place where too much depended on you.

"I know that you feel like you failed at some point in the past. I don't know any of the details, but you wouldn't have come to help Carson last time if you didn't feel like you owed him something."

Grayson let silence fill the line for several seconds before he finally responded. "You seem to think that you know an awful lot."

"Maybe, maybe not. I'm building guesswork on top of supposition here, but I'm doing it because I need you. The people we lost last time were on me. Their deaths were my fault because I went ahead with the operation despite knowing that we didn't have enough people to cover all of the contingencies. I need you here because I don't want to repeat that mistake.

"There have been other...developments...since the last time I saw you. I can keep my people safe from most of what I can see coming our direction, but I need people I can trust to back me up in case I get caught off guard again."

"You almost had me." Grayson's voice was bitter. "You were doing so well—right up until you said that. The whole point is that you can't trust me. We're done here."

"I'm offering you redemption! This is your chance. Maybe you won't earn it this time, maybe you won't earn it next time, but eventually you're going to be the deciding factor on one of the battles we're headed into. Every time you save one of my people you're buying yourself redemption.

I'm the only one who can offer it to you, and this is the only time I'm going to make the offer."

I couldn't have said for sure where the words came from—they'd just felt right—but they got through to Grayson at least enough to stop him from hanging up on me. He wasn't saying anything, but I could still hear him breathing on the other end of the line.

"Fine. I'll be there in six hours."

"That's not possible. I want you here, but I want you to travel safely—this all falls apart if they track you here."

"They won't track me. Our mutual acquaintance isn't the only one who can call in favors. I'll be on a plane within the hour and nobody will ever know I was on it. Text me the address where you want to meet."

I looked at the phone for several seconds after he hung up.

"How did you know that was going to work, Carson?"

"I didn't. I wasn't sure it was possible, but you said exactly the right things to him. You couldn't have done better if I'd coached you beforehand. I'll text Grayson our location using a cypher that he's familiar with. What do you want me to do after that?"

"Can you please talk to all of the rest of our people and let them know that they need to be ready to go at a moment's notice? I want people sleeping in shifts, and I want them all well-rested."

"You're not planning on leaving after your deadline to Jaclyn expires, are you?"

"No, I'm not. We aren't going to get a better chance than this, Carson. We may not be able to convince Jaclyn that she's about to be attacked, but we can make sure that we're near enough to hit the Coun'hij's forces just minutes after they attack the Tucson pack. There's still no guarantee that we'll be able to save any of her people, but we can make sure that the Coun'hij loses every enforcer it sends after her.

"We're going to lay a trap, and then once we've killed the Coun'hij, we're going to send photos and video to every single pack in North America. They all need to know that the Coun'hij isn't playing by its own rules anymore, and they need to know that we're the ones who can save them."

Carson nodded. "I'll talk to our people, and then I'll go find Isaac and get his buy-in as well. What are you going to be doing?"

I held up my phone. "I'm going to be securing the other half of our trap."

I waited until Carson was gone and then activated two more privacy boxes before dialing Shawn's latest number.

"Is this the friend who threatened to rip down my door?"

"Yes—you should get your electrical system re-inspected so that our next meeting doesn't have to be so adversarial."

Now that we both knew who we were dealing with despite the masking programs running on our phones, Shawn laughed.

"I'd say it's good to hear your voice, but under the circumstances that's neither accurate nor appropriate. How are things going down there?"

"We talked to the target. Nobody saw us arrive or leave, so if there's a leak it has to come from her or her daughter. She doesn't believe that the threat I told her about is real. What can you do to send your evidence her way?"

Shawn was silent for several seconds. "There are a number of things I could do, but my dad isn't going to agree to any of them. It was all I could do to get him to agree to come out into the open with you. He's never going to agree to blow our cover with our friend from the border."

I smiled, a cold, humorless expression, because I knew it would help the emotions behind it make it into my voice even despite the masking.

"I came down here on nothing more than faith. I want to trust you, but you've played your hand as far as it can go without you putting more skin in the game. You say you want to help, but so far all you've done is send me and my people into what could be a gigantic trap. You're going to have to do better than that. Either get that intelligence over to our favorite headstrong female, or give me another sign of your commitment to the cause."

Shawn was slow to respond, but even so I could tell by his voice that he wasn't surprised by my demand. "What did you have in mind?"

"I want more bodies down here, but I don't want just any bodies. You said that your dad's best people all report directly to you. Send them—the best of them—down here where they can help out if we run into a group that I can't deal with by myself."

"Okay, it's a deal. I'll have eight of them down there before tomorrow morning. Believe it or not, I was actually considering suggesting something like that to you already. We're getting reports of...hoover...activity down there."

Hoover was code for vacuum, which was what we shape shifters called werewolves. Shawn sounded like he thought the negotiations were all over, and we were headed into the closing pleasantries, but I wasn't done.

"I want your bodyguard on that plane. She comes too, or the deal is off."

"I can't do that. My father will never agree to leaving me uncovered."

"Then don't ask him."

I'd nearly decided that Shawn wasn't going to go for it when he finally responded.

"How did you find out? We've done everything conceivable to keep her ability a secret."

"Call it a hunch. The first time we met she reacted even before the lights went out. Add in the fact that your dad wouldn't let anyone but the best serve as your bodyguard, and it was obvious she had to be exceptional in some form or fashion."

"She's not your equal. She can't wipe out dozens of people all at once."

"That's okay, I've got plenty of those kinds of weapons. I need something that can go toe-to-toe with any one single foe and come out on top."

"She's your girl then. She'll be on the plane—just know that my dad is going to make things unpleasant for you at some point down the road as a result."

"I'd expect nothing less."

I hung up on Shawn and turned to go back outside, but a knock on the door pulled me up short before I could take more than a step or two.

Adri looked up at me as the door opened, and I was suddenly incredibly grateful that this meeting wasn't happening inside of a dream. I could smell her here, could hear her heart racing. There was still no guarantee, but out here I at least had a chance of getting through to her—assuming I still wanted to.

I examined my feelings as she climbed up the stairs, and found that I still wanted to patch things up between us. More than just me, my beast seemed to want it too. With anyone else who had caused us so much grief he would have been a growling, crackling ball of anger, but he was remarkably quiet right then.

"I can come back if this is a bad time…"

"No, your timing is fine. I just finished the two most important calls that I'm going to make all week. I was just headed back outside to check on my people, but it's nothing that Carson can't take care of."

She nodded hesitantly, as though unsure if she was happy that I had time to talk rather than just brushing her off. I could feel her nervousness, smell her worry. I wanted to reach out to her, but I didn't know what to say, didn't know what might save her or what might set her off.

"They went well? Your calls, I mean."

"Yes. The first one got me exactly what I wanted, without any subterfuge. The second one required asking for something I knew I wouldn't get in order to get what I actually wanted, but in the end I got the assistance we need, and the other party seems happy still."

"Is it hard to play those kinds of games?"

I nodded. "I'd give a lot not to have to play them, but right now it's the only way to get us what we need. There are dozens of packs scattered all across North America, and all of them are scared of the Coun'hij, all of them are worried about making the wrong call and giving up their power to someone who will get their people killed. I have no choice but to unite them in any way possible. Maybe once the Coun'hij is gone there will be a chance to destroy the old order and create something that has a chance of letting us trust each other. Right now everyone is too scared."

"You seem awfully sure of that."

"I am. I know that they are scared because I'm scared. Being a hybrid—being an alpha—doesn't mean that you're not scared, it just means that you have to find a way to function around the fear."

"What are you scared of, Alec?"

"I'm scared of letting everyone down. I'm scared of making the wrong decision and putting us in a position where even my power isn't strong enough to get us out alive. I worry that this fight is one that we can't win, and most of all, I worry that I'll end up becoming my father."

She shook her head. "That's not possible. From everything I've seen, you're nothing like your dad."

I shrugged. "From what people have told me, my dad didn't used to be like this. There's no way of telling what will happen to me with the passage of enough time."

"It's not going to happen, Alec. You're too good for that."

She was becoming a better liar than the girl I remembered from my dreams, the girl who had come to me wondering whether it would be safe to trust Dream Stealer with the secret of her identity. If she'd been dealing with someone else she probably could have gotten away with her most recent lie, but I could hear the falsehood in a dozen different ways.

"Once upon a time I think you probably believed that, Adri. You're not so sure now, are you?"

For a moment I thought that I'd gone too far. She looked up at me with anger flashing in her eyes, but somehow she brought it back under control.

"You're right. I'm not as sure as I was once upon a time. I saw you do things to your father that I never expected out of you. The guy I met so many weeks ago couldn't have tortured anyone—not even a monster like Kaleb."

Part of me wanted to respond with anger. My beast even seemed to be waking up and getting into the game, but I clamped down on him and forced my voice to remain even.

"I did what had to be done, Adri. I didn't enjoy it, and I would have gladly taken another course if I thought one existed, but I didn't see any other way, so I took the only route that offered me a chance to keep my people safe."

"I'm not questioning your intentions, Alec, just the results."

We weren't just talking about me torturing Kaleb anymore, this was about her parents.

"I'm sorry for how things turned out with your parents, Adri. I've thought about every single choice I made that day. I've reviewed each of them at least a hundred times, and there are a host of things that I would have done differently in hindsight.

"If I'd known that my power was going to fully manifest that day, I would have taken one or two wolves to watch my back and gone in after your parents while you and everyone else went after Cindi. I could have stopped that vampire from ever raising that piece of machinery above your mom and dad's heads, and you guys would have outnumbered the bad guys holding Cindi by such a big margin that you would have easily been able to free her.

"If I'd known exactly what we were up against—and known that I could easily neutralize the biggest threat—then everything would have been straightforward, but I didn't and it wasn't. I don't know what to say or do to make things better between us."

I'd been able to smell Adri's mounting distress as I'd been talking, but I was still surprised to find tears running down her face. Somehow my mental picture of Adri didn't include someone who could cry silently like that. To me she'd always been the tough-as-nails fighter who'd saved me from Brandon.

"I know that there isn't anything you could have done differently, Alec. You didn't know that we were up against two of the most powerful vampires that any of your people ever remember hearing about. You didn't know that we were going to be frozen in place by her powers, helpless as she started executing us, and you didn't know when you came through that door and neutralized her power that she had twenty tons of machinery dangling above my parents.

"You saved Cindi, which is more than I had any right to expect, and you saved the rest of us. Nobody else in the world could have managed even one of those feats, and the really amazing part is that you were willing to sacrifice your life to make that happen."

I opened my mouth to tell her that she didn't have to thank me again, but she talked over the top of me.

"I'm grateful for what you did, Alec, but you had no right to keep me in the dark like that. If you wanted to offer to risk your life in a single-handed rescue attempt that would have been fine, but you were supposed to offer instead of just making the decision for me.

"You have no idea how conflicted I am right now. It was my responsibility to choose which members of my family lived and died, but you took that away from me. I understand why you did it, but that doesn't make it right."

"I was trying to save you from the guilt of having to choose between them, Adri. I've seen that kind of guilt before, and it would have destroyed you."

"Maybe it would have, but at least then it would have been my choice. I would have felt the guilt, and it would have been on me to deal with it, just like it had been on me to make the choice in the first place. Instead you made that choice and I'm left with an impossible mixture of anger at you for doing so—and getting my parents killed—at the same time that I'm trying to sort out the gratitude I'm feeling for you at having saved Cindi and guilt over the fact that you went into that building fully intending on dying. How am I supposed to process all of that, Alec? You were ready to lay your life down for me. Not even to save my life, just to spare me from making a hard decision."

"I'm sorry, I never meant to add to your difficulties."

"Didn't you? If everything had been different and you died failing to save Cindi while the rest of us succeeded in saving my parents, it wouldn't have changed any of my feelings. I would still be tangled up in gratitude and guilt. The only difference is that you wouldn't be around to watch me try to work through it all."

"I'm sorry, Adri. You're right, I never thought about the other side of the coin, never considered just how hard it would be for you to be whipsawed back and forth between those particular feelings."

It pained me to make that admission, but I made it because it was the truth and because it was what I thought Adri needed to hear, but she wasn't done.

"You didn't respect me, Alec. You probably still don't, but I know for certain that you didn't in that moment when you decided to take away my choices. If you'd really respected me then you would have let me choose. It's what everyone else does. Taggart, Isaac, Heath, they all trust me to recognize when I need to lean on them for help making a decision. You, on the other hand, didn't.

"I don't know where things are headed between us right now. I don't know if I'll ever be able to work through everything I'm feeling right now, but I do know that I can't see myself ever being with someone who doesn't look at me as an equal partner."

She turned to go, but I captured her wrist. "You don't get to yell at me like that and then run off without hearing my response—not if you want to be treated like a strong individual who can make her own decisions."

I hadn't grabbed her with a strong enough grip that she couldn't break free if she'd wanted to, and for a second that was exactly what I thought she was going to do, but then my words sank in and she nodded.

"Fine. If you want to have a chance to respond then you can."

"You're right, I didn't treat you like you were capable of making your own decision, and now that you've pointed that out to me I'm even angrier at myself for how things went down. What I did to you was exactly the kind of thing that everyone else in my life did for years until I took Rachel and ran away from home. That wasn't fair to you, any more than it was fair to me. You're the one who was going to have to bear the cost of whatever we decided to do about your parents, and it was only fair that you pick what we did there."

Her eyes started to soften, and I took hope that my admission would gain me enough credit with her to get me through the rest of what needed to be said.

"What I did was wrong, but I did it because, at the time, I thought it was a way of taking the worst of those consequences and putting them on me. I understand now that it wasn't my place to do that, but I'm not working in a vacuum, Adri. I make decisions every day that have the potential to cost people their lives, and that is only going to get worse now that I've manifested my ability.

"I don't have any equals outside of that door—not with regards to raw power, not now. Even before, true equals were very few and far between. I respected Carson and Isaac, just like I respected many of the rest of my friends, but for weeks now I've been the alpha of my pack and one of the key players in our alliance. Respecting those people doesn't mean that I don't keep secrets from them. I have to keep secrets or even more people would die."

She frowned, eyes flashing. "I wasn't just an associate, Alec. I was…"

"What you were to me is exactly the question. I cared about you, but that is true of many people. We never defined what we were to each other—every time we tried something came along and upended everything. As my girlfriend you would have had the right to know things that the rest of my people didn't know, but I haven't been sure of your feelings toward me for weeks now. For every step forward we take, we take at least two more either to the side or backwards."

She ripped her arm away, but she didn't turn to go. "This is a lousy time to be pressing me to make a stronger commitment to you, Alec."

"That's not what I'm trying to do. I've acknowledged the validity of your position, and now I want you to understand where I'm coming from. My emotions going into the decision to save Cindi were a snarled mess too. It's a lot harder to separate our relationship as 'coworkers' from all of the personal stuff. I'm sorry for not giving you all of the relevant information before you had to decide what to do with Cindi, and I'm trying to meet you halfway."

"I understand, Alec. Like I said, I've never doubted your intentions, just how things end up as a result."

"I know that now is a bad time for you, Adri, but it's bad for me too. I've got a lot going on, and if I make the wrong choices none of us are going to survive to learn from my mistakes. If you know right now that you're never going to be able to forgive me, then just say so and release me from having to constantly worry about trying to make things right between us."

She took a deep breath and stepped into me and wrapped her arms around me.

"I don't know for sure either way, Alec. I wish I did, but all I can do is continue to try to work through things. Thank you for bringing Cindi back to me."

I returned her hug like she was a porcelain doll. It wasn't the same kind of hug as what we'd shared in Minnesota, but it was a start.

Interlude

Coun'hij Agent
Caravan RV Park
Tucson, Arizona

The being was walking across a parking lot when it happened. Puppeteer's presence had been a near-constant distraction in the back of the being's head for decades now, but every so often the jumped-up mongrel tried to take more direct control over the reins.

The being never liked that, but it was even worse at times like this, times when the being was in public. Puppeteer was capable of exerting control over individuals like the being over distances of hundreds of miles, but he would never be capable of doing so while accessing the being's more unique abilities. Puppeteer had tried dozens of times, but it was like watching a blindfolded child try to replicate a Picasso using nothing more than their feet. The hybrid simply didn't have the control or finesse required.

The being was grateful for that fact—it was the only thing that kept it from complete enslavement to Puppeteer. The hybrid knew that the being's abilities were too precious to be wasted on brute-force search-and-destroy missions, so the being was allowed a much greater degree of latitude than the rest of its captured fellows.

Not all of them had been captured, but many of them had been, and none of them were happy about it. The only thing that made their servitude tolerable was that Puppeteer's existence was no more than a speck on the continuum of their long lives. Eventually Puppeteer would die—of old age if for no other reason—and they would be free to go back to doing what they did best.

Puppeteer's presence inside the being's mind made it stumble, but even more concerning, it made the being's seeming—its illusion in the modern parlance—flicker. The being's lips drew back in a snarl. It didn't want to have its cover ruined. Puppeteer was very good at placing the being in situations where it could feed, but the meal it had been dining on these last several weeks had been a masterpiece of sorrow. It was a meal that wouldn't be easily replaced.

The insignificant wolves around the being were unlikely to be able to kill the being—even if they realized what it was—but the being wasn't anywhere near ready to give up its current food source.

What do you want?

A report. You haven't checked in since before you left your last location. I wouldn't even know that you'd moved if not for the fact that I can feel your position.

There is nothing to report. All is as you indicated it would be. I have continued to plant the seeds we discussed, and now just await your order to bring them to fruition. Besides, reporting has become more dangerous given my current surroundings.

I thought you weren't scared of my kind.

I'm not, but despite their inability to kill me, them finding my communications to you would be...inconvenient.

Very well. You have permission to implement the next stage of my plan. Make them wish that they'd never been born.

The being smiled as Puppeteer's influence receded back to the furthest reaches of its mind. This was going to be particularly enjoyable.

Chapter 10

Alec Graves
The Socorro Motel
Tucson, Arizona

Grayson was just as good as his word. He arrived within hours of our phone call, and then after reporting in to me, he retreated to one of the spare rooms we'd rented in the motel and went to sleep.

He was an odd individual, but it went beyond this taciturn manner. He seemed made up of intense flashes of emotions that disappeared as quickly as they arrived. Given just how useful his power made him, I was more than ready to overlook that particular oddity though—especially with how rare it was for him to let his flashes of emotion override his normal, steady manner.

Grayson had been the easy part of the last twenty-four hours. I'd made no secret of our efforts to bring him on board, so there was no reason to conceal his arrival from any of our people. Vicki and the rest of Shawn's people were a whole different matter.

Shawn hadn't explicitly told me that our alliance would be over if I allowed the rest of my people to know that Vicki and the rest of her fellows were in town, but the implication was clear. In one sense, the individuals who'd flown here from Chicago were completely expendable. If it became common knowledge that they'd taken part in my efforts against the Coun'hij, then Ulrich—and even Shawn—could disavow their actions, but I knew full well that neither of the top dogs in Chicago wanted to lose the services of so many hybrids all at once. They especially didn't want to lose Vicki—which was a big part of the reason that I'd asked for her.

I didn't like leaving the rest of my people all by themselves, but once I received a text from Shawn indicating that his people had arrived, I slipped away from my RV and drove over to the motel where Vicki and the rest had set up shop. It was less than three miles from where my command RV was parked, but that didn't provide a terrible amount of reassurance—not given just how much could go wrong in the slightly less than ten minutes it would take me to cross the distance back to my people.

Vicki met me at the door to my SUV, appearing out of the darkness like she'd teleported there.

"That's quite the trick—are you going to tell me how you do it?"

She shook her head at me, obviously biting her tongue, but that didn't do anything to hide her scent, which made sure that I knew just exactly how unhappy she was to be there.

"My brief didn't include anything about revealing the secrets of my pack, Mr. Graves. I've been commanded to come down here and assist you, and that's exactly what I'll do, but I won't go one millimeter beyond what is specified in my brief."

"Okay, maybe it would be helpful to understand what's included in your brief—you know, just so that we can avoid any misunderstandings."

"I brought along a complete copy of our intelligence briefs and current force estimates for the area. I'm to provide you with that information and then serve as your bodyguard as much as is possible while remaining out of sight where your people are concerned. In extreme situations I'm allowed to reveal myself and the presence of my people if it is required in order to preserve your life, but other than that, I'm to maintain my pack's official position of neutrality."

"Thank you, that's very helpful. I have to admit that is about what I expected. I'm not going to lie and say that it doesn't complicate things for me, but at this point I don't have any other choice but to accept Shawn's terms. Can I see those intelligence files?"

Vicki nodded. "Right this way."

I followed her into her motel room and started thumbing through the thick stack of paper that she handed me. It took me less than five minutes to find what I was looking for. The file on the estimated positions and numbers of werewolves in the area was just as detailed as the information I was used to receiving from Jack. I read through the file twice, matched it up with the map of the area that I was carrying around inside of my head, and then dropped the file on Vicki's bed.

"Okay, we'd best be going if we want to finish up and get me back to my people before sunrise."

"What are you talking about? I need to get you back to your people now and then take up a position close enough nearby that I will be able to intervene if something happens."

I cocked my head to one side. "Is this the first time that you've been loaned out as executive protection?"

"No. It doesn't happen often—Ulrich doesn't like to leave Shawn uncovered—but it has happened a couple of times before."

"Great—that means that you've got a clear playbook that you're operating from. I'd ask you if you're prohibited from assaulting your principal, but it actually doesn't matter because I could drop you where you stand without even working up a sweat."

"You could try, but not even you are unbeatable, Mr. Graves. I'm unlike anyone you've ever faced off against before now."

Nearly any other shape shifter—hybrid or wolf—would have taken my words as a sign that I was getting ready to fight them, but Vicki seemed completely relaxed. I smiled at her, and then stepped backwards as I cracked open the cover over the miniature black hole that I carried around inside of me.

It wasn't enough to force her to the ground—it probably wasn't even enough for her to feel—but it had exactly the effect I'd been hoping for.

"What did you just do?"

Vicki's yell was that of someone who was ready to rip out my throat, but she looked like she wanted to turn and run away. She looked like someone who'd just been deprived of one of their senses.

"I'm making a point. I have no doubt that you're one of the single most deadly hybrids within a thousand miles, but you're not ready to force me into doing anything I don't want to do—not unless you're ready to kill me, and even then your odds aren't great. I can take your gift away at any moment, and there isn't anything you can do to stop me."

"Okay, you've made your point. Give it back to me. Now! Anything could happen at any moment, and I'm defenseless to stop it."

I closed my power up tightly again, and then gave her a sad smile. "Welcome to the world the rest of us deal with, Vicki. Now please go get your people. I'm going werewolf hunting, and I suspect that you're going to want them along if you're really serious about keeping me alive."

It took us just over half an hour to make it to the location that was most likely the current home base of the werewolves. It was a town so small that it didn't even show up on the map on my phone until I'd zoomed it in to nearly its highest resolution setting.

Vicki didn't speak to me even once on the drive there. One of her people drove the SUV we were in, while the rest of her people had crowded into the other two vehicles she'd rented at the airport.

Once we arrived at our destination, Vicki dispatched her people with an expertise that told me she wasn't any stranger to hunting werewolves—that or she'd had some very good teachers over the years. Either way, I was glad to have her along. It was like being accompanied by a younger, more attractive version of Jack, a version that I suspected was much more deadly than any three Jacks could have been.

Vicki's people disappeared into the darkness and then it was just the two of us. She threw me a challenging look, and then started stripping out of her clothes. I shot her a wry smile and then turned around and started pulling my clothes off. Unlike us, the Chicago pack still didn't use ha'bits, and regardless of what the custom was in her pack, I wasn't going to stand there and ogle her.

A few seconds later we were both in hybrid form and moving through the darkness. I'd felt a multi-pointed rush of power while we were shedding our clothes, so I knew that her people were already ready to go. I hadn't, however, anticipated what came next.

Vicki's people didn't have radios or phones—not that they could have used them while on four legs—but instead they reported in with pulses of energy at regular intervals. It was genius.

We weren't getting all that far away from each other, but wolves probably couldn't have managed pulses strong enough to be felt this far out. Luckily our team was comprised solely of hybrids, which meant that we could communicate—at least in a rudimentary manner—by pulses of energy, pulses that served as a kind of sonar to keep Vicki and me apprised of exactly where the others were.

"This is incredible."

Vicki shrugged massive hybrid shoulders. She was darkly furred and only slightly smaller than I was. She blended in almost perfectly with the night.

"Hunting werewolves is prohibited, but we have the single largest pack in the world, and Ulrich doesn't recruit just based on raw physical power. We have some of the best tactical minds in the world, and we've had decades to game out simulations. This wouldn't work against other shape shifters, but we've had people pretend to be dispossessed for long periods of time. They used this tactic to great effect against werewolves."

I nodded. "Of course. It probably doesn't even matter whether the werewolves can feel the pulses. If it attracts their attention it's all the better since we have to lure them out of hiding."

"Yes. My people are all well-trained enough to maintain adequate separation between us—if there are any werewolves out here they should engage with our scouting elements well before they sense the rest of us."

Vicki cut loose with a surge of power to provide a reference point for our people, and my beast tried to respond with a burst of his own, but I stopped him. She looked over at me in surprise.

"You're not what I expected, Mr. Graves. Most dominants struggle to avoid responding in kind—it's part of why all our signals don't attribute any meaning to a second pulse from the same location."

"I guess I'll take that as a compliment since this isn't the first time that we've met. I do try to keep people guessing. We're on the same side for now though, so if there's something on your mind go ahead and ask."

She waited until we'd received the next round of pulses from the perimeter before speaking again. "Why are we out here? You're leaving your people exposed—every minute you're gone is a minute that they have no real defense against the Coun'hij enforcers if they arrive in overwhelming numbers."

That made me chuckle. "It's like you're reading my mind. I was worrying about the same thing on my way over to your motel, but the truth is that my people are much better equipped for this battle than Shawn realizes. As of right now, you and I are the fourth and fifth hybrids with effective combat abilities down here on our side. Things might get a little sticky without the two of us, but my people are far from defenseless."

She nodded, seemingly unsurprised. Maybe Shawn's intelligence was even more comprehensive than I'd assumed it was.

"I ask again—why? Just because your people might survive an attack while you're away from them isn't a good reason to leave them to face it without you."

"We're out here for two reasons. Partly we're here because I want to see just how good all of you are, but mostly we're here because I need to see if my ability works on werewolves. I've tested it on vampires and other shape shifters, but I've never taken it into battle against any of the earthborn."

It went without saying that testing her people was shorthand for testing her, but she didn't seem angry about that—not even after having refused to explain her power to me earlier.

"You'll be able to make sure that your power doesn't interfere with mine if we do get into a fight?"

I shrugged. "I think so, but we won't know for sure until we try. My power will be focused on an area of ground around the werewolf, but I've never done any testing to determine how much bleed-through there is out into the surrounding areas. Your power seems somewhat...fragile. It didn't take much for me to short it out earlier. Based on that, you're going to want to avoid committing too deeply until after you've confirmed that I'm not going to cause you problems."

I'd seen Vicki face down several times her number in hybrids from within her pack and she'd never even blinked, but she was scared now. Even if she hadn't showed fear earlier, I could smell it coming off of her now. She was scared—terribly so—but she wasn't letting it cripple her. I found myself suppressing flashes of envy. Shawn had an incredible find in this one. Even without her ability she would have made a fine bodyguard. With it, she was in a league all her own.

"Try to give me a few seconds to try out my ability on any werewolves before you kill them."

"That would have been useful for my people to know before we sent them out where we can't talk to them."

"I know. I considered saying something, but I didn't want to make them hesitate. I'd rather lose the opportunity to test out my new toy than have one of them killed because they retreated when they should have attacked."

I could smell the approval coming off of her. It made me wonder if her other assignments had been cavalier when it came to her life or the lives of her people, but that was a question for another time. I felt three pulses of power come from up ahead of us.

"You're about to get your chance."

Even as the words left her mouth, Vicki threw herself into motion, but I was only half a step behind. She cut loose with three bursts of power before we'd even managed to cover the first dozen feet, and I felt single pulses of acknowledgments come from the other teams.

Vicki was fast—startlingly so—but it wasn't the product of her ability, it was nothing more than the preternaturally strong muscles of a hybrid combined with someone who obviously trained on a regular basis to make sure that she had every edge possible.

Before I'd spent weeks moving between St Louis and the Mexican border I wouldn't have had a chance of keeping up with her, but I'd toughened up since I'd left home, and Carson's unrelenting weapons training had taught me a bit about commitment. I threw myself forward, right to the point of falling forward, and then dug in with everything I had to keep my center of gravity from tipping to the point where I would fall.

It took us less than ten seconds to get close enough to our team to see the fighting. Two on one was the bare minimum for engaging a werewolf. Vicki's people were obviously good, but they were struggling against a tower of bone and muscle that outweighed the two of them combined.

I itched to unleash my power, but we were still too far away. Aiming in three dimensions was a lot harder than aiming a gun, and if I misjudged the distance between us I might clip one of our operatives and knock their legs out from under them at precisely the wrong time.

Vicki and I were both starting to breathe heavily as our secondary circulatory organs kicked in to try to take some of the load off of our hearts. One of our people darted forward in an effort to score a long slash on the werewolf's arm, but they weren't quite fast enough, and the werewolf caught them with a backhand that threw them into the side of a building with enough force to go through the bricks.

I winced—hitting anything that hard wasn't pleasant, but the real danger was the back edge of the werewolf's claws. Unlike our claws, they were sharp on both edges. There was a decent chance that Vicki's person was already dead.

The other hybrid from the team backpedaled in an effort to stay out of the werewolf's reach, but the legs on werewolves were jointed exactly the same way as ours. We were designed to go forward, not backwards and the monster ahead of us had several inches of height on our comrade.

Vicki bent down and picked up a length of steel pipe without missing a step. Our guy was losing ground. He reversed direction and then threw himself to the right in the hopes that the werewolf was moving too fast to match his lateral velocity.

It wasn't going to work—he was fast, but nobody was fast enough to beat a werewolf in a one-on-one fight, not once the werewolf was that close. I reached down for more speed—even though I knew it wouldn't be enough to save our guy—and then Vicki planted and hurled her length of pipe through the air like a javelin.

I'd spent weeks learning how to use a sword, but Vicki managed to pick up something that hadn't ever been meant to be thrown, and turned it into a spear, a spear that hit the werewolf with enough force to bury itself six inches deep into the werewolf's arm.

It was little more than a flesh wound for something that big, but the attack did its job—it knocked the werewolf's blow just enough off track that our hybrid took a glancing blow to the shoulder rather than a fatal blow to the chest.

I let out a roar as I pounded past Vicki, who'd lost her lead on me when she'd planted to throw the pipe. The yell had been more instinct than anything else, but it served to bring the werewolf around in a charge at me rather than finishing off the hybrid who was even now spinning across the blacktop in a spray of blood.

I let it take two steps in my direction, and then I ripped the cover off from the rift inside of me. I'd learned my lesson in the past. Opening my gift all of the way up usually resulted in me spending the next several hours on my back, so I normally used only the barest amount of power possible. That all went out the window this time.

I took off all of the stops and I landed my absorption field directly on the werewolf as the sparse streetlights around us momentarily flickered back on.

It was like trying to drink down a hurricane using a straw. It should have been impossible, but somehow I managed to get my metaphysical hooks into the werewolf enough that I felt the stream of energy start to ground out in the center of my body.

It was worse than standing at ground-zero for a lightning strike. The energy that I'd sucked out of the vampires had stressed my ability to the very limit. It had been a raw, angry kind of power, but it had nothing on what I was pulling away from the werewolf.

The energy I was sucking down from the werewolf was distilled malice. It burned my insides, but it was coming down, and that was all that I cared about until I felt the rift start to destabilize.

Up until that moment I'd never worried about where all of the energy I was absorbing went. I understood physics better than the average layperson, but I'd forgotten one of the most fundamental rules of the universe. Energy doesn't just disappear. It can be redirected and it can be transformed into another form, but it doesn't just vanish.

I'd somehow thought that I could just dump an endless amount of energy into my rift without any concern for anything other than how wide I could crank that rift open. Before now, the strength of my absorption effect had been the limiting factor, but something had changed over the last few days.

Maybe it was a result of the practice I'd put in experimenting on Carson and my friends. Maybe it was just a new level of power brought on by raw need. Either way, I opened up the portal inside of me wider than I'd ever managed before, and for the first time I noticed that the energy was going somewhere else, somewhere that had limits of its own.

The rift inside me wasn't destabilizing because it couldn't handle the flow of energy I was feeding into it, the rift was destabilizing because whatever place I was sending that energy into couldn't accept it—at least not that much, not so quickly.

The werewolf missed a step and nearly tripped. I could see it in its eyes, the savage orbs that usually conveyed only the most violent of emotions. The werewolf had been taken off guard by the sensation of me stealing its energy away, but as the werewolf righted itself my rift slammed shut, and it was me who was falling.

I was dead. There was no other possible outcome—not with more than a quarter-ton of deadly werewolf crashing toward me—but Vicki didn't function under the same constraints as the rest of us.

She shot past me in a blur, a blur that defied all common sense by arrowing in straight at the werewolf rather than dodging to one side. The werewolf had all of the cards. It was bigger, heavier, had a longer reach, and was faster than Vicki.

No hybrid could go toe-to-toe with a werewolf and survive more than the first pass, but Vicki did. The werewolf moved like barely-leashed lightning, but no matter how fast it struck, she always managed to be a fraction of an inch ahead of the blow.

My legs were weak. I knew I needed to get back to my feet and help Vicki, but I couldn't seem to get my body to respond. Vicki danced in, claws scoring on the werewolf's arm, and then threw herself over the counterattack, body clearing the deadly claws that otherwise would have ended her life.

For a second I thought she was moving faster than she'd been moving on the way into the fight, but that wasn't the case. She wasn't moving any faster than I could have moved if I'd been able to get up. The difference was that there was no wasted movement to anything she did.

It didn't matter what the werewolf did, or how fast it moved, Vicki always moved from wherever she was to wherever she needed to be in order to avoid its attacks. She chained together combinations of movements that were unreal. She was using techniques that should have gotten her killed several times over.

Her fighting style was all of the commitment that Carson had spent weeks beating into me, but it was reckless in ways that he never would have condoned. A slip, a hesitation, if anything had gone wrong in the first three seconds of her fight she would have died a dozen times over, but time and time again her crazy, reckless actions proved to be exactly what she needed in order to survive against an opponent that she had no hope of beating.

The sound of wolf pads on asphalt told me that the rest of Vicki's people were only seconds away from joining the fight. A surge of relief crashed through me at the knowledge that Vicki wouldn't be forced to continue fighting by herself.

Somehow my mind hadn't been able to process what I'd been seeing ever since Vicki had engaged the werewolf. I still thought that she couldn't win, still expected her to back off and wait until the rest of her people joined the fight.

The way to take down a werewolf was the same way that wolves took down hybrids. Surround it with greater numbers and harry it until it made a mistake that let one of the smaller combatants get into position to kill it from behind.

As if reading my mind, Vicki did exactly the opposite of what I'd been anticipating. She didn't fall back, she upped the intensity of the fight. She charged forward into deadly, foot-long claws, and it was like she was made out of nothing more than air.

The claws flashed by, passing within millimeters of her, and then she lashed out, a single impossible blow that ripped out the werewolf's throat. The death throes of something as big and dangerous as a werewolf were more than capable of taking an unsuspecting hybrid with it, but Vicki danced back out of range shrugging off blows that should have opened her up from hip to collarbone.

She watched the werewolf bleed out to make sure that it wasn't going to lunge forward and kill her, and then turned as though planning on going to check on her downed hybrid. In the heat of the moment I'd forgotten all about the hybrid who'd been backhanded by the werewolf, but I looked over to find three of Vicki's people clustered around their teammate.

Vicki was halfway over to the group when one of them turned around and gave her a thumbs up to indicate that they'd managed to stabilize the injured hybrid. I was astonished—very few hybrids would have survived that kind of blow.

Apparently Shawn hadn't been kidding when he said that he would be sending down some of his very best.

Vicki sighed in relief at the confirmation she hadn't lost anyone, and then turned back to me.

"I assume we passed muster?"

Chapter 11

Alec Graves
The Socorro Motel
Tucson, Arizona

I managed to walk back to the SUVs under my own power, but it was a close thing. Under other circumstances I probably would have been worried about showing so much weakness in front of a hybrid I didn't know very well, but the idea that Vicki might decide to take advantage never crossed my mind. She was the consummate professional.

Getting back to Vicki's motel was easy. The challenge arose when it was time to discuss me getting back to my RV.

"You've got tinted windows, Alec. Drive me back to your RV and just leave me in the car."

"They'll be able to smell you—not well, not with the small amount of airflow in and out of the vehicle, but well enough that James, Jess and Jasmin will recognize you if they get close enough."

Vicki scowled. "You're right. I'm not used to being in a location where someone outside of the pack will recognize my scent. You'll have to relocate your operations here. I'll send one of my people out for food, and then we'll hole up inside of our rooms so that nobody has a chance to see or smell us."

Now it was my turn to frown. "I can't uproot my entire operation and move them here. That would look incredibly suspicious to anyone watching a satellite feed. We worked really hard to make sure that we arrived in staggered waves precisely to avoid that."

"I can't protect you from all the way over here, Alec. That's not the way that my gift works."

"Then tell me how your gift works, Vicki. I need something to go off of if we're going to figure out a solution that puts you close enough to help out if things go south without blowing your cover if they don't."

She waved the rest of her team out of her room before speaking.

"I'm doing this under protest, but I suspect that you already have a pretty good idea of what I'm capable of now that you've had a chance to see me fight. I can see the future."

"That's incredible!"

"Not as incredible as you might think. I can't predict stock market crashes or tell you who's going to win the Super Bowl. All I can see is the next few seconds. It's enough to give me advance warning when something big goes down around me, and if I'm really concentrating I'll know what an opponent is going to do before they do it."

The possibilities were incredible, and with every second that I continued to think about her gift, additional uses unfolded before me.

"I was suspecting something like that, but to be honest I was leaning towards some kind of telepathy to explain what you were doing earlier. No wonder you were freaking out earlier when I cut off your power. You're used to knowing everything that's going to happen before it happens. Losing that would be worse than going blind."

"It wasn't pleasant, but it probably wasn't as bad as all of that. I don't see everything that happens, but I'm used to knowing if I'm in danger with plenty of time to react and get myself and Shawn out of trouble."

"How do you process all of that information? Is it like light or sound, or something completely different?"

Vicki looked at me oddly. "Nobody has ever asked me anything like that."

"Sorry, I didn't mean to pry. I'm just still in the middle of figuring out the limits of my own power, so I'm extra curious right now. An ability like the one you've just described is fundamentally different than something like Brandon Worthingfield's. His is solely an increase in his physical attributes, yours has nothing to do with your speed or strength and everything to do with receiving a completely separate feed of information, one that normal brains aren't equipped to handle."

She shook her head. "I wasn't angry, just surprised. Most people just want to know what I can do rather than how I can do it. In answer to your question, I get...premonitory sensory feeds from all three major senses. Sight, sound, smell, I constantly get information coming in from all three of those senses that tells me what's going on in real-time and what could happen in the future."

"Could happen?"

"Yes, the concept of destiny is a bunch of rubbish—at least in the short term. Every action I take causes ripples in the possible futures that I sense. Right now the future I'm sensing indicates that we're going to spend the next few seconds just talking, but if I threw myself at you and tried to rip your head off, all of that would change."

She said it so calmly that I almost failed to react, but my beast was more on the ball than the rest of me. He lashed out with the energy required to trigger a transformation to hybrid form, but I managed to intercept the surge. I wasn't fast enough to stop the flare of energy completely, but I grounded enough of it out to stop from transforming.

Vicki smiled. "That was also a possibility, but it wasn't very likely until I said what I said just now."

"And you can see all of it at the same time?"

"I wish. No, it's like you said, our minds aren't really designed to handle an infinite stream of information coming at us. In theory I could see all of it at the same time—the information seems to be there—but I discard most of it. It's like standing in a normal room and picking out a single conversation from all of the background noise. It's taken a lot of practice, but I've mostly managed to train myself to pick out the most important bits and ignore everything else."

"You had a hard time when you first manifested your gift, didn't you?"

"If by hard time you mean I was borderline catatonic for more than a month while my mind tried to put itself back together after being fractured by more information than any mind was ever supposed to be exposed to at one time, then yes, it was a hard time.

"It was Shawn who helped me. We'd known each other since we were kids, but we weren't that close until then. He sat at my bedside for weeks. More importantly, he ordered everyone else to leave me alone. The fact that he was Ulrich's son meant that he had enough pull to make an order like that stick. That was when I first started to be able to cope with things.

"He'd reduced the number of futures facing me, and then as I started being able to tell him what was happening, he moved me even further away from people. It took another three months of gradually exposing me to more and more varied environments before I could function more or less normally, but even now I sometimes have to shut down one or more of my senses in order to focus on the futures headed at me. While I was fighting that werewolf I shut down my sense of smell and my sense of taste. That bought me almost a full second of extra foresight."

"So you just see the future play out in your head alongside the present?"

"No, it's more like a series of ghost images that play along in real time. The most likely events are more defined, but the further you get into the future the harder it is to pick things out."

She'd just given me part of the secret to beating her, and we both knew it. I hated myself for doing it, but I added that piece of information to the files I kept inside my head detailing the weaknesses of all of the hybrids with known powers. In a one-on-one fight Vicki was going to be nearly unbeatable, but if I could throw her into the middle of a bigger fight where she was up against more opponents, she would have a harder time dealing with all of the stimuli coming at her.

She sighed. "So that's why I need to be nearby. If I'm three miles away from you, I'm not going to be able to see anything smaller than a bomb going off. I considered just phoning in this particular guard assignment, but I've never let Shawn down before this, and I don't want to start now."

"Okay, the closer you are to me, the better you're going to be able to protect me. I'm sure we could find a way to mask your scent from everyone if we were to stick you in an SUV, but it wouldn't be a comfortable solution. I can only see one other way to do this. I'll go back and get my RV, and meet you a mile or two away from our camp. You'll spend the next few days in my room until I can get someone to pick up another RV for you. We'll stick some air fresheners out in the main living area, and I'll just keep everyone out of my RV between now and then."

"They'll know that something is up. They'll know that you've got someone in there with you."

"Yeah, but they won't know who."

Vicki considered the plan for several seconds and then nodded. "Okay. I'm not sharing your bed though—you'll be sleeping on the couch."

"Of course. I'll get started back now—my phone has been off for long enough that people are going to be worried about me."

Chapter 12

Alec Graves
The Caravan RV Park
Tucson, Arizona

When I stepped into my RV, I found Jasmin and Jess both clustered over Brindi, giving her motionless form CPR.

My mind was whirling as I sprinted over to the three of them. I couldn't remember for sure when I'd last seen Brindi—when she'd last gotten the fix she needed. I'd thought that she still had a few hours before she would be getting to the critical zone, but it seemed I'd somehow lost track of time and not been here when she'd needed me to be.

"Have you called 911?"

Jasmin shook her head as she continued with chest compressions. "We didn't know if that would be okay. You were pretty clear about the need to keep a low profile out here."

BURNED

I already had my phone out and was dialing.

"How long has she been like this?"

"We've been here for ten minutes—she's not cold yet, so she can't have stopped breathing very long ago. Check her pulse, Alec, I'm having a hard time getting back into position after taking my hands off of her to check."

I grabbed Brindi's wrist right as Jasmin stopped compressions and Jess leaned back down to resume mouth-to-mouth, and felt a shock that was an order of magnitude more powerful than just static electricity. I recoiled instinctively from the spark, but Brindi started gasping for breath and my insides started to unknot.

"Alec, you came back."

Jasmin was trying to take Brindi's pulse now, but she batted Jasmin's hands away with one hand while reaching for me with another.

"Of course I came back. I'm so sorry I wasn't here when you needed me. I thought we still had time before you were going to need me. I guess I lost track of an hour or two in there somewhere."

She looked around disorientedly, searching for a clock. "I thought we did too. I would have called you otherwise. I was starting to get nervous, but I wanted to give you your space. I was feeling so tired. I sat down to rest my legs—I guess I fell asleep."

I was trying to fit the pieces together, but nothing was matching up with our experience so far. Brindi had fallen asleep dozens of times leading up to needing her next fix, but before this she'd always woken from the shaking that accompanied the onset of the severe withdrawal symptoms. If she was getting to the point where she was going to slip into the danger zone without actually experiencing the shakes, then we'd just entered dangerous new territory.

"How are you feeling, Brindi? Do we need to get you to a doctor?"

She shook her head. "No, I actually feel pretty good. My ribs are a little sore, but other than that I think I'm okay. How come?"

I closed my eyes, wishing I could clone myself. There were too many pieces in motion right then for any one person to give them all the attention they deserved.

"I have something I need to do right now, something that shouldn't wait. If you need to go to the doctor then I'll take you right now, but if you think that you can wait, then we need to go do that thing."

"I'm okay—Jess or Jasmin can wait here with me. If something starts to go wrong they can drive me to the hospital."

I shook my head. "Which will do absolutely no good. Until we figure out what's going on, you're not leaving my sight. If you're to the point where you don't start shaking before you collapse, then it's too risky to let you get more than a few feet away from me."

Jasmin finished checking Brindi's pulse, and stood. "Don't they have heart rate monitors that people can wear on their wrists? We should outfit Brindi with something like that so that you'll get an alert if she stops breathing."

"That's a good idea, Jasmin. Jess, can you please see to that? Jasmin, I'm going to need you to let Carson and Taggart both know that Brindi and I are leaving camp for a few minutes. We should be back before anything bad happens, but I don't want them relaxing their guard right now just because they heard that I'm back in camp."

The girls both started toward the door. I could tell that they were curious about what would make me drag Brindi away so soon after she had such a terrible episode, but they knew that most of what I did these days was need-to-know.

Before either of them could disembark, Adri opened the door. "Alec, can we talk? I wanted to…"

She trailed off as she saw my arm around Brindi, hand pressed up against the bare skin of Brindi's waist in an effort to both support her and make sure she didn't fall back into withdrawal so soon after having her heart stop.

I opened my mouth, unsure of how to respond to Adri, but before I could come up with the right words Carson stuck his head inside of the RV.

"Alec, I'm sorry to interrupt, but we're starting to see odd power outages along the southeast edge of the Tucson pack's territory. It's possible that the local utility is just having problems in that area, but if not it has all of the normal signs of a large werewolf pack. We've got maybe twenty minutes before they arrive here—assuming that there isn't another group ahead of the one that we're seeing."

I walked past both of them and helped Brindi into the passenger seat. "I've got to leave for a few minutes, but with any luck I'll be back here before they arrive. Pull all of our people back here. We want the biggest deterrent we can muster."

"That isn't going to work if Puppeteer is controlling this batch—they'll attack regardless of how many of us there are."

I nodded. "I know. Even if Puppeteer isn't involved, it could still backfire on us. Sensing this many wolves and hybrids together in one place could scare them off, or it could just make them hang out in the area until they feel like they have a big enough force to overwhelm us. Unfortunately, it's our only option until I get back."

Carson shook his head. "I know that you wouldn't be planning on leaving us without a good reason, but we need you here. Your presence could make all the difference in this fight, Alec."

I knew that he meant my ability could make all of the difference. He was wrong about that, but he was right in thinking that I was more valuable than most of our hybrids—even without my ability. The massive sword I'd stolen from my father had originally been created to give hybrids an advantage when they fought against werewolves and the more powerful jaguars out of South and Central America.

Carson had spent untold hours with me forging me into a fighter capable of using my weapon. I still probably wasn't quite a match for a single werewolf all by myself, but I would be close—much closer than any of the rest of my people.

"I'm sorry, Carson, but I have to do this. My ability doesn't work on werewolves. If it did we'd probably be having a different conversation altogether, but it doesn't. The help I could provide with my sword isn't as valuable as the help I'm headed off to get."

Carson hesitated, obviously full of questions, but he knew that our relationship was changing. The days when he could do more than respectfully suggest an alternative course of action had come to a close.

"I'll get everyone rallied together and have them ready for whatever is headed our way."

Adri shook her head. "We still need to talk, Alec. If Brindi is going with you then I should be able to go too."

"I'm sorry, Adri. I know that this is terrible timing, but you can't come with me. The help that I'm headed out to pick up isn't going to like Brindi being with me, but there isn't any choice—Brindi could die if I leave her here without me."

I could smell her anger starting to rise, but even without that I would have known she was unhappy—it was obvious in her stance and expression.

"No, you can't do this. If she goes, I go."

My beast was unhappy with the way that she was contradicting me, but I was having a surprisingly easy time separating my emotions from his. I was angry too, but my anger was a cold, controlled thing.

"Don't do this, Adri. If you want to talk about Brindi then we can talk about her, but not right now. I should have been on my way thirty seconds ago, and every second we're sitting here puts our friends—my people and yours—in more danger. You can go happily, or you can go pissed off, but right now you're putting your feelings ahead of the lives of everyone out there. It wouldn't matter how much I cared for you, that isn't a contest you can win."

I turned away from her and started flipping switches to bring in the pop-out sections of the RV. I could hear her shift around, torn between her anger and her common sense.

"Fine, I'll go, but we are going to have a conversation about Brindi. I'm not okay with another girl living with you like this—you're going to have to come up with another solution to keep her alive."

I didn't respond. I knew that ignoring her wasn't going to help my case when we did finally sit down to talk, but with my anger in the forefront like it was, there was too much of a chance that opening my mouth would just make matters worse.

Twenty seconds later we were on the road. I looked back in the rearview mirror just before we turned onto the main road. Adri was still standing there watching us drive away.

Chapter 13

Alec Graves
Halfway between The Caravan RV Park and
The Socorro Motel
Tucson, Arizona

I called Vicki on my way to the motel where she was staying and asked her to meet us at the halfway point. I didn't say anything about Brindi, but I knew how she was going to respond when we arrived.

Saying that Vicki wasn't happy about Brindi's presence in the RV was an understatement. I think the only thing that saved me was that I'd had Brindi go back into the bathroom and lock herself in just before we arrived.

That meant that I could escort Vicki back to the bedroom without Brindi seeing her. Vicki's scent was full of barely-leashed anger, and her body language promised that there would be an accounting at some point in the near future, but apparently she could see that I wasn't in the mood to brook any kind of argument. My people were in danger and between Adri and Carson I'd already wasted too much time getting Vicki and her people back to our base of operations.

I got Vicki safely back to my bedroom, waited for her to lock the door, and then helped Brindi back up to the front of the vehicle. We got the RV back in motion in near-record time, and Vicki got her people to follow us in two of their SUVs. It meant that we were leaving more of a trail for anyone watching by satellite than I would have liked, but there wasn't anything that could be done about it.

As we pulled back into the RV park, I turned to Brindi. "Could you dig around back there for something to spray in the air to mask our visitor's presence? We need to make sure that nobody can figure out their identity."

"Sure thing, I grabbed some air freshener when we stopped for groceries."

I parked the RV and did a quick survey of the area as I unbuckled my seatbelt. It was still dark, but there was a hint of light off to the east. That might not save us if Puppeteer was controlling the werewolves to the north of us, but if that wasn't the case then the threat of sunrise might be sufficient to prevent the attack we were worried about. Werewolves tended to only shift forms at night.

It was one of the things that nobody understood about the earthborn. They didn't seem intelligent enough to understand the dangers inherent in humanity knowing that they were more than just a legend, but they still kept a surprisingly low profile.

I opened up the door to the RV and stepped out, leaving it open so that I would be able to hear if Brindi collapsed again. Carson materialized out of the darkness a second later.

"We're still getting reports of electrical grid issues up north, but they don't seem to be getting any closer. It's looking like it might have been a false alarm."

I rubbed my eyes. It was long past the point where I should have gone to sleep. "Okay, there are some SUVs headed this way. They'll be pulling up behind my RV and stopping there. They won't get out of their vehicles unless we're attacked, and I don't want anyone approaching closer than twenty yards of them."

"Your help?"

"Yeah, but the kind of help that is trying to keep a low profile so that the Coun'hij doesn't find out they are working with us."

Carson nodded. "I'll pass the word, but you may want to speak to Isaac and Heath directly. That kind of thing always comes best from someone inside their own chain of command."

I tried to suppress a yawn, but didn't quite succeed. "Okay, that's a fair point. I'm running on empty right now though. I'll give them a call, and then if nothing materializes in the next few minutes I'll send that part of the help home and go get some sleep."

"That part?"

"Yeah, the other part of our help is going to be staying in my RV. It's not ideal, but I don't know of another way to keep their identity a secret while still keeping them close enough that they'll be able to help if we get attacked."

There was a stubborn set to Carson's shoulders that told me I'd better let him say his piece.

"Alec, that's a very bad idea. How sure are you that you can trust whoever is back there? If they are in the RV with you, then you're going to be incredibly vulnerable while you're sleeping. Let me post some guards in there with you."

I shook my head. "I'm sorry, Carson. I understand your concerns. If I'm completely honest with you, I even share them, but this alliance is too important to risk having it go sideways because I let the wrong person figure out who I've got back there with me. Brindi will be with me, and I'll make sure that we sleep in shifts so that I at least have some forewarning if that operative tries anything. With my ability being what it is, I only need a fraction of a second to get it into play—that will just have to be enough."

Carson still didn't like it, but given all of the secrets he was still keeping, he didn't have much room to throw stones at me for keeping a few of my own.

"Okay, Alec. This is your show." He turned as the SUVs carrying the Chicago pack pulled up. "Those are the ones you want left alone?"

I looked down at my phone as it chirped with an incoming text. It was Vicki, confirming that it was her people who'd just arrived.

"Yes. I'll keep an eye on them for a few minutes while you go spread the word."

Carson nodded and then headed off to the closest RV. I waved to the SUVs, and then dialed Isaac's number. He answered on the second ring.

"You're back. That's good—you'd never believe the rumors that started flying around this place when your vehicle left."

"I can only imagine. I'm sorry about not giving you more of a heads up about that before I left."

"It's okay. Our favorite human dreamer made it back here within a few seconds of your departure and told me that you were going to pick up some help."

"Yeah, that's actually what I'm calling about. There are two SUVs parked right behind my RV, and they are full of that help, help that needs to remain anonymous if at all possible. I'll be sending them away once the sun finishes rising, but until then it would be helpful if you could ask your people to give them a wide berth."

"Sure thing. We're trying to keep our people out of sight right now for the most part so that we don't tip off the Coun'hij as to just how many people we've got here. If we're lucky it will help keep them from realizing that this is our HQ."

I nodded, even though I knew he couldn't see the gesture. "Yeah, and if we're unlucky it should still cause them to underestimate us."

"Right. That means that there isn't any reason for most of them to be over there anyway. I'll pass the word to the dreamer and the illusionist—I'm sure they'll honor your request."

"Thanks. I've got another operative in my RV right now. They'll be there for the foreseeable future, which is going to create some difficulties with regards to conferences for the next little while, but it can't be helped."

I could sense Isaac's curiosity, but he was one of the most even-keeled hybrids I'd ever met. He wouldn't let his questions push him into doing something that would cause the two of us to have a falling out.

"Right—I'll make sure that everyone knows to give your RV some space as well. Anything else?"

I hesitated. I wouldn't have said that I wanted anything else from Isaac, but his question made me realize that there was one more thing he could do for me.

"I was up late hunting down a werewolf and I haven't gotten a chance to get any sleep yet. Adri is pissed at me for leaving without talking to her first, but I'd like to get some shut-eye in before we start yelling at each other. Do you think that you can find something to keep her busy for a couple of hours?"

Isaac was quiet for so long that I checked my phone to make sure that our call hadn't dropped.

"I don't know, Alec. This feels like something that I should stay out of the middle of."

"Yeah, you're probably right. Forget I asked. I'll power through until the sun comes up and then I'll crash and just hope that I can manage to get my forty winks in before she comes over looking for a fight."

Chapter 14

Alec Graves
The Caravan RV Park
Tucson, Arizona

I stood outside the RV, exchanging texts with Vicki to confirm what my nose was already telling me. Her people had rounded up some industrial-strength air fresheners and hung them liberally inside of their vehicles. It probably wouldn't stand up to a concerted effort by someone who was willing to get right up next to the SUVs, but given the fact that they could always just drive away if someone violated the safety perimeter I'd ordered established, it would probably be enough.

I watched as the sun started up into the sky, and marveled at the contrast between what I saw in my surroundings and what I felt. To a human, the RV park and attached motel would have looked quiet. There were a couple more people wandering around than I would have expected for such an early hour, but not so many as to make me suspicious that something important was going on.

The unseen plane was another matter altogether. I could feel bursts of energy as people's beasts acted up in frustration at being trapped inside four walls when there was the possibility that we were going to be attacked before the morning was out.

I'd known that keeping so many shape shifters cooped up inside of motel rooms and RV's was going to be a challenge, but I was feeling a lot more tension than I'd been counting on. There were too many of us packed into much too small an area, and the question of dominance hadn't been settled to our beasts' satisfaction.

It was yet another problem that I didn't have a good solution for. We couldn't let everyone walk around at the same time, and we couldn't afford to have large numbers of our people trying to rip each other's heads off, but I was going to have to think of something soon.

I waited for an extra thirty minutes after the sun cleared the horizon, and then told Carson to let people relax a little unless he got new intel that indicated an attack was imminent. By then my beast was trying to wrestle control away from me, so I knew I needed to get inside and get some sleep.

Brindi was asleep when I went inside, but she woke up when I went to cover her up with a blanket.

"What do you think you're doing?"

"I was going to make sure that you didn't get too cold."

Brindi shook her head at me. "We both know that you've gone too long without sleeping, Alec. You should have just kicked me off the couch."

"You need your sleep too."

She shook her head as she yawned. "I'm not likely to rip someone's face off if I have to go another few hours without getting my sleep. Go ahead and get some rest—I'll stay up to make sure that your friend back there stays a secret."

Her words were innocuous enough, but the slight lift to her eyebrows told me that she knew I wouldn't like the idea of sleeping with someone new so close. I debated telling Brindi to go back to sleep, but she was right. If I didn't sleep soon I was going to become dangerous to everyone around me, and if that happened Brindi was going to be especially at risk. Not only was she physically close to me, she also couldn't defend herself if I did lose control.

I nodded and lowered myself down to the couch. Brindi sat down on the floor—close enough that she could touch me if she wanted to, but just far enough away that she wouldn't actually be getting another hit.

She hadn't acted this vulnerable for weeks now. It was probably just the result of nearly dying earlier, but I made a note to keep an eye on more than just her physical state over the next little while. It had been a small thing given everything else that had been going on, but I'd really appreciated Brindi's efforts to lighten my mood as I'd headed off to rescue Cindi. She hadn't had any way of knowing that I wasn't planning on coming back, but she'd still made a concerted effort to make me feel better.

She wasn't just a burden anymore—hadn't been for a while now.

I went to sleep fully expecting to have Adri barge in and wake me up, but woke up feeling remarkably refreshed considering the metaphorical sword poised above our collective necks. Brindi's head was bobbing, so I moved off the couch and slid her onto it, putting a light blanket over her. I waited until she was asleep, and then went over and knocked on the bedroom door to let Vicki know she could take a bathroom break if she wanted to.

Ten minutes later I locked the RV's doors behind me and headed towards Adri's motel room. It was less than a hundred yards, but I got stopped no fewer than five times by people who wanted advice, resolution to some conflict or another, or an updated set of orders.

The last person to stop me was Taggart.

"Alec, I think that Adri has put enough weight back on for us to take another run at Kaleb tonight."

"You're sure? At this point I'd rather wait another day or two than rush things again and fail a second time."

Taggart nodded. "It will depend on how she does with her calorie intake today, but she's on track to have added a couple extra pounds over what she was carrying when we went after him the last time. If you add in the fact that this time she'll be going to your dream rather than pulling you to hers, I'm fairly confident she'll be able to control the outcome. We can wait and see what she says when she gets back though. If she says she's not up to it, we'll give her more time."

"She left?"

"Yeah, as far as I know. Isaac said that he was sending her out with a wad of cash to buy groceries. There's a limit to how much food preparation we can realistically do here, but feeding our entire force by going out to eat for every meal would be both expensive and sabotage our efforts to keep a low profile."

I instantly felt bad about not having thought about that particular issue. My people were all being taken care of with some of the funds I'd stolen from Kaleb, but I'd failed to make the same arrangements for Isaac's people. I knew that Taggart and Adri had netted a nice payday when they'd taken out that nest of vampires in Wyoming, but that money was hardly inexhaustible.

"I'd like to help out there, Taggart. I've only got so much I can do without making another trip to bring physical cash across the border, but I was planning on having someone go purchase another RV. That will give us another stove so that we can give people some variety in their diet, but really it's not fair to expect you all to pay for your food out of your own pockets while you're down here helping me out. I'd like to provide a war chest to fund your half of the operation."

I could smell Taggart's reluctance. I was a product of the current generation, but growing up with two- and three-hundred-year-old shape shifters had given me more insight than most guys my age into how things used to be. Taggart didn't want charity. He wanted to make his own way in the world, which I respected, but I suspected that the real reasons went even deeper than that.

Once he accepted my money, it would be that much harder for him to refuse me if I asked for something he didn't want to do. He was worried about me tying strings to him, strings that could eventually become chains.

"I…I think that the girls, Tristan and I are all okay for now, but you may want to float the idea past Isaac. I've been helping out a little there, but his people are probably the ones who are feeling the most pinch."

I gave Taggart a smile that I hoped was understanding. "Perfect. I was headed over to talk to Adri, but since she's gone I'll go over to Isaac's room instead. That way the trip won't be a waste."

We shook hands, and then I took a right turn into the main courtyard of the motel. Isaac's room was only four doors down from Adri's. I was headed past Adri's room when I suddenly heard the unmistakable sound of voices from inside.

I nearly stumbled when I realized *who* I was hearing. It boggled the mind that they would be doing what they were doing inside a motel room with shape shifters all around, shape shifters for whom mere walls and windows did little to impede sound waves.

There was a split second where I thought that I'd been mistaken, that I wasn't standing outside of Adri's room, that it wasn't her I could hear in there. Taggart had told me that she was gone, and he hadn't given off any of the usual signs of someone who was lying.

I nearly had myself convinced until I heard her gasp and call out Tristan's name.

My beast surged up with such force that it was all I could do to stop myself from transforming right there in broad daylight. I clamped down on the tsunami of power crashing through me. I managed to funnel it all into my right hand, which exploded outward with the deadly claws of a hybrid, but I had zero desire to do anything about the anger coursing through me.

The rage coming from my beast was because he viewed Adri as his. He felt like she was his mate, and he didn't want anyone else claiming her. The human part of me knew that people weren't possessions, that Adri was perfectly free to choose someone else, but that didn't change the fact that she'd given me nothing but crap about Brindi.

Time and time again she'd acted as if we were together. Time and time again she'd expressed her displeasure when it came to just about anything in my life that took precedence over her. I'd come over here intending on apologizing for being so curt and instead heard her cheating on me with the guy she'd claimed was nothing more than a friend.

I put my hand through the door. It was every bit as sturdy as I would have expected from an exterior door to a place like this, but it still wasn't a match for the rage-fueled muscles of a shape shifter. I shattered the locking mechanism, and stalked forward on legs that were trembling with the need to shift.

They were there, just like I'd imagined based on the sounds that had made it past the door. Tristan and Adri were lying together on her bed, his shirt already off and hers pulled up high enough that it was obvious it would be joining his on the floor in a matter of seconds.

I'd moved so quickly that they were only just separating from each other by the time I made it to the foot of the bed. Tristan was scared—the fear coming off of him was unmistakable—but that only egged my beast on. I grabbed him by the throat and slammed him into the wall with enough force to leave a body-shaped impression in the sheetrock.

I used a lot less force than my beast wanted to, but Tristan still mewed in pain as his legs hit the wall.

I turned to Adri and sneered at her.

"After all the times you complained about Brindi—Brindi, who I've never kissed—you really thought I wouldn't mind if you made out with Tristan? You told me that you didn't want him, that you wanted him and Cindi to get together. You lied to my face and I believed you. You didn't just betray me, you betrayed Cindi too."

Adri smirked at me. "You believed what I wanted you to believe. I don't care about Cindi any more than I care about you. She's treated me like trash over and over again—this is nothing more than she deserves. As for you, I got tired of waiting for you to give me access to the reins of power. I didn't go through everything I've been through in the last few months just so that I can hold your coat while you make all of the tough decisions."

"That's what you were in this for? You're nothing like the person I thought you were. How could I—"

"How could you be so wrong about me? Simple. You're an idiot. Every decision you've made since you left home has been one catastrophe after another. You're not fit to lead one pack, let alone the entire rebellion. The only reason you haven't died yet is because people like Jack and Carson continue to bail you out."

I sagged back against the wall. It felt like she'd hit me. The urge to just give into the rage and hurt pouring through me was almost overpowering, but something didn't feel right. Try as I might, I couldn't get all of the pieces to fit together. Unless this wasn't about what she was claiming it was about.

"Your parents. This is about your parents, isn't it? I told you I was sorry. I don't know what else to say."

"How about that you're completely incompetent? I've been trying to pretend that everything was okay, but nothing's been okay since before I met you. Everything you touch wilts and dies, Alec. Get out of my room before I call for Isaac and the rest to come kick you out. They all feel the same way I do, they are just better at hiding it."

My fist had tightened in step with my anger, and Tristan had stopped being able to breathe seconds ago. Killing him would have been the easiest thing in the world. I considered it for the briefest of moments. It might hurt Adri, but I doubted it. The monster sitting on that bed with her clothes halfway off didn't care about anyone, not really.

More importantly, Tristan hadn't done anything worthy of death. He hadn't done anything but fall for someone who would use him up and spit him out. He'd done exactly the same thing I'd done. I dropped him on the bed and then turned and walked out of the room without looking back.

Chapter 15

Adriana Paige
The Crazy Cactus Motel
Tucson, Arizona

My stomach felt like it was going to explode from all of the food I'd crammed into it while we were shopping. I didn't understand why Isaac had asked Cindi and me to go along on the shopping trip with Dominic and Heath, but I was incredibly grateful to have had a chance to get out of my room.

Actually, I was more than a little surprised that Alec had been willing to have Heath leave our base, but maybe his new asset—the one he'd blown me off to go pick up—had made Heath redundant.

I'd tried to convince Nellie to come along. Having another person with shape shifter strength along to help carry the heavier boxes and cans of food would have been welcome, but she'd bowed out. I expected to miss her while we were gone. For the last few weeks I'd never been more than a few dozen feet away from her, but it was actually refreshing to spend some time with other people—Dom especially.

It made me feel bad for not having sought her out when we'd first arrived in Arizona. Dom had been the best friend I could have asked for, but somehow I'd let everything else that was going on distract me from spending time with her. As we pulled back into the motel parking lot, I promised myself that I was going to do better—and not just with regards to Dom.

I'd been witchy towards nearly everyone in my life. Dom, Cindi, Taggart and Tristan all deserved apologies, but Alec deserved one most of all. I'd been impossible lately, but even before that I hadn't made things particularly easy for him.

Before I'd blamed him about my parents, I'd been attacking him for not cutting Brindi loose. Even lately it had been all I could do to avoid bringing her up. I needed to just start trusting him. If he said that he and Brindi were just friends, then I needed to either accept that or move on. This weird, halfway state of existence wasn't fair to either of us.

I helped unload the food we'd brought back, and then headed out to make my first apology, the hardest, most important one.

The walk over to Alec's RV flew by too quickly, and I found myself standing outside of his command center without a clear idea of how I was going to open our conversation. The door was cracked, which surprised me—Alec usually kept doors closed as a way of helping the privacy boxes defeat eavesdroppers—but my surprise quickly turned to horror.

The sounds coming from inside of the RV were unmistakable. I didn't need shape-shifter hearing to pick out the moans—not when I was this close to the door. I stood there for several seconds trying to tell myself that it was a mistake, that I couldn't be hearing Alec, but I knew that wasn't possible. Nobody from either group would have dared use Alec's RV for something like what was going on in there.

Shape shifters were all possessive by nature, and Alec's beast would take something like that to be a demonstration of insubordination that would have to be punished. It was Alec in there, I knew that without a doubt, but that wasn't enough for me.

Alec and I were through, but I had to know who he was with. My bet was that it was Brindi, that my suspicions had been right all along, but it could have been anyone. Jasmin, Jess, even Nellie. Even before Alec had manifested his power he'd been one of the single most eligible bachelors in the shape shifter world. Now that he had a top-tier ability at his beck and call, he was capable of protecting his future children from anything up to and including the Coun'hij. He was the perfect mate.

Almost as though working without any input from my brain, my fingers slowly pulled the door to the RV open. It was ludicrous to believe that Alec wouldn't hear me coming, but I didn't care about that. He could pull away from whoever he was with, but that wouldn't change the fact that I knew what they'd been doing.

It was going to infuriate him that I'd come inside of his RV, but I just had to know who he'd cheated on me with. I needed to know who I was going to hate as much as I hated him.

I stepped into the RV and saw the two of them. It was Brindi. Her shirt was off, showing a lacy black bra, and her pants were unbuttoned, showing the top of a matching set of underwear. Alec's shirt was off, but for once I couldn't appreciate his impressive muscles.

Brindi was on top. She spun around when she heard me, but any hope that she'd been the aggressor, that she'd somehow forced Alec into a compromising situation, evaporated when Alec reached up and pulled her back down against him. He met my eyes without shame.

"Don't look at me like that, Adri. You can't have really expected me to continue waiting around for you, not given the way that you were beating me over the head with the death of your parents."

I ignored him. I wanted to explode into a screaming, clawing mess, but instead I just looked at Brindi calmly.

"You have to know that this is wrong. I was told that you were starting to get over your addiction to him—this isn't because you don't have any other choice."

She was obviously uncomfortable, but I watched her push past that, watched her settle down against Alec's chest.

"You've treated Alec like garbage for as long as I've known him. He's right, you should have been thanking him for saving your life. He went in to save Cindi fully planning on dying, but you've been so stuck on yourself that you couldn't see what an amazing catch you had."

I shook my head. "That's nothing more than a justification. You know this is wrong. If he did this to me, then he'll do it to you too—it's just a matter of time."

Brindi's lips were quivering as she wiped away a tear. "He told me that the two of you were through."

Alec nodded. "We are. I told Adri that things weren't going to work out—it's not my fault that she's having a hard time coming to grips with it. Are you going to believe her, or are you going to believe me?"

She didn't respond. She just turned away from me, burying her head in Alec's chest, and I knew that she was too far gone to recognize that she'd just become the other woman.

I turned and left the RV without saying another word. Tears were streaming down my face, but I still somehow managed to make it across the blurry landscape that separated the RVs from the motel. Taggart intercepted me before I made it to my room.

"Adri, what's going on?"

"It's Alec. He...he isn't the guy I thought he was. It was just like you warned me—I caught him with Brindi. He's been lying to me for weeks, saying that he wasn't interested in her."

Taggart went stiff. "I don't understand. I didn't get any of that from him—not once in all of the times we've talked to each other. How could he have concealed that from everyone?"

"I don't know—go over there yourself if you don't believe me. You'd better hurry though, based on the way they were acting when I left, it won't be very long before they'll both be naked. I just don't understand why he would do that now of all times."

"I'm so sorry, Adri. I told him that you were gone. He was over here just a little while ago. He asked about you and I told him that you'd left to pick up food. He told me that he was going to talk to Isaac, but he didn't."

I laughed bitterly. "Of course not. Instead he headed right back to his RV so he could screw that slut."

I pushed away from Taggart and walked into my room. Tristan was sitting on my bed, looking like his entire world had just been turned upside down.

"Adri...I'm sorry about Alec. I know I'm not supposed to say anything, but I just feel so bad about everything..."

I'd never seen Tristan struggle to get words out—come to think of it, I'd never seen him conflicted about anything before this. Tristan had always just gone after whatever he wanted.

I followed his gaze over to the dent in the wall and then turned around and re-examined the door that I'd just walked past. It was obvious to me what had happened.

"You saw Alec earlier, didn't you, Tristan? He was here, wasn't he?"

Tristan looked miserable, but that was exactly what I would have expected out of someone who'd been threatened by the most dangerous person within a thousand miles. Tristan was the one person in my life who hadn't been taken in by Alec. He'd never been vocal about his dislike, and I'd always put it down to simple jealousy, but I'd been wrong. Tristan had seen through Alec's ruse, and Alec had obviously come by and told Tristan not to say anything to me.

I'd never given Tristan's opinion where Alec was concerned enough weight, and now I was paying the price. Tristan slowly nodded, and then opened his mouth, but I cut him off.

"I don't need to hear anything else—I know exactly what happened. I don't want you to ever speak of it again."

Taggart was looking back and forth between the door and Tristan, but he looked up when I started throwing clothes into my suitcase.

"Where are you going, Adri?"

"I can't stay here, Taggart, not as long as Alec is going to be here. I know it's dangerous, but I've got to go. As long as I can manage to get a couple hundred miles away from here, I'll probably be okay. Kaleb and the rest are probably so focused on this little corner of the country that they won't even be keeping an eye out for me anywhere else."

That wasn't the way that facial recognition worked, and we both knew it. Every time I drove under a traffic camera or stepped into a store with video feeds, there was a chance that I would throw an electronic flag somewhere and bring half a dozen Coun'hij enforcers down on myself. I was taking my life into my own hands, but I couldn't bring myself to stay where I might have to see Alec again.

"I know that you're hurting right now, Adri, but leaving our group isn't the answer. You need to stick with Heath and me. We can't guarantee your safety, but we can come close."

I opened my mouth to argue with him, but he talked over the top of me.

"We'll go with you—all of us. That way you'll be safe and never have to see Alec again."

"I appreciate the offer, Taggart, but we both know that can't happen. I'm mad as hell, but that's not a good reason to let the entire Tucson pack die."

Taggart was already shaking his head. "You're missing the bigger picture here, Adri. Whether we go with you or not, this coalition is finished. None of us can afford to ally ourselves with someone who can lie with impunity. If Alec can do this to you after telling everyone that Brindi was nothing more than an obligation, then we can't trust anything he's said to us up until now. Everything—including the intelligence that brought us down here—could be nothing more than a ruse to lure us into a position where Kaleb and the rest can kill us.

"Whether you want us to leave or not is beside the point, Adri. We're all leaving here—within the hour. It's just a question of whether or not you'll agree to come along."

Chapter 16

Alec Graves
The Caravan RV Park
Tucson, Arizona

I left Adri's motel room at a run, and I didn't slow down until I was out of sight of the main road and all of the buildings. Even then I slowed only long enough to strip out of my clothes and shift forms. Back home I would have been risking punishment for shifting out in plain sight, but that was the last thing I was thinking of as I tore away from the RV park, all four legs a blur.

I ran without paying any attention to where I was going, or how far I'd traveled. I couldn't get lost, not with a nose that was sensitive enough to retrace a trail that was days old, but I needed to get away from everyone. I couldn't bear the thought of looking anyone in the eyes—not after Adri had made such a fool out of me. She was right, my inability to see her deception before now called into question my very ability to lead the wolves and hybrids I'd gathered together down here.

I ran for nearly half an hour before my conscience started bothering me. My anger and shame hadn't grown any weaker, but with every step I took I knew that I was carrying myself further away from people who were depending on me to defend them. Maybe I would ultimately lose control of both groups of shape shifters, but for now I owed it to them to get them all out of Tucson alive.

I fought off the guilt for another twenty minutes before I finally turned around. Every step I took was a dagger being driven into my side, but once I got started moving I knew I had to keep pressing forward. If I stopped there was just too much chance that I would turn and run away.

Part of me had been hoping to be able to sneak back to my RV without being noticed by anyone, but I knew that wasn't going to happen as soon as I crested the small rise just outside of the RV park. My RV was surrounded by people, and they all seemed to be demanding that Brindi move to the side and let them enter. As I got closer I was able to hear them.

"He's not in there, and before he left he made it clear that I wasn't supposed to let anyone inside."

Jasmin bristled at Brindi's words. "You don't get to tell us what we can or can't do. You're less than nothing. You have no standing inside of our pack. You're nothing more than a dirty sk—"

Carson grabbed Jasmin by the arm and pulled her back out of reach of Brindi. "He's not in there, Jasmin—his scent trail clearly left here an hour ago and didn't return. If you want to know where he is, then track him—his SUV is still here so he can't have gone very far."

Jasmin ripped her arm free and turned on Carson with a fury that would have gotten her into a fight if she'd been dealing with someone less even-keeled than Carson.

"That's what I've been trying to tell everyone. I tried to track him. He walked away from here and headed off to the motel, but then his trail just disappeared."

"Somebody picked him up in a vehicle?"

"No—I'm not an idiot. No vehicles crossed over his trail at any point in the last hour. He disappeared. I've never seen anything like it. That's why I want answers out of this human skank. Isaac's people have been gone for more than twenty minutes and when I tried to find out what was going on, that Nellie chick threatened to rip my face off. She's a submissive through and through, but she was ready to go eight rounds with me if I pressed the issue."

Jess moved over to stand at Jasmin's back. "I got more than that out of Dominic. They are leaving because Adri caught Alec getting ready to screw Brindi. They are all freaked out because nobody knew that Alec could lie that well. He's told all of us that he didn't return Brindi's obsession."

Shock at what I was hearing had slowed my pace, but the fury and fear that the wind was carrying to me weren't the kind of thing I could let fester. I needed to be down there dealing with the rumors.

Even now I was having a hard time believing that Adri had started such a nasty rumor about me just to hide her own transgressions. She hadn't seemed the least bit concerned about me walking in on her and Tristan at the time, but she must have had second thoughts about what that information would do to her relationship with Taggart and the others.

I raced down to my people and threw myself into the air, changing between one heartbeat and the next.

"Everything you've heard in the last hour has been a lie. Earlier today I walked in on Adri and Tristan making out in Adri's room. I...it was too much for me to deal with so I left. I've spent the last hour and a half running in the hopes it would clear my head. I'm sorry that I left you all here like that—it was the wrong thing to do, but I won't be repeating that mistake again."

I expected everyone to nod and relax. Instead everything from their scents to their body language was screaming that they were getting more confused and distrustful by the second.

James pushed his way through to the front of the crowd, and when he spoke there was a pleading note to his voice that I hadn't ever heard out of him before.

"So you walked in on them, and then came back here and made out with Brindi as a way of getting back at Adri?"

"No, of course not. I walked in on them and then I left directly from Adri's room. I haven't been back here since I woke up. I never made out with Brindi—that's just a red herring that Adri threw out there to convince Isaac and the others to leave. She must have thought that would be enough to keep everyone from finding out what she did, but I'm not going to let her get away with it. I'm going to call Jack and get him to send over the satellite feeds for this area. We're going to track Adri and the rest down, and I'm going to make her acknowledge what she did in front of everyone she cares about."

Carson was shaking his head. "You can't force Isaac and the rest to bend knee to you right now, Alec. They'll fight you on it. I'm not even sure—"

"No. They don't get to play the free will card on me—not right now, not after abandoning our operation on nothing more than Adri's say-so, on nothing more than a bald-faced lie that would have taken less than two minutes to confirm or disprove."

"It's not a lie."

I rounded on Rachel, quivering with rage, and only the fact that she was my sister and a human stopped me from throwing her into the side of my RV.

"How dare you. Is this why you wanted to rejoin us? So you could undermine me? It's not going to work, Rach. The fact that you're the only other heir to the monarchy isn't going to carry any water with the packs. If you were a shape shifter it might be enough, but a bunch of hybrids aren't going to agree to follow a human."

Rachel looked as terrified as she smelled, but she refused to back down. "You're not listening to us, Alec. It's not a lie. Look at everyone, and then look at Brindi. You're right, I'm not a shape shifter, but even I can tell she's got a guilty conscience."

Rachel was right. I looked at Brindi, and the guilt streaming off of her was so intense that I couldn't believe I hadn't smelled it already. She looked like she wanted to crawl into a hole somewhere, but she squared her shoulders.

"It's true. I'm sorry, Alec. At one point I would have done just about anything for you, but I'm not that person anymore. I want to be with you so badly I can barely think sometimes, but not like this."

I shook my head, trying to understand what I was hearing. It didn't make any sense. I knew Brindi. We'd spent an incredible amount of time together over the last few weeks. She wasn't a very good liar. She did okay for a human, but I'd caught her in several lies early on in our acquaintance, and she'd had a lot more on the line back then than she did right now.

Even more mind-boggling, all of the incentives were pointing the wrong direction. By lying and telling everyone that we'd made out—that Adri had caught us making out—she was cutting herself off from everything she'd seemed to like about her life lately. Adri and Taggart couldn't possibly keep her in spending money forever, and even if they could, she was risking her life by doing this. She was addicted to me—so much so that she'd nearly died just a few hours ago.

"Have you found someone else you can transfer your skin addiction to? It's the only rational explanation for why you'd be lying right now."

"What? No. I'm not lying, Alec. You came back a few minutes after you left, and you kissed me. We…we were making out, and then Adri walked in on us."

My beast was getting angrier by the second, but my emotions weren't that straightforward. I felt like someone had pulled the rug out from under me.

"I don't know what is going on here, but I promise you all that I haven't kissed Brindi. I walked in on Adri and Tristan and then I left. That's it. I know that Brindi smells like she's telling the truth—maybe she really believes that's what happened, but it's not."

Carson shook his head. "Isaac and Taggart wouldn't have pulled their people out like that unless they were convinced that Adri was telling the truth. When you add in Brindi's testimony it becomes all but impossible to believe your version of events."

Grayson had been standing quietly in the back of the group, but now he spoke up. "It's a lot more likely that *you* are an expert liar than that both Brindi and Adri are both capable of lying with impunity."

His voice was incredibly dispassionate for someone who had flown down here in the hopes that I would be able to offer him the redemption he needed. His calm delivery was more convincing to the rest of my people than any impassioned accusation could have been.

I tried to put the pieces together. Was Grayson in on it? It had been hard enough to believe that Brindi would be working with Adri on an effort to discredit me.

In the human world, the world where everything was more straightforward, the possible explanations for all of this would have been limited, but we didn't live in that world. I suddenly realized just how blind I'd been.

"It was Heath. I walked in on Adri and she realized that she had to convince everyone that I was the bad guy. He came here pretending like he was me, and then she walked in on the two of you. She planned it from the start, and his ability to control what people see and smell meant that there wasn't any way you could have known it wasn't me."

I had them—not all the way, but there was finally an explanation for what had happened, an explanation that would mean they could still trust me. They needed that hope almost as badly as they needed to breathe. We were all wanted men and women, and there was a limit to how long any of us could survive simply by running. They needed me, needed me to serve as a focal point just as much as they needed me to help fight their battles.

I had them right up until Brindi opened her mouth again. "It was you, Alec. I want it to be Heath, but I've brushed up against Heath before and he doesn't feel like you do. It *felt* like you. It was the same buzz, the same everything...just more."

I shook my head. "No, this is the answer. I can't explain it all—not yet—but somebody used their power to set me up. Maybe Heath's power is broader than we've been led to believe—maybe it wasn't even him. I don't know for sure what happened, but that wasn't me."

Between one breath and the next it hit me. "Go to Adri's room. I put a big hole in it, and my scent will be there from before Adri came over here. There's hard evidence that my story is the truth."

James took off without waiting to see if anyone was going to join him. I pulled out my phone and walked several steps away before dialing Jack. Based on the way that everyone was shifting around as though unsure if they should be stopping me from making that particular call, I didn't want them overhearing Jack's half of the conversation.

"Hey, it's me. I need you to get your hands on a satellite feed from this area for the last hour. Half of our force packed up and left without telling me what was going on. I need to track them down—the sooner the better."

"Okay, I'll see what I can pull up, but it's going to take some time, and it will be expensive. Hacking the NSA isn't something that happens at the drop of the hat."

Jack didn't sound thrilled at being handed another impossible assignment, but he also didn't sound like he'd heard Adri's version of events down here yet.

"I don't care about the cost—just make it happen as quickly as you can."

A second after I hung up from Jack, my phone rang again. It wasn't a number I recognized, but that was hardly unusual these days.

"Yeah?"

"I know that you have every reason to hang up on me, but I implore you to listen."

I knew that voice. It was the man who'd been in the background of most of my childhood memories, the man who'd supported my mother time and time again, the man who'd still believed there was good in her even after she'd been willing to let Kaleb sell Rachel off to Vincent. It was Donovan.

"There is one reason, and one reason only, that I haven't already hung up on you. The last time we saw each other you did something that could have gotten you killed. I haven't forgotten that. I do, however, want to know how you got this number."

"This call is encrypted—we can use names, Master Alec. As to the how, your father has deeper penetration into the phone companies than you might imagine. His people have been analyzing the phone traffic in Arizona for days in an effort to track you down. They identified this number as belonging to you less than an hour ago."

Donovan sounded tired, like he was feeling every one of his two-plus centuries of existence. I didn't blame him—right then I wanted nothing so much as to just curl up in a ball and go to sleep in the hopes that when I woke up all of my problems would prove to be nothing more than a bad dream.

"I'm dealing with a host of problems right now, and you've just told me that every single communication I've had with any of my allies is now suspect. This better not just be a social call."

"You're dealing with problems because the Coun'hij—your father—has an operative down there. I'll deal with the fact that your number has been compromised. Kaleb has a virus that can go after specific numbers—I've already loaded it up to the phone company and by this time tomorrow your call history on that number will be wiped clean—even the backup files will be corrupted and unusable. That's not your real problem."

"You're right—my real problem is that operative. They've already created massive issues. Do you have confirmation who it is that's been turned?"

"No. Mistress Samantha put together the intelligence based on something minor your father said in passing."

I wanted to rub my eyes, but appearances were especially important right then. "Okay, thank you for the heads up—I hope that you didn't take too great of a risk in reaching out to me. Thanks for deleting my call history as well."

"Of course, Master Alec. May I ask what you're going to do about your father's operative?"

"There's only one person it could be. I'm going to hunt them down and kill them."

After everything else that had happened I shouldn't have been surprised by the reaction I got out of my people as I hung up my phone. Jasmin was the first to protest—even though she knew that she had no chance against me if I took exception to her challenge.

"No. I refuse to be party to that. Heath has always been decent to all of us. You can't just execute him—not without more proof than this."

"I just got a call from someone in Sanctuary, a contact who gets bits and pieces of Kaleb's plans. They just confirmed that Kaleb has an operative down here, an operative Kaleb is overjoyed is making life hard for us."

"That's awfully convenient. You needed independent confirmation of your implausible theory, and then within seconds of hanging up from your call with Jack, you have it. We're not stupid, Alec. You had some kind of code word in there that told Jack you'd been compromised and needed him to call back to back up your story."

She turned to leave. I let her take three steps—just far enough to confirm that everyone else was going to follow her—and then I ripped the cover off of the black hole in the center of my being. They all collapsed between one breath and the next—even Carson.

"You will hear me out. I'm not going to tell you who just called me, but it was the one person still living in Sanctuary who hasn't lost my respect. I believe them, and I'm going to act on their information. You may not like that, but I don't need your help to execute one hybrid—not even a hybrid as formidable as Heath. I'm not asking you along because I need your permission to kill him, I'm ordering you to accompany me because we still have a mission to finish up down here.

"You want to go your separate ways? Fine. You can leave after we're done with what we set out to do. We're either going to extract Jaclyn and all of her people, or we're going to spring whatever trap Kaleb and the rest are trying to close around her neck. You leave now, and our operational security will be even more blown than it already is."

"And if we refuse?"

There was a level of hatred in Jasmin's eyes that I'd never seen her direct at anyone but Brandon and Vincent before now.

"If you leave there is a very good chance the Coun'hij's enforcers will pick you up before you make it out of the state. If that happens you'll be dead, but if you somehow manage to get past them, I'll hunt you down once I've finished up with our mission down here."

I'd just crossed a line that couldn't be uncrossed. Not with Jasmin—maybe not with any of them—but it was Jasmin I was having the hardest time dealing with. Somehow I'd never seen it. For years she and I had been best friends. Neither of us had ever shown any evidence of wanting to take the relationship beyond that.

Apparently Jasmin hadn't been as happy as she'd seemed about that state of affairs. It was too late to do anything about it now. I had to keep focused on the bigger picture or people were going to die.

James skidded to a stop, eyes wide at the fact that everyone else was lying on the ground.

"What's going on?"

"They were going to leave before you came back to tell us all what you found."

The rift inside of me was starting to oscillate as I reached the limits of how much energy I could absorb. It was all I could do to avoid snapping at him, but I knew I needed to keep my anger leashed. James was the only person so far who seemed ready to believe that I might have been set up.

"It was just like you said. Adri's door was all busted up, and you'd obviously been there—your scent trail headed straight away from the motel."

I released them all—I had to or I risked losing control of my ability and making it obvious just how hard it was to keep so many people immobilized at once.

"You've all heard me out. Stay or go, it's your choice—just remember that there will be consequences if you run out on me right now."

I turned just in time to see Brindi's legs collapse. I caught her just before she hit the ground.

Chapter 17

Alec Graves
The Caravan RV Park
Tucson, Arizona

I knew exactly what they were all thinking as I carried Brindi up into my RV and closed the door behind me. I would have invited some of them in so they could see that I wasn't going to do exactly the kind of stuff that Adri claimed I'd been doing earlier, but that wasn't a possibility—not given how pissed I knew Vicki had to be by now.

I was right—she didn't even let me get Brindi to the couch before she came hurtling out of the bedroom. I cracked open my ability while she was still several feet away from me, and prayed that I still had enough juice left to stop her from killing me.

With someone else it probably wouldn't have worked. My first instinct had been to try to stop her from transforming so that I could deal with her in a less deadly form, but there just wasn't enough capacity on the other end of my rift to absorb that much energy. There was however enough of an absorption effect to shut down Vicki's gift.

I felt her start to transform, felt the energy ratchet up, and then she realized just how dangerous it would be to escalate like that without her ability to see into the future. Instead of shifting to hybrid form and ripping my throat out, she punched me in the face.

She was winding up for another blow when I captured her wrist and pushed her down onto the couch.

"I know you're pissed that I would leave you stuck inside the bedroom while I was out here making out with Brindi, but that wasn't me."

"It sure sounded like whoever it was had Brindi fooled."

She practically spat the words at me, but she hadn't shifted yet, so that was better progress than I'd been expecting.

"Yeah, he did have her fooled, but that doesn't change the fact that it wasn't me. I walked in on Adri and Tristan an hour and a half ago. All I can figure is that she decided her best bet was to start a nasty rumor in the hopes that it would keep me too busy to tell everyone else that she was playing me this entire time."

Vicki did a double-take. "That's much more sophisticated than I would have expected out of someone who didn't grow up among our people."

"Yeah, apparently we've all been underestimating her ability to deceive. For all I know, my people are leaving right now in the hopes that I'll be too busy chasing everyone else to come after them. I'm surprised you didn't hear all of that already."

"I've had three privacy generators going in there—the last thing I wanted to hear was you and Brindi going at each other again. Once was quite enough. What are you going to do?"

"I'm going after all of them. I got a call from someone just now warning me that the Coun'hij has an agent down here—an agent who has reported back saying they've managed to disrupt our operations—but I don't know for sure who Adri is working with."

"Heath. If you're telling the truth, it has to be him. Nobody else could have convinced Brindi like that."

"Yeah, that was what I thought too, but something like that is supposed to be beyond even him. Right now it's still just my word against theirs though. I need some proof—I don't suppose Shawn has a satellite feed of this area for the last couple of hours that he can send over? I've got Jack trying to get hold of that intelligence, but he said it's going to take a while, and every minute that passes puts Adri and the rest that much further away from us."

"You think that was their plan all along, to split your forces up and then send you off to chase them down, thereby creating a window of opportunity for them to take out the Tucson pack?"

I shrugged. "I don't know. I've gone from thinking that Adri is behind all of this, to thinking it's all Heath, and then back again just in the last five minutes. There are too many pieces that I can't get to fit together quite right."

Vicki sighed. "I should probably wait to tell you this until after Shawn gets me the video feed that proves it really wasn't you in here with Brindi, but what the hell—you only live once. Adri and the rest are back at the motel where I left my people. I got a text from them forty-five minutes ago asking me if they needed to be worried."

I wasn't sure whether to feel relieved or even more worried. We hadn't been spread across a thousand square miles, but I still had to find a way to get to the bottom of what had happened.

"Get on the phone to Shawn right away, please. We're going to need that video."

I should have known that things weren't going to be that easy. Fifteen minutes later—as I was out trying to get the rest of my people ready to move our operations to the motel where the Chicago hybrids were staying—Vicki texted me to let me know that the only satellite in the area had mysteriously stopped transmitting earlier in the day.

Kaleb and the rest had obviously known that something was going to happen today and they'd wanted to make sure that I wouldn't have a provable alibi. Five minutes after I got Vicki's text, I was back in the RV and the big vehicle was moving.

Brindi was still unconscious, which meant that Vicki came out of the bedroom as we pulled onto the main road. She obviously had something to say, but I got my question out first.

"Did you guys bring one of those portable EMP devices that Ulrich developed to keep people from flooding the internet with videos of hybrids?"

"Yeah. I'm assuming that you want us to use it to knock out all of the phones and cameras at the motel before we get there?"

"Yes, please. If you can target it carefully enough to avoid breaking all of the vehicles in the parking lot that would be ideal, but one way or another we need to make sure that the humans in the area don't leak what's about to happen to the outside world."

Vicki nodded. "Okay, I'll have my people deal with it, but I have a condition in return. Don't kill anyone, Alec. If you want to keep Shawn and me as allies, then that's the price."

"You're afraid that I really was the one in here with Brindi and I'm going to kill whoever could prove that."

"Not to put too fine a point on it? Yeah. That's exactly what I'm worried about. It wouldn't be the first time that some despot used a situation like this to eliminate a rival."

"I'll do my best, but you know how situations like this get—it's going to be a mile past volatile."

She didn't respond to that—we both knew that she was putting me in a difficult situation. If I'd had any other choice I would have been delaying this confrontation, but I was working against a clock this time.

Vicki was worried about me disposing of evidence and witnesses. I knew I was innocent, but that just meant that *I* needed to be worried about someone else disposing of whatever hope I had of clearing my name. Not only that, the satellite coming down like it had was another straw in the wind, another indication that the Coun'hij was gearing up for something. They wouldn't want their massacre of the Tucson pack caught on tape—not unless it was footage that they were a hundred percent sure they could control.

I could feel the noose tightening around my neck—around all of our necks—and the only chance we had of surviving against a massed force of werewolves was if we were all in the same spot when the attack came.

I half expected for my people to scatter once we were on the road—it wasn't like I was going to be able to run them down in an RV—but they all fell into formation behind me, and a few minutes later we were all pulling into the motel parking lot.

I tucked a blanket around Brindi, and then as I exited the RV, James stepped up behind me.

"I can't explain what's going on, Alec, but I believe you. Everyone else has had a chance to go check out Adri's door, but most of them are still pretty unsure what to believe."

"What's tipped things for you, James?"

"You saved my mom. I haven't forgotten that, even if she seems to have. I know her well enough to know that she's back there masterminding a whisper campaign to keep everyone convinced that you're the bad guy here, but she's wrong. I've got your back—just try to remember that your plan hinges on keeping all of Isaac's people alive."

"Yeah, I haven't been able to think of anything else."

It wasn't a surprise that Isaac's people had formed up in front of the motel by the time that my people had finished gathering at my back. They'd had scouts out, and based on how jumpy they all looked, they knew just how sticky things were probably about to get.

"You're not wanted here."

It was Taggart who'd spoken. He was standing there front and center looking like he wanted to tear me in half and watch me die.

"I know I'm not wanted, but you all need to hear my version of events, Taggart. After I talked to you, I fully intended on heading over to Isaac's room and making the offer you and I discussed, but as I passed Adri's room I heard her and Tristan in there making out."

"That's a lie!"

Taggart was shaking now—obviously having a hard time stopping himself from transforming and coming after me.

"A lie. Yes, that's exactly what I was thinking when I heard them, Taggart. You had just finished telling me that Adri left to go pick up food, and yet there they were. All I could assume at that point was that you were covering for her, that you knew all along that she and Tristan were an item."

Isaac grabbed Taggart's arm, stopping him before he could take more than one step toward me. "Hear him out, Taggart. Too much is riding on what happens over the next few minutes."

"I'm not going to sit here and listen to him call me a liar."

Isaac's knuckles went white on Taggart's arm. "We have more people than he does, but you and I both know that we can't take them—Heath is not a match for both Alec and Grayson. Even if he was, us killing each other just does the Coun'hij's work for them."

Taggart shook off Isaac's grip, but he didn't move any closer to me. I looked out over the rest of the people standing in front of me, and continued.

"I heard Adri and Tristan making out, so I put my fist through her door and stepped in to make sure I was really hearing what I thought I was hearing, and then I left. I knew staying around was going to result in me killing Tristan, so I put as much distance as I could between the two of them and me. Imagine my surprise when I got back a short time ago and was told that Adri was telling everyone that she caught me making out with Brindi."

"I told everyone that because it was the truth."

Adri had been standing in the back of the crowd—I hadn't even been able to smell her back there. Now she stepped forward.

"I caught the two of you, Alec. I saw you both with my own eyes, and no amount of lying on your part is going to change that. During the time that you claim to have seen me with Tristan, I was getting food—just like Taggart said. Isaac watched me get into the SUV with Heath, Cindi and Dom—they can all vouch for me. Who can vouch for you?"

Isaac, Heath, Dom and Cindi were all nodding, obviously ready to swear that Adri had been with them. I could feel things starting to spiral out of control. I'd come into all of this ready to deal with the fact that Adri and Heath would back each other up—I never imagined that I'd be dealing with Dom, Cindi, and Isaac too.

"My people went to your room, Adri. Everything was just like I told them it would be. Your door was damaged, and my trail led off into the desert. I wasn't lying, but it's interesting that you bring Heath up. From the moment I got back and heard everyone talking about your revelation, I realized that there was only one person I knew who could make people believe that I'd actually been there with Brindi—only one person who could make themselves both look *and* smell like me.

"I don't know if you're the one behind all this, and you dragged Heath along with you, or if he's the one putting you up to it, but one way or another he's involved, and that means that nobody here can trust anything they've seen."

Adri snorted. "Okay, we've heard you out, now let me explain what really happened. You're right, you were at my room before I found you and Brindi together. You even broke my door just like you said, but you didn't find Tristan and me together because that never happened. You found Tristan and you nearly killed him for some reason known only to you. Then you went back to Brindi. I don't know how you ever thought your word would stack up against mine, Heath's, Cindi's, Dom's and Tristan's but it's not going to happen. It's time for you to leave."

It was my turn to start shaking now. I needed an opponent I could hit, something that I could defeat through pure brute force, but instead I was being verbally backed into a corner by the fact that she had all of the witnesses. Or did she?

"Fine, get Tristan out here so he can tell his side of things, and then I'll leave."

"Absolutely not! I'm not going to let you brutalize him again. If you're not going to believe all of the rest of us then it isn't going to do any good for us to add one more witness to our side."

"You're not adding another witness to your defense, I'm adding another one to mine. Tristan is the only other person who can confirm that I was there at your room and saw the two of you ripping each other's clothes off."

"No. I'm not saying it again, Alec."

I smiled as the balance started shifting in my favor. "It almost sounds like you're hiding something when you say it like that, Adri." I turned to James. "Go get him. Don't worry, I won't let any of them interfere."

Things started happening almost too fast for even a shape shifter to follow. Taggart and Isaac both stepped in front of Adri as though trying to shield her from me, at the same time that their people started to spread out so that they could stop James.

That would have been bad enough all on its own, but at that precise instant I saw Heath and half a dozen other people flicker out of sight. My hand had just been forced.

I opened up the rift inside of me, dropping a circular absorption field around Isaac's people. I'd mostly been concerned about stopping Heath, but I couldn't afford to leave the rest of them unrestrained. I didn't just get Heath, I got a lot more than I bargained for.

Heath popped back into view as my ability shuddered from the effort to draw in more power than I'd ever tapped into at any one point. I thought it was just the sheer number of shape shifters I was trying to immobilize that was causing me problems—right up until the illusion around Nellie dropped.

One second she looked like a normal human girl, and then in the next she was replaced by a black-skinned man who was at least two inches taller than me. He was shirtless, revealing massive muscles, but that wasn't the most astonishing thing about him. As we all watched, tendrils of glowing black energy unfurled from behind his back.

There were dozens of them, all moving independent of each other, but all fanning out into a pair of wing-like masses to either side of him.

"I have to hand it to you—I didn't think that you would find me out. I've been doing this for thousands of years, and you're the first to manage it. It's a shame really—the feast the two of you were on track to provide me was going to be the best meal I'd ever tasted."

There was an undertone to the creature's voice that made me think of tearing fabric, fabric that was rotted and failing. He was corruption incarnate.

I'd never seen anything like him—not even in my darkest nightmares. Part of my mind was comparing him to fragments of legends that had been handed down by both the humans and my people, trying to find a match, but the rest of me had already started responding to the presence of a new threat.

I shrank my absorption field down, shifting its focus to the creature at the same time that I ramped up the strength of the draining effect it created. I hit whatever it was with everything I had, and the entire time I was worried that I'd already used up the bulk of my ability holding Jasmin and the others in place until James could get back.

The energy tendrils—the wings—on its back flickered ever so slightly, but it didn't drop to its knees, didn't evidence any other sign that my ability was even working. Instead, it casually whipped one of the tendrils around and slammed it into one of Isaac's wolves.

She never even had a chance. It was a toss-up whether it was the blunt-force trauma or the discharge of electrical energy that did her in, but there was no question in my mind but that she was dead based on the way her chest had been crushed and the scorch marks visible in her clothes and skin.

I threw myself forward even though I knew I wasn't any kind of match for whatever we were up against, and to my relief I heard my people spring forward to follow me. I shifted forms and took my second step as a hybrid, fully aware that I wasn't going to make it there in time to save either of the next two victims—I was just too far away.

I checked my ability, expecting to find that the rift—the conduit—was fine and that I was failing to stop the creature because the reservoir on the other end of the conduit was full. As I took my next step I realized that wasn't the case at all. The reservoir had been full earlier, and I could still feel the energy I'd drained off of Carson and the rest raging on the far end of the conduit, but somehow the reservoir had expanded exponentially—was still expanding. I was failing because no conduit in the world was big enough to drain the energy coming off of those wings. I could feel them whipping through the air, strands of power that seemed like they originated from the creature's back, but which actually came from somewhere else, a place of limitless, titanic forces.

I shut off my ability as I heard a crash from behind me, and then I was close enough to engage and it was too late to worry about anything other than just staying alive. Isaac's people had cleared the area enough to deny the creature more easy targets, and the bravest were already shifting and coming back to help me, but I knew I was going to have to deal with the first couple of attacks by myself.

I feinted forward, trying to force the creature off balance, and then had to throw myself to the side to dodge one of the tendrils. I'd learned a lot about committing to attacks and evasions from my time with Carson, and I didn't hold anything back, but I still almost wasn't fast enough.

DEAN MURRAY

Despite my best efforts, the tendril hit my shoulder with enough force to throw me into the side of the closest building more than thirty feet away. It was like being hit by a wrecking ball. I'd fought dozens of hybrids, telekinetic vampires and more than my fair share of werewolves, but I'd never been hit by anything so hard.

The closest match was being backhanded by a werewolf, but even that didn't hurt as bad. Werewolves were strong—maybe even stronger than whatever this was—but they were still all organic. When they hit you there was still some give to whatever they used to deliver the blow. The tendril of energy had no give to it, and I winced as I felt my shoulder dislocate on one side and ribs crack on the other side from hitting the brick wall I'd just demolished.

I expected to look down and find my chest blackened and my heart destroyed, but somehow my beast had absorbed the jolt of electricity and funneled it off somewhere else. I still should have died right then and there though, because the creature had followed me, intent on finishing the job it had started.

I hit the ground in a three-point stance, favoring my injured shoulder, and then surged back up to block the first attack, but I was operating at an even bigger disadvantage than I'd been under before. I deflected an energy tendril over my head, but the force of the blow staggered me and there were two more already headed my way.

I dug my talons into the asphalt underneath me and slammed my claws home against one of the tendrils, fully expecting the other one to snap my neck, but it never landed. Vicki arrived at my side in the nick of time and deflected the other tendril into the ground with enough force to pulverize the asphalt where it struck.

The next attack came barreling in with a pulse of darkness, but Vicki wasn't there where it was supposed to land. She dodged to the side, moving even before the tendril had started forward, and then our backup arrived.

Wolves darted in at the same time that hybrids stepped forward to try to knock the darkly glowing threads out of the way. They managed to chase the creature off of Vicki and me, but nobody was getting in close enough to land anything on that dark skin.

I tried to move in and reengage, but Vicki shoved me back into the building. "I can't keep you alive if you're in the middle of that—it's all I can do to keep myself alive."

She was right, we outnumbered the creature more than seven to one, but we were still losing. The creature didn't seem to be able to move all of the energy tendrils at the same time, but they still moved around enough on their own to make it hard to get through them. I watched as the creature fought and finally understood how it was able to generate so much force with its blows. Every attack involved at least two tendrils—one to do the striking and another to push off of something to help stabilize the creature.

It felt like we'd been fighting forever, but barely a dozen seconds had passed. I was still looking for options that would let us take it down when everyone around me flickered and went translucent.

Heath. I saw the creature realize it at the same time I did. It might be able to hold a dozen of us off as long as it could see the blows coming, but the odds had just shifted entirely to our side—as long as Heath was still alive to keep us masked in invisibility. Heath had made himself invisible before extending his power out to shroud the rest of us, and he'd started moving away from where he'd been when the creature had revealed itself, but with all of the other shape shifters still milling about he hadn't had a chance to move far.

The creature spun around, looking for Heath, but I was already in motion, and luckily Vicki's power had told her exactly what I was trying to do. The black, pulsing wings swept past me and then shot downwards, generating the thrust needed to launch the creature into the air. The creature's plan to throw itself across the distance between it and Heath would have worked perfectly, but at that instant I opened up the black hole inside of me and fed one of the tendrils into it at the same time that I slammed into another at full speed.

A few feet away, Vicki collided with a third tendril, and the results were everything I could have hoped. The tendril I attacked with my ability flickered and then disappeared, while the other two deformed under the force of several hundred pounds of desperate hybrids moving at more than thirty miles per hour.

They didn't collapse completely, and the claws on my good hand struggled to get any kind of real purchase on the oddly smooth substance of the energy tendrils, but without the support of three of the tendrils that the creature had been relying on, its wing-assisted jump went off course.

One of the other tendrils clipped me, but we'd succeeded in our objective, and the creature landed more than a dozen yards away from the last place where Heath had been. Black tendrils of energy lashed out in every direction, a buzzsaw of destruction that killed another of Isaac's wolves, but Heath was more than fifty yards away by that point, and a second later Adri opened up with her handgun.

The first bullet creased the creature's shoulder, but then it shielded itself with its wings and a second later Adri's magazine was empty and the creature was headed in her direction. It couldn't see her, but given just how much reach its wings had, it didn't need to get very close to be able to kill her.

Adri was desperately backpedaling, but she was making too much noise—the creature was using it to track her. I was running toward the two of them, and I wasn't the only one, but we'd all started moving too late and even if we managed to get to Adri, there wasn't any way we were going to be able to get past the flailing mass of tendrils that had turned the air around it into a kill zone.

My emotions were a confusing mess where Adri was concerned right then, but I didn't want her dead—not if this might have all been the result of the Coun'hij's machinations. My heart jumped up to my throat as the creature closed to within a few yards of Adri, and then Vicki was there behind it, but she wasn't looking at the creature, she was looking at me.

My mind spun. She'd started racing toward Adri even before the creature had landed. Her ability had told her that this moment was coming, but she seemed just as stymied by the furiously slashing wings…only she wouldn't have bothered running all that way if she couldn't see a future that might allow her to save Adri.

She needed me to make that happen. My gift had shut off again as soon as we'd thrown off the creature's jump, but I opened the rift wide open again and focused all of that absorptive power on one single tendril again.

Vicki was moving forward again even before the strand of energy disappeared. She leaped between two more tendrils that would have ripped her in half if her course had been off by as much as a few inches, and slammed her claws home in the creature's back.

The wings rippled as the creature screamed out, throwing Vicki clear with such force that I was worried that I would arrive to find her dead. Adri was out of the danger zone and Heath continued to silently fall back, carefully keeping the rest of us in sight so that he could maintain our invisibility shrouds.

By the time I made it over to Vicki she was struggling back to a sitting position. She was rattled, and if she'd been anyone else she would have been killed, but she must have thrown herself free of the creature a split second before the wings would have torn her off of him. That had been just enough to soften the blow.

I helped her to her feet and turned to see Isaac and Taggart both silently positioning themselves to attempt capturing some of the dark energy tendrils in the hopes that they would be able to replicate Vicki's feat. The creature was injured—bleeding profusely—but it wasn't dead, and none of us wanted to let it get away. We'd already paid too steep a price to let it come back and attack us another day.

It either divined our intent or had access to some kind of shadow precognitive ability of its own. It used its wings to throw itself more than fifty yards away from us and then turned back around to mock our efforts.

"You'll all be dead before the day is out. Even now a force closes in on those you came here to defend. They will be wiped off of the map and then the enforcers will come for you. A pity really—I could have feasted on this group for months."

The creature sprang away, using the strength of its wings to move faster than any wolf or hybrid could have run. Some of my people—our people—made as if to follow, but I called them back.

"Following it will just give it a chance to pick us off one by one as we spread out trying to chase it down. Come on—we need to get to the Annikov estate."

Chapter 18

Alec Graves
The Annikov Estate
Tucson, Arizona

The next few minutes were a blur of activity as we tried to get the wounded stabilized and load them and our dead into vehicles. Less than five minutes after the fight ended, we were all back on the road and I was praying that we would be able to make it to Jaclyn's in time.

My RV was more than a little worse for the wear—Vicki hadn't slowed down to open the door when she'd sensed my impending death—but it was still one of the best places to treat the injured. Unfortunately that included me.

Brindi was awake again—a little disoriented—but other than that okay. She wrapped my ribs while Vicki set my shoulder and taped it into place. It would all have to be re-done once I shifted back to human form, but I couldn't keep fighting with the breaks unstabilized and I wasn't going to go into whatever awaited us in human form.

"I left my guys behind to try to contain the situation, Alec. Everything happened too quickly for them to get out and assist in the fight, but hopefully they can tranq all of the humans who might have seen our throwdown with the Coun'hij's own personal dark angel."

"That wasn't an angel. It can die—we just couldn't figure out a way to hit it hard enough."

"Fair point. You do realize if we all show up at Jaclyn's estate and there isn't actually an attack underway that you'll have painted a big target on her back, right?"

"Yeah. In for a penny, in for a pound, I guess. Besides, it was your boss who told me that this was going down. What's the matter? Don't trust him?"

"No, I trust Shawn, but that doesn't mean that he can't be wrong. I guess more than anything I'm worried about the fact that I had to reveal myself to everyone back there."

"My people are trustworthy, and now that we've exposed Nellie—or rather the thing that was pretending to be Nellie—as the spy, Isaac's people shouldn't leak either."

"Yeah. I had that same thought, but once a secret like this is out there isn't any putting it back in the box. Shawn's involvement will get out eventually—it's just a matter of trying to figure out how long we have so that he can stay ahead of the retaliation headed our direction."

"Yeah—hopefully we can send a message of our own here in the next few minutes. If we can wipe out a significant chunk of the Coun'hij's enforcers it will go a long way towards making sure that Kaleb and the rest won't be able to come after anyone. Make sure that your people don't waste any time. I want them on the road as soon as possible—the sooner they join up with the rest of us, the safer they'll be.

"Put up signs saying that the motel is closed, drug all of the humans up, and then lock them in a room somewhere. If we survive the next couple of hours then we'll go back and deal with figuring out who saw what."

"And if we don't?"

"If we don't then it's the Coun'hij's problem."

My RV, James at the wheel, was in the lead so I got a firsthand view of the flurry of activity from the estate as we drove up to the gates around Jaclyn's house.

I was tempted to leave myself in my hybrid form. It would make dealing with the pain so much easier, but it would also escalate the situation out there in ways that didn't need escalating. There was no sign that the estate was actually under attack yet, so I shoved my beast further back into the corner of my mind where I normally kept him. A second later I'd shifted back to human form and was getting scowls from both Brindi and Vicki.

"You realize that you just ruined all of our work, don't you?'

"Yeah, sorry. Couldn't be helped."

I pulled myself to my feet with a groan, and then peeled off the tape as I exited the RV. "You need to open the gates and let us in—I have reason to believe that you're about to be attacked by an overwhelming force."

The guy behind the gate, a short, musclebound guy who looked like he was in his fifties, shook his head. "The only invading force I need to worry about right now is the one trailing along behind you. I'm not letting you inside."

"Get Jaclyn down here."

"Ms. Annikov doesn't come running for the likes of you. You can turn around and leave, or I'll have your entire group arrested."

It boggled the mind to think that this guy didn't know who he was dealing with. Even if he didn't recognize my face, the simple fact that I was shirtless and wearing a ha'bit should have told him that I wasn't just another random human.

I lashed out with a surge of power that forced him back a step. "If you call the police you're going to have an even bigger mess on your hands than if you make me come in there after you. I'm going to say this once more. Get Jaclyn down here in the next five minutes or we'll rip your precious gate down and beat you with it."

I turned around and walked away without looking back to see how he would respond. I headed down the column of vehicles until I found Carson, Taggart, Isaac, Heath and Grayson. Adri joined us as I started talking, but I didn't acknowledge her presence. We weren't fighting inside of a dream, so this wasn't her area of expertise, and things were still too raw between the two of us to risk starting a conversation with her—there was no telling where it would go and I couldn't deal with another distraction right now.

"I just gave them a time limit. They've got about four and a half minutes to get Jaclyn down here. After that, I want those gates open. I'll neutralize anyone in the guard post. Heath, can you take a group and go over the wall? I don't think that Jaclyn has any snipers working the top of the house, but there's no way to know for sure and I'd feel a lot better knowing that our people aren't sitting ducks up there."

I couldn't tell if Heath was carrying a grudge about my having accused him of being a Coun'hij agent—he was too reserved for that—but he nodded in all of the right places, and Isaac seemed to trust that he was professional enough to do his job regardless of his personal feelings toward me.

"Grayson, I know that your power is somewhat hit-and-miss, but can you be ready to deal with anyone further out?"

For the first time I could remember, Grayson looked agitated. "Yes. After what we just saw back at the motel, I think I'll be able to muster up the mojo to do what needs to be done."

I turned to Carson, Isaac, and Taggart. "I need the three of you to coordinate the rest of our forces. I'll be too busy using my ability to give orders once the fur starts flying, but I want this to be as bloodless as possible. We go in and neutralize people rather than killing them. I've got a stash of high-strength tranqs in the storage compartment in the second RV. Tranq anyone that gives us any problems, but use small enough doses that we have a chance of getting them back on their feet if the Coun'hij shows up."

The other two agreed right away, but Carson studied me for several seconds before nodding. "You're not going to give them any choice, are you?"

"I'll give them as much of a choice as I can, but let's not be under any illusions. I came down to Arizona because I have good reason to believe that Kaleb and the others are planning on executing every member of this pack. I'm not going to just walk away and let them all die. In a very real sense, their choices disappeared when we showed up at their gate—the line member over there just doesn't realize it yet."

We split up, and I arrived back at the gate just in time to see Jaclyn hurry up to the gate.

"Are you out of your mind, Graves? You just signed our death warrants! Once word gets out that you showed up on my doorstep the Coun'hij is never going to believe that I'm still a neutral party."

I laughed. "I should have known that I could trust you to both see the reality of the situation and still delude yourself into thinking that you could play both sides, Jaclyn. The Coun'hij knows that you're not independent, but you're right, I just took away the slender pretext that you've been hiding behind. I have very strong intelligence indicating that there's a group of Coun'hij enforcers on their way here as we speak, or I wouldn't have come, but you're right. It's time to make a choice."

"You're putting me in a very difficult spot, Alec. I tried to warn you away, but you're as stubborn as your father and nearly as certain of the rectitude of your cause as he is. The only way for me to offer my people a life other than constantly being on the run from your dad is if we attack you now."

"You'll regret that, Jaclyn. Your pack won't last five minutes against my people. I'll try to save as many of them as I can, but you're too dangerous for that. If you turn this into a fight, you'll be the first to die."

She nodded. "I'm under no illusions about my ability to get my claws in your throat before you take me down, Alec, but you've forced me into a situation where no matter which option I choose I'll be faced with regrets. The only real question is whether I think my people have a better chance going up against you or going up against your father."

The tension ratcheted up to the point where all it would take was a blink for both sides to explode into violence. Even as I reached for my ability, I refused to look away from Jaclyn's gaze. If I ended up having to kill her I was at least going to do her the honor of looking her in the eye while I did it.

A split second before the violence started, Vicki appeared at my elbow. "Don't do this, Jaclyn. Your people can't beat us."

Jaclyn's eyes narrowed. "You—I recognize you. Does this mean that Ulrich has finally picked a side, or is this just another of Shawn's youthful indiscretions?"

Vicki looked off into the distance as though trying to read the future, and at that moment I realized that she was wishing she could read more than just the next few seconds of what was going to happen.

"I can't talk about all of that out here in the open, Jaclyn, and you know it. If you want to let us inside, then I'll tell you what's going on. Otherwise we'll just have to let things play out as they would if my boss wasn't in the picture at all."

Jaclyn had been ready to die a few seconds before—now she was faced with a possibility that offered survival for both her and her people. If Vicki had just given her a yes or no response, Jaclyn probably could have made her decision in a split second. She'd doubtlessly fantasized about the idea of the Chicago pack finally coming out in open rebellion. The question of whether or not to let us inside her walls was a completely new problem though, one that had just been drastically complicated by the promise of inside information.

The question of what she was going to do next hung in the air between us for several seconds, and then I felt Vicki relax. I thought that meant that we were in—Jaclyn's sigh took me completely off guard.

"No, even if you tell me that Ulrich is finally picking the side of the rebellion it still wouldn't be enough for me to put my people at risk like that. He's a long ways away, and Kaleb has people less than two hundred miles from here. Ulrich is strong, but even he doesn't have as long of a reach as the Coun'hij."

Jaclyn turned—to give the order to prepare for our attack—and then Tasha came running into view. "We've got reports of a motorcade headed this direction, Mom. They're coming from the west. Stack and Nick are putting it at ninety-five percent probability that it's Worthingfield and his people."

I couldn't blame Jaclyn for swearing. I'd been expecting something like this—hoping for it really—for days now, and I still felt like cursing.

We could take the people that Brandon had stationed on the border, but there was always a chance that he was just one prong in a much bigger attack—an attack that could include everything from other enforcers and members of bootlicker packs to werewolves and another creature—a dark angel—like the one we'd just finished fighting.

I looked back at Isaac and the rest to make sure that they'd heard, and then turned forward to face Jaclyn again. "You can't run—not now. I've got arrangements made to help you disappear, but it will take time for you to make it to the extraction points. If you leave now you'll never manage to fall off of their radar."

She nodded. "Get the gates open. Tasha, get the word out to the rest of our people—we need them all here, and they need to come ready for a fight. How long do we have before Brandon arrives?"

"Less than ten minutes. The satellites are all down. Our information came in from one of our human contacts on the other side of town—we're lucky we have even this much warning."

The gates opened and our vehicles started pouring into the estate. Vicki's people weren't going to make it here in time—even some of Jaclyn's people weren't going to be able to get here before the fighting started.

I grabbed Brindi as she came down the steps from my RV and sent her towards Vicki. "Tell Rachel that I want her to coordinate with Vicki's people, and then go find Tasha. Ask her for an alternate assembly point outside of the estate for any of her people who are too far away to make it here in time. If they can all meet up there with Vicki's people there's a chance that they'll be able to fight their way out even if things go badly here."

The next few minutes flew by in a frenzied blur. We got everyone inside the walls of the estate and then we closed the gates and backed both of my RV's up against them from the inside and engaged the brakes.

It was the equivalent to burning the boats we'd arrived in, but I wasn't going to take any chances that the gates weren't as strong as they looked—having Brandon's people run us down in three-thousand-pound SUVs was one of the worst things we could have happen. This way they would all have to come over the walls, which would mean that we would have a chance to pick them off as they tried to reform before engaging us.

I tried to coordinate with Jaclyn, but she simply told me to hold the north and west sides of the estate and her people would hold the other two sides. Before I could break through her stubbornness, Brandon's people started arriving. It quickly became apparent that Tasha's network of observers had missed at least one group of incoming enforcers. The motorcade that arrived outside the wall was much bigger than

I'd been expecting. I counted more than two dozen cars before the field of vehicles had filled up the drive and started parking out of sight.

Jaclyn's estate was on the very outskirts of the city, surrounded by more than three hundred acres of private, unoccupied land, but I was still surprised that the local police hadn't showed up. All I could figure was that the enforcers must have come in mostly as smaller groups and only reformed into a single cavalcade once they were within a short distance of the estate.

I asked Heath and Grayson each to anchor one side of our defenses, and then left Isaac and Carson to finish splitting up the rest of our people. Jaclyn and Tasha were both standing a few feet back from the gate, waiting for whoever was in charge to step forward.

I should have known that it would be Brandon. He approached to within a dozen yards of the gate, followed by Vincent and a few other bruisers.

"I'm here in the name of the Coun'hij to deliver judgment for the treasonous act of providing shelter to Alec's band of misfits."

Jaclyn's expression was grim, but apparently she'd decided to play the hand she'd been dealt to the best of her ability.

"That's interesting timing considering that Alec just showed up at my gates a few minutes ago, but you would have had to have started driving hours ago."

Brandon shrugged. "They may have only arrived at your gate a short time ago, but they've been inside of your territory for days. If you're not able to police the ground your pack has claimed, then you should have petitioned the Coun'hij to allow you to move or at the very least you should have reduced the area you claimed."

Jaclyn laughed. "I don't even know why I'm bothering to have this conversation with you. If Alec hadn't come down here you would have come up with another pretext for being down here. As much as I hate to admit it, Graves was right all along. Your masters have decided that they need to make an example out of someone, and they're too stupid to realize killing us will only force them to patrol this section of the border themselves in addition to all the other demands on their time."

Brandon showed his teeth at the reminder that he was there as little more than a hired gun, but other than that he maintained his composure much better than I would have expected.

"You're wrong, but I've been down here long enough to know that's par for the course. It's true that your pack is guilty by association, but the Coun'hij is willing to be merciful. I'm not here to kill all of your people, just you and your second in command. I will then take over the pack to make sure that there aren't any dissident elements left."

It wasn't a half-bad plan. With a bigger pack, one that was less united, it might have even worked, but looking around at those of Jaclyn's people within visual range, it was obvious to me that they saw it for what it really was. They would be buying themselves a few more months of life, but once Brandon was their alpha it would just be a matter of time before their lives would be spent against some enemy of the Coun'hij.

I stepped forward and clapped. "Brilliant. Kaleb kills two birds with one stone. He pays you off for murdering a few hundred innocents by giving you your own little fiefdom down here, he purges the most dissident elements of the Tucson pack, and he secures a new batch of cannon fodder. Too bad it's not going to work."

Brandon resumed talking as though he hadn't heard me. "Of course your...guests...will be killed. Alec and everyone with him have proven themselves beyond redemption. It is with great regret that Kaleb signed the order for them to be destroyed, but sometimes terrible sacrifices must be made to protect our race."

I turned to Jaclyn. "I know this is your home, so if you want to be the one to kill him I'll let you, but I was really hoping to be the one to finally put him down."

Jaclyn's grin showed too much teeth to be mistaken as a human expression. "Let's make a contest of it. Whoever kills him gets to call the shots from here on out?"

I shook my head. "He's a threat, but he's still not much more than an errand boy. In order to justify those kinds of stakes you'd have to bring down the entire Coun'hij."

She shrugged. "You can't blame me for trying." Jaclyn turned her back on the gate. "I think we're done here."

I started to respond and then all hell broke loose. Something hit on the other side of the house hard enough that the ground shook, and then hybrids started coming over the wall. I froze for a second, looking back and forth between my people and Jaclyn's, but she waved me off.

"Go take care of your half of the battle."

I shifted forms and for the first time since we'd arrived, felt a measure of relief from the pain of all my broken bones. I tore across the grounds and rounded a corner of the house to see exactly what I'd been afraid I would find.

The creature—the dark angel—was back. My people were being forced back away from the wall by the maelstrom of glowing black energy tendrils, tendrils that were shredding everything within a dozen feet of the creature.

The sound of running off to my right brought me around just in time to see the third prong of the assault come sailing over the wall. I opened my mouth to give orders, but Carson was already ahead of me. He dispatched a team of six hybrids—along with Heath—to keep the dark angel busy, and brought the rest of our people running in my direction.

With most of our hybrids detached to fight the creature we were drastically outnumbered, and most of our remaining people were wolves, but we still had a couple of cards to play. I was ready to hit the first group of hybrids with my power, but Grayson was a half-step ahead of me. Most of them were still in midair when their bodies started convulsing.

It was the perfect response. My ability would have kept them down, but I would have been forced to then kill them one at a time—all by myself. Grayson being in play meant that all of our people—every wolf and hybrid—swarmed over the first wave of opponents. They were all dead within seconds.

The battle sounds coming from the other side of the estate were growing—our prong of the attack hadn't ever been meant to face real opposition. Brandon and the rest had all come over the other wall.

I grabbed Isaac and turned him back toward the blur of motion around the dark angel. "Grab half our people and go help contain that—take Grayson with you in case they launch another wave at us from this direction."

I spun around and took off at a sprint, Carson, Vicki and James at my back. The ten seconds it took us to get far enough around the house to see the fighting stretched out forever, and the vista of destruction awaiting us made something inside of me recoil in horror.

Brandon had brought even more warriors than I'd expected, and the Tucson pack was fighting a rear-guard action against more than twice their number. Jaclyn had seemed confident in her ability to beat Brandon in a one-on-one fight, but even from so far away it was obvious to me that he was toying with her.

Carson pushed past me—faster than I was in my injured state—and then he lit up like a signal fire on whatever wavelength of sight my beast bestowed on me. He was far enough ahead of me that I only caught the very edge of what he threw at the combatants, but it still drained me of much of the anger that had been powering me. I managed to retain my shape and continue stumbling forward, but the people it had been directed at weren't nearly as lucky.

A ripple of change swept through the battle, momentarily robbing the combatants of the emotional peaks they needed to maintain their transformations. Some of them still pressed forward, trying to kill each other with their bare hands, but most just collapsed to the ground in a daze.

Whatever Carson had done wasn't as targeted as what Grayson had done, but it still seemed to hit the Coun'hij forces harder than it did Jaclyn's people, who managed to kill several of their opponents before Carson stumbled in exhaustion and dropped his emotional damping-field.

Between one heartbeat and the next the battlefield re-erupted with violence, but he'd bought us nearly three full seconds. It had helped, but it wasn't going to be enough to save Jaclyn—not against a monster like Brandon.

I reached inside and for the third time that day opened up the conduit inside of me as far as it would go. What I found shocked me. As long as I could remember I'd been told that Brandon had the potential to manifest a gift like nothing that had been seen among our people in thousands of years. Somehow I'd lost sight of that in the face of his blinding speed and unbelievable strength.

I'd seriously underestimated him. I reached out intending on using my ability to bring the fighting to a halt once again. I hadn't expected to be able to maintain the absorption field indefinitely, but I only needed three more seconds to make it to the fighting, and then every second that passed would mean one more dead enforcer, one more person who wouldn't be able to threaten my people.

Instead of bringing the *fighting* to a stop, *I* was nearly brought to a stop. The energy crashing into me before being sucked down into the rift inside of me was unbelievable. In the aggregate, it was every bit as fearsome as what I'd felt coming off of the creature. Inside of my mind I could see a map of the people in front of me. The hybrids shone brighter than the wolves, Carson and Jaclyn both shone much brighter than the other hybrids, and Brandon was like staring into the sun.

I felt something inside of me start to tear as I exceeded the limits of my gift, and immediately narrowed down the focus of my attack. I pulled back the edge of my field, shrinking it down so that it didn't include Brandon and Jaclyn, and then threw myself toward that dead spot on our end of the fighting.

My people didn't know as much as they would have liked about my ability, but they all knew enough to stay out of the area I was targeting. Jaclyn's people weren't as knowledgeable. Several of them lunged forward intending on savaging a fallen opponent and instead joined their targets on the ground.

I brushed past the two hybrids between me and the dead spot, trusting James and the others to distract the enforcers from taking swipes at my unprotected back. It was risky, but I could feel the black hole inside of me starting to destabilize—I needed to eliminate some of the power sources that were overwhelming my ability.

I buried my right fist in the chest of my first target while he struggled to pull himself back up to his feet. I knew I would regret what I was doing later—regret killing defenseless enemies—but right then I'd locked my emotions safely away behind a thick wall. Sorrow, fear, pain from my broken ribs and damaged shoulder—it was all inaccessible.

The second and third targets were close enough for me to kill them less than a second later, and then a flicker of motion brought me around. My people were streaming around the edge of the circle of immobilized bodies and in our little corner of the battle we had numerical superiority. Coun'hij hybrids were falling to groups of three and four wolves working in unison or to paired hybrids, but the real destruction was being dished out by Carson.

No living thing could cross the invisible line in the ground created by my ability, but Carson had figured out a way around that. He stalked along the perimeter of fallen figures and his sword licked out with nearly every step, crossing the boundary and killing with each stroke.

I almost yelled for him to stop. I'd been focused on my targets, on killing the enforcers as quickly as I could, but what flashes I'd seen of the rest of the battle told me that Brandon was tearing his way through the Tucson pack like they were nothing more than immobile paper dolls. Carson was one of the few opponents Brandon couldn't just mow down and part of me wanted him out there fighting the biggest menace on the battlefield, but he was right. My usefulness on the field of battle was limited by how quickly I could dispatch immobilized foes.

That was the main weakness that made someone like Grayson or Heath so much more effective in most situations. Carson was doubling my usefulness and killing enemies even faster than he could have in open battle. It was a stroke of brilliance, but it wasn't enough.

I yelled for Jess and Jasmin as I saw them take down another hybrid.

"Follow along behind me and kill any stragglers while they are still disoriented and weak!"

I centered my ability on myself so it would move with me, and then I took several steps forward as a fresh wave of hybrids came soaring over the wall. My forward motion brought new enemies into my sphere of influence at the same time that it let me get to another target.

Some of the newcomers realized what was going on too late—after they'd already stumbled into the dead zone that surrounded me. The shock of so many new bodies—new power sources—nearly brought my absorption field down and I was forced to shrink it.

Carson paced me on one side—now enveloped in fighting as some of the hybrids I'd been immobilizing staggered to their feet—and I could hear Jas and Jess behind me wreaking nine different kinds of destruction on the hybrids that I'd bypassed, but all of that was secondary to Brandon's bellows.

"Overwhelm him—there are only so many he can affect at one time. Pile on and bring him down now!"

He was right. It was a replay of my experience with Shawn all over again. I'd strolled into battle thinking that I'd thought through all of the ways in which I was vulnerable, but I'd been gravely mistaken.

The fighting behind me intensified as some of Jaclyn's people were free of my ability and joined Jas and Jess, but the new arrivals among Brandon's people were spilling around now and engaging the wolves behind me. My ability wobbled again, and I was forced to reduce the radius I was affecting once again or risk losing control altogether. I was sprinting from target to target, trying not to be pushed back into Carson, but seeing that moment approaching all too quickly.

In another second or two my limit was going to be reached and then I'd be forced back against the house and any of my people caught up in my field would be set upon as soon as I'd passed them by, before they could gather their strength again.

I desperately looked for a way out that would allow us to survive what was coming, and then I heard the first shot.

It was Adri. She'd come out through the front door of the mansion and she was calmly putting round after round into the shifting pile of shape shifters who'd thrown themselves into the circle of my power.

She fired with the precision of a metronome, emptying her magazine and then reloading and resuming with barely a pause. I'd seen action movies where the shots weren't as close together as she was managing, and even shape shifters couldn't endure that indefinitely. Things balanced on the edge of a razor, my ability trembling from the strain of draining so much power, as Carson, Adri and I killed hybrids by the dozen. Two more seconds dragged by, and then suddenly the enforcer and loyalist hybrids were streaming around my dead zone in an effort to get at the rest of my people.

As the pressure came off of me, I stopped moving and let the area I was affecting shift around more freely. I'd been thinking of this all wrong. It wasn't about dropping people and pinning them in place until I'd managed to kill them myself, it was about dropping large numbers of enemies and then pulling my ability back far enough that my people could kill them.

Carson figured out what I was doing even before I announced the change in my strategy. He watched me temporarily immobilize half a dozen hybrids and then darted in once they began moving again, and killed them in a series of lightning-fast strikes that took less than three seconds.

Jasmin and the rest of the wolves at my back figured things out as I yelled for them to alternately fall back and then attack. They'd been a fearsome bunch even before that, but now they were four-legged reapers who were felling enemies many times their size with each pass, killing with near impunity.

A scream from up ahead of me pulled my attention back to the wider battle, and what I saw chilled my blood. The dark angel had fallen back around the perimeter of the estate and had joined up with the cadre of enforcers that Brandon had formed up around him.

The fighting over there mostly involved members from the Tucson pack, and they were even less prepared to go up against a creature like that than our people were. Heath had moved around far enough that large chunks of our people were flickering in and out of sight as he extended his ability to its limit, but even that was only slowing the rout that was developing on that side of the fight.

I tried to push forward faster, tried to get over to where I could influence that side of things, but more and more of my people had been peeled off of my side of the fighting and forced to shore up Jaclyn's forces. The only way to move through the press of people between me and Brandon would be to turn my ability off altogether, and run through the horde of semiconscious enforcers ahead of me. I could do it, but Jasmin, Jess and the rest behind me would fall in seconds against those overwhelming numbers.

I moved forward anyway, trying to expand out my sphere of influence, and as an ever-increasing torrent of energy roared through me and into the semi-tame black hole inside of me, I realized something for the first time.

The energy I was siphoning off wasn't going somewhere, it was going *somewheres*. My ability didn't just form a single conduit. There was one big conduit, but I could also sense smaller threads heading off in other directions. The reservoir where my ability was sending all of that energy wasn't a single reservoir, it was one big reservoir and more than a dozen smaller reservoirs.

I'd been right in fearing earlier that I'd reached the limit of how much power that reservoir could absorb. I had. The bigger reservoir was nearly tapped out—or maybe just my ability to use it had been reached. The smaller reservoirs though still had capacity.

I reached down one of the threads between me and a secondary reservoir, and to my inner eye it was a brilliant golden thread. It disappeared into the ether, impossible to follow, but all of a sudden I somehow knew where the thread went. It went to Carson, tireless, deadly, loyal Carson.

I followed other threads, felt them go off into other dimensions that somehow terminated in people I knew. Rachel was there, a tiny thread that was so slender I almost couldn't see it inside the landscape of my mind's eye.

Brindi was there too, a thread that was nearly as big around as the one leading to Carson, but the reservoir she represented was no bigger than the one inside of Rachel. I expanded my awareness into each of them, and there was one thread that was different than all of the rest. I tracked it to its destination and found James, locked in combat alongside Taggart and others against Brandon.

Heath had warned me about the fact that his ability didn't work on Brandon, but I hadn't been prepared for what that really meant. Brandon was fighting some of our best warriors and it was obvious that he was just biding his time, waiting for one of them to make a mistake that would let him start picking them off.

Each and every hybrid fighting him moved with the speed and precision that was only found in the most deadly of our kind, but they were no match for him—not individually, not even collectively. Brandon moved with a speed and strength that allowed him to dodge out of the way of multiple attacks all at once and check the blows that he couldn't avoid.

There was a thread connecting me to Taggart too, but it was James my attention was pulled towards even as I killed the enforcer at my feet. The thread to James was the biggest around of any of them, and his reservoir was big—just like the reservoirs of all of the hybrids I was connected to, but there was more to it than that. He was nearly full to the brim with energy, but I could feel something balancing on the edge of becoming something else.

More power flowed down the link between us, and I felt it get that much closer to becoming that other thing. A group of wolves came racing around the inside of the wall, and I was momentarily forced to extend my ability out to them, cutting their legs out from under them in an effort to buy Jasmin and the others time to fall back to Carson.

The surge of power coming into me was too much, and I felt my ability momentarily short out, but not before James' reservoir hit some critical mass. James stumbled and went down on one knee, and I knew that I'd just killed him without meaning to. He was still breathing, his heart was still beating, but I'd just created the opening Brandon had been waiting for. He moved forward to dispatch James, and there was nothing I could do to stop him.

Taggart and the others threw themselves at Brandon with renewed energy, but he beat them all back, and then there was nothing between him and James but the tawny body of a wolf that had come out of nowhere to throw herself at Brandon. I was too far away to be able to confirm the identity of the wolf, but I didn't need to be able to see her to know that it was Addison.

Brandon tore her out of the air in a shower of blood, and continued forward intent on killing James, but James wasn't where he'd been a split second earlier. James spun to the side and slammed his fist home into Brandon's side with a force that lifted Brandon up and threw him into the wall.

It was an impossible blow—not just the strength of it, but the speed. I'd known James since before he'd become a hybrid, and I'd never seen him move that quickly. He followed up his initial strike with a series of attacks that were nothing more than a blur to me. The only time I'd ever seen anything even remotely like that had been when Brandon had been fighting the Ancients down in Mexico.

James wasn't the equal of Brandon—nobody living was—but the margin of difference had just shrunk down to the point where few beings who weren't as fast as them could have hoped to tell them apart.

Brandon scored several deep blows against James, but he didn't manage a killing strike, and that was unheard of. Nobody had stood against him in single combat since before he'd first manifested his power. Brandon surged forward in an attempt to end the fight and dispatch James, but now James' allies had arrived and Brandon was being driven backwards.

The hybrids all around me were struggling back to their feet, and for the next several seconds my attention was fully occupied with trying to keep myself alive. Carson and a few others fought their way to my side, and for a long eternity we all traded blows with our adversaries in an endless round of violence.

Somewhere along the way I realized that I was using both arms, that my ribs didn't hurt, but there was no time to wonder at the miraculous healing I'd experienced. One of my opponents hit me with enough force to send me reeling backwards, and I was convinced I was going to die right up until the Coun'hij enforcers started falling to invisible foes. Heath had just arrived with help.

I stepped back as a horde of bodies—some seen and others still invisible—pushed past me, eager to get in on the final kills. A scream brought me around in time to see Adri fall to the ground. I crossed the distance between us without even considering if I should be focused elsewhere. Despite everything else that had happened, part of me was still more concerned about her than almost anything else.

A battle still raged around us, but less than five feet from her were the bloody remains of the fallen angel, and it was obvious that we were going to win. Adri was kneeling between Taggart on one side and James on the other, and her sobs precluded anything approaching speech.

Both men had shifted back to human form because of their wounds, which was never a good thing. It meant that they didn't have long. Their wounds were bad enough that I was surprised that they'd lasted this long.

I didn't realize that I'd shifted back to human form until I took each of their hands in mine. Their body temperature had both already started to plummet, but I didn't try to administer first aid—their injuries were mostly internal, the kind of thing that even a surgeon couldn't have fixed in the time they had left.

James was trying to say something, but struggling to breathe past the blood. I leaned down close enough to hear him and my heart dropped as I realized he was asking about his mother. I didn't have the heart to tell him that she was already dead—resting less than a dozen feet from us.

"I've never seen anything like it." Vicki was standing at my back. "The two of them chased *Brandon Worthingfield* off and then crashed into the damn angel like it was just any other enemy. I tried to get in there to save them, but there just weren't any openings. The wings provided it with too much coverage."

I nodded. "I suspect that they knew that—they were trying to create that opening for you. They knew that it had tied too many of our people up for too long, people we needed over on the other side of the battle. It looks like you managed to get it though. It's a relief knowing that it's gone. There will be one fewer of those things that we'll have to deal with in the future."

"You don't think it's the only one of its kind, do you?"

I shook my head. "The only way it would be the last of its kind is if there's something else out there that's even more scary hunting them down. There are more of them, and at least some of them are allied with the Coun'hij. We're going to run into them again, which means that we're going to have to find a better way of fighting them."

Vicki looked down at my arm and did a double-take. "How did you heal that so quickly? I thought it would be days still before you'd be moving around without wincing at every step."

"I'm not sure. It's a good thing though—I would have been dead a dozen times over out there without the use of both arms. I..."

I suddenly had a suspicion how I'd done it. I reached out to the closest pocket of fighting and brought all of the shape shifters to their knees. Enforcers, Tucson pack members, Isaac's people, my people, I hit all of them with my power without even pausing to consider the fact that I wasn't sure if my ability was still working.

I sucked down a torrent of power as intense as anything else I'd ever accessed, and this time I didn't let it just flow down the threads as it willed. I reached out to the threads that were still rich and vibrant, and I pinched them off, forcing the energy into the fading threads that led into Taggart and James.

Their threads resisted the energy—there was no capacity in the fraying vessels inside of them, but I refused to be thwarted. I poured energy, poured life into them and seconds passed by as pain-filled hours until I saw the bones underneath their skin start to shift back into place. James started breathing again, and the hole in Taggart's chest sealed itself, flesh surging upwards until there wasn't even a scar left.

It was good, but it wasn't enough. I reached for more, pulling in more and more of the people around me. The ocean of energy raging through my body threatened to consume me. It felt as though the rift that was the interior manifestation of my ability was going to tear free of the fleshy moorings that made it part of me, but I forced it wider open in an exercise of pure will and sent the resulting power racing outward, exploring the limits of my new domain, the invisible realm that comprised individual universes of possibility.

People started fainting on all sides. Some of them lost consciousness from having their vitality drained away, some of them lost consciousness from having too much power forced into them, but still I pushed.

I reached the end of the network of golden threads. None of them were like James, teetering on the edge of a transformation to something else. I pushed energy into the ones that were hurt, and then grabbed all of the remaining energy and tried to push it into Addison.

I owed James. It had been my fault that he'd stumbled and his mother had been forced to sacrifice herself, I needed to bring her back. I continued to suck down more energy at the same time that I crimped the golden threads. I kept hoping that if I built up enough of a voltage differential the energy would jump from me to Addison, but it stubbornly refused to respond to my will. Something inside of me started to tear, and then I lost my grip on everything and the energy shot outward from me to all of my people and I lost consciousness.

Chapter 19

Alec Graves
The Socorro Motel
Tucson, Arizona

We won, not that I was conscious to see the last of our enemies put down. I woke up an hour later inside of my RV surrounded by a combination of wounded and unconscious individuals. Rachel hurried over to check on me when she saw that I was awake, but I waved her off. Physically I was fine.

I made my way outside and found that we'd returned to the motel where Vicki's people had been stationed. It was Vicki who was waiting for me, which shouldn't have surprised me. She'd been close enough to me not to get caught up in my ability when I'd started draining people, and she hadn't been connected to me by one of the golden threads, so she'd avoided being affected by the backlash of all that power at the very end.

"We've got things under control now. As people wake up I'm sending them out to establish a perimeter. If Brandon shows back up he'll encounter stiff resistance, but I have to admit that I'm glad to see you up and about. I've never been completely confident that I could take him by myself. With you back in the picture to drain away some of that unnatural energy, my chances of taking him down are a lot better."

I grunted. "I don't think Brandon will be coming back. They didn't expect to lose today. Brandon isn't going to come back against us unless he's confident he can win. He'll fight against terrible odds when he has to, but having James stand against him like that will have unnerved him. I don't suppose we managed to get Vincent?"

"No. Once Brandon realized he was outclassed he pulled back over the wall with a core of his most trusted people. Vincent was one of the ones who got away."

"How many did we lose?"

"About a third, but we lost a lot fewer than we should have and we killed several times as many as we lost. What's left of the Tucson pack will go a long way towards replacing the people we lost."

I shook my head. "Not replacing. Replenishing our numbers, yes, but nobody is going to replace the ones we lost. What about Ulrich? He can't hope to remain on the fence—not now, not after Brandon and his people saw you."

She gave me a sad smile. "I've been disavowed. As much as Ulrich would have liked to be able to keep me around, I'm a liability now. If anyone asks, he and Shawn will say that I and my men were part of a splinter group inside of Shawn's movement, one that was trying to make the world think that the Chicago pack had sent me as a way of forcing Ulrich's hand."

"Kaleb will know that's a lie."

"Yep, but they won't risk going after him for it. The Coun'hij is going to be running scared right now. The majority of the people they just lost were hybrids from bootlicker packs, but they still lost a ton of enforcers. They are going to be trumpeting Ulrich's continued neutrality as proof that they haven't lost control of things."

"Ulrich is playing a very risky game. I wouldn't put it past Puppeteer to decide that he needs to be taken out regardless, and when that happens the last thing he and Shawn are going to want is for me to doubt their true loyalty."

That made Vicki mad, but I'd known it would even before I'd said it. There was no gold thread connecting her and me—Ulrich might have officially cut her loose and told her to play the part of one of my people, but she was still Shawn's woman—would always be his. I'd said what I'd said because I wanted her to pass that message on to Ulrich and Shawn.

Vicki saw Jaclyn and Isaac approaching, and used that as a reason to leave. I nodded a greeting.

"Are the two of you ready to swear fealty to me?"

Jaclyn didn't even wait for the words to fade away before she shook her head. "I'll be joining Isaac's group. He's got plenty of experience running a team with disparate power levels while keeping them under the Coun'hij's radar."

I should have known better. Jaclyn didn't have a thread connecting her to me. There was no loyalty there. Isaac on the other hand was connected to me by a thin filament of gold.

"I'm surprised, Isaac. I know that our history isn't without hiccups, but you of all people know how dangerous things are going to get if we continue to operate as separate groups. You've got Heath in your court, and Jaclyn too apparently, but there is only so much the two of them can do if Kaleb or one of the others decides that he wants your heads on a platter."

Isaac shifted uncomfortably. "I'm sorry, Alec. If it were strictly up to me, I'd fold my people into your organization and back your play, but it's not just my call. I owe it to my people to see things through with them, and a lot of them don't like the way that you used them as some kind of metaphysical power source to heal James and Taggart. Your people walked away without so much as a bruise, while many of my people are going to be limping for days. They don't think it's fair."

A hundred responses whipped through my mind, but in the end I just nodded. "There is a reason that they weren't healed, Isaac. It's just the other side of the reason that you were healed. If you ever change your mind there is a place for you in my organization along with whoever you want to bring along."

I could smell James and Taggart standing just inside of my RV, but they saw Adri approaching at the same time that I did, and apparently decided to give us at least the illusion of privacy.

"I came to see Taggart—I wanted to make sure that he's okay."

"He's fine. The backlash from having his wounds healed put him down for a while, but he's awake now and none the worse for wear. Please feel free to go inside and check on him."

She turned to go and then stopped. "That wasn't you I saw inside the RV with Brindi, was it?"

"No more than it was you that I saw making out with Tristan in your room. That creature...that dark angel...played all of us for fools. It knew that you were headed out, so it lured Tristan to your room and waited for me to come by."

She stood there in silence for several seconds, refusing to meet my gaze. "I suppose that you think I overreacted."

Yes. If I was going to be entirely honest, I did think that she'd behaved rashly. That wasn't what she needed to hear though.

"You had your reasons. To some extent, both of us played directly into that thing's hands. If I hadn't disappeared for more than an hour then it never would have had a chance to implement the second half of its plan. Luckily we were able to right things in time to expose the creature and then get here and defeat the Coun'hij's forces."

"That sounds like a polite way of avoiding my question."

"I'm not sure what you want out of me, Adri."

"I want an apology. That would be a good starting point."

"An apology for something that I didn't actually do?"

She'd been unhappy before, but now she was furious. I could smell the anger coming off of her in waves.

"An apology for creating a situation in which such a transparently obvious ploy could drive a wedge between us. I shouldn't have had any reason to doubt your loyalty, Alec. I should have *known* that you were faithful to me, but I didn't. I didn't know because you've made that nearly impossible by keeping me in the dark. You've got Brindi sleeping in the same room as you, you're driving off minutes before we're supposed to come under attack, and then to top it all off, it turns out you had another girl hidden inside your bedroom for the last twenty-four hours. Anyone would have thought exactly what I thought when I saw Brindi lying on top of you like that."

My beast was starting to act up, and for once where Adri was concerned, I wasn't completely inclined to rein it back in.

"You're free to think whatever you want to think, Adri. I've explained the fact that there are certain secrets that I have to keep, certain obligations that I assumed when I stepped up to lead this cell of the rebellion. Those obligations aren't going to go away regardless of how you might feel about them.

"You had every right to be hurt by what you saw—I was definitely hurt by what I saw—but you didn't have the right to split our forces in half while we were in the middle of hostile territory. You probably didn't have the right to risk your people, and you *certainly* didn't have the right to risk the lives of my people."

"You left! When you thought you saw me there with Tristan, you left. By doing that you put everyone depending on you in more danger than they would have been if you'd stayed."

We were standing only inches away from each other now, practically yelling at each other as we each refused to back down.

"I already acknowledged my mistake there, Adri. The difference though is that I didn't split our coalition wide open. I left our people without my ability, but still protected by Heath, Grayson, Taggart, and Vicki. No, I take that back. The real difference is that you've refused to take one iota of responsibility for anything that's happened.

"You want to throw stones? Fine, I'll throw stones. You've led Tristan on for weeks. I could see it in the way he looked at you in Minnesota, and based on how quick he was to jump into bed with the creature when he thought it was you, nothing has changed there. I get that you've been through a lot lately, but that doesn't excuse your errors in judgment. You're not the only one hurting right now. Your parents are dead, but at least they died being the people that you loved and respected. My parents tried to sell my little sister off as some kind of sex slave.

"You've ignored all of the people who died in an effort to help you out—simply by making this all about you at every single step. At this point my biggest regret is the fact that I was willing to throw my life away and reinforce your bad behavior. This is no more my fault than it is yours, and the fact that you're unwilling to even acknowledge that possibility tells me that you're not worthy of the sacrifices that it's taken to get you here."

She looked like I'd hit her. Her lips were parted, stuck between shock and indignation, but I didn't wait around to see what she was going to say. I turned, fully intending on leaving, until I felt her hand on my arm.

"Wait, Alec. I...I'm not going to pretend that I'm happy about what you just said, but maybe there is something to it. I...I'm sorry for coming out of the gate swinging. I'll try to do better—to be better—but you have to understand how hard this is for me. Knowing that Brindi is there with you every hour of every day is killing me. I want to get past this and have things go back to the way that they were, but I don't think that I can do that while she's still part of your life."

Her words hung in the air between us, and I knew that there wasn't any going back. I stretched out my newfound sight, taking in the golden threads leading away from me in all directions. There were more of them now than there'd been a few hours ago, but they were still precious few in the face of what I knew was coming for us.

I touched the one that led inside the RV to Brindi with the faintest tendril of thought and confirmed something that I'd started suspecting just recently. The threads were designed for conducting energy, but the flow wasn't as one-directional as it had seemed during the battle. Energy was flowing inwards from some threads and outwards along others.

Brindi was one of the ones selflessly giving of her energy—painfully weak as it was—sacrificing so that energy could be fed into someone else. She didn't do it for that other person, she did it for me. It was something below the level of conscious control for either of us, a soft, calm power that I knew had to be related to James' sudden manifestation of an ability where Mallory had always said none would ever exist.

Brindi was part of that—a critical part of it. Without her energy—and without her willingness to serve as a reservoir—any number of fights might have gone very differently—with a catastrophic result.

"I would like to stop by and see Tristan if he'll agree to meet with me, Adri."

"Don't try to turn this around on me! This is about Brindi, not Tristan."

I continued on as though I hadn't heard her. "I owe him an apology. I'm not okay with the way that he behaved, but I shouldn't have reacted the way that I did. Please let him know that is the reason that I would be stopping by. He's welcome to have whoever he would like there to watch his back if he's concerned about his safety. It's too bad really. In a lot of ways he and Brindi both got the raw end of this deal. They both got to taste the thing they'd been hoping for and then found out that it was nothing more than an illusion."

I started walking away from her, and this time Adri didn't try to restrain me.

"That's it? Brindi's more important to you than I am? You do realize that you're proving exactly what I've suspected all along, right? Are you really going to throw everything away?"

That made me pause, and once again I traced each of the threads leading out from my center.

There was no thread leading to Vicki, no thread leading to Jaclyn, no thread leading to Shawn, and most heartbreakingly, there was no thread leading to Adri.

"I'm sorry, Adri, but loyalty deserves to be rewarded. It's not like you think it is, but I can't explain it beyond that. I'm not forcing Brindi to leave—not after everything she's done for me."

I heard her turn and run away, but I didn't try to stop her. I'd made my decision. Taggart and James met me at the top of the stairs, and I could see the conflict inside of Taggart's eyes. I reached up and clasped him on the shoulder.

"Go and be there for her. That is where you need to be—and not just for her sake. I'm going to need allies, and you are uniquely placed to be the voice of reason in Isaac's inner circle, to say the things that he can't say."

"I won't be a double agent."

I nodded. "I wouldn't ask it of you. To be honest, after the last two days, I want nothing less than to become the next king, but that is the only way that our people have a chance of surviving in a world where things like that dark angel are feeding on us. I need loyalty, Taggart. More than bodies or abilities, hybrids or wolves, I need people who believe in me, who believe in what I'm trying to do. You can help with that."

He nodded hesitantly, like his conscious mind wasn't quite prepared to accept the implications of what I was saying, like he wasn't ready for the knowledge his subconscious was already trying to tell him, and then he left.

I turned to James and bowed my head in a gesture that few dominants ever would have granted one of their submissives.

"I'm sorry about your mother, James. I never meant for her to die...I—"

He stopped me. "She did what she felt like she had to do, Alec. I know what you did—I felt it. I could get all indignant about the fact that you transformed me in the middle of a battle, but the truth was that we were all dead men. It was just a matter of time before Brandon was going to kill us—we all knew it—but you changed that. You gave me the power I needed to stand against him."

That surprised me. James had never been the most intuitive of my friends. "How much do you know?"

"Enough—enough to realize just how dangerous it would be for the full nature of your gift to become common knowledge—enough to know what you tried to do for my mother after you healed Taggart and me. You have my allegiance, Alec, but what are you going to do if the packs continue to refuse to recognize you as their leader?"

I looked over to Brindi, still sleeping the peaceful sleep of a child, and I smiled. "I will find the support I need elsewhere."

Acknowledgements

I continue to rely on an outstanding group of people to help me bring these books to market. RJ Locksley and Amy Jirsa-Smith, my editors, both did a phenomenal job working over the initial manuscript, and thanks to their tireless efforts, the draft that went to my advance readers was much cleaner than I could have possibly managed on my own. Thank you, RJ and Amy!

My advance readers continue to do yeoman work in catching items which either slip past my editors, or which I introduce while trying to fix something my editors flagged as being wrong. Additionally, they often keep me from accidentally letting characters do impossible things like enter the same building twice without ever exiting it. A big round of thanks to Heather, Mei, Janelle, Jenine, Mom, Dad, Matthew, Shalese, Lachele, Mark, Mimi, Kim, and Merissa!

My readers collectively deserve a heart-felt expression of thanks for continuing to trust me with their time and money in the hopes that I'll be able to deliver an experience that will leave them wanting still more Alec & Adri (thank you all!) but I also need to express a special, separate thanks to my Launch Team for being so willing to make extra efforts to spread the word about my books. You're too numerous to list out separately here, but you know who you are (and I do too)—so thank you one and all!

Lastly, as she always does, my wife Katie deserves special mention in a paragraph all by herself. In 2014 we released 7 novels, which was a herculean undertaking, but heading into 2015, we resolved to try and do even better than that. We both knew it was going to mean more time spent in front of the computer writing, but it's also meant a lot more work for Katie as she's continued to serve as my first reader and cover artist. Without Katie none of this could happen, and I'm more grateful than words can express for her unwavering support. Thank you Katie!

About the Author

Dean Murray is a prolific author with dozens of titles across multiple pen names and more than half a million copies of his work currently in circulation.

Dean started reading seriously in the second grade due to a competition and has spent most of the subsequent three decades lost in other people's worlds.

Things worsened, or improved depending on your point of view, when he first started experimenting with writing while finishing up his accounting degree.

These days Dean has a wonderful wife and two lovely daughters to keep him rather more grounded, but the idea of bringing others along with him as he meets interesting new people in universes nobody else has ever seen tends to drag him back to his computer on a fairly regular basis.

Keep up to speed on Dean's latest projects at www.DeanWrites.com.

Reborn

True love never dies.

A new arrival at Selene's high school is about to turn her entire world upside down. She's never met anyone so attractive—or so mysterious—before this, but Jace's unyielding insistence that they've known each other for decades can't be denied—not given how familiar he feels to her.

In the hidden world of gods and fairies what you don't know can get you killed faster than anything else and only those you love have any chance of saving you.

Stone Heart

Dani's new home isn't just another stopover in a long chain of places she'll never see again, it's the home of both Caine and Jerek, two guys like nobody she's ever met before. One represents the best friend she's been hungering for, and the other represents something much more.

It should be the perfect recipe for a fairytale, but Caine and Jerek live in a dark, shadowy world and one of them is hiding secrets that will change everything, secrets that relate directly to Dani.

The Society

People need to be monitored, or they'll repeat the mistakes of the Desolation, a centuries-old war that killed billions of people and destroyed civilization.

Skye is part of the Society, the hi-tech, nanite-endowed group responsible for making sure that the millions of surviving people—grubbers—are confined to the ancient, decaying cities where they can be watched to ensure they aren't redeveloping the weapons technology that came so close to extinguishing life on the planet.

When the Society's monitoring programs pick up troubling developments in one of the grubber cities, Skye is ordered in to deal with the man responsible, but what—and who—she finds once she arrives will change everything.

The Greater Darkenss

Dean writing as Eldon Murphy

Something powerful is stirring in the darkness. Something so ancient that even creatures who've been alive for hundreds of years have long since discounted this new threat as nothing more than myth.

Normal humans will be caught in the crossfire, but then that's always the way of things. Geoffrey has no memory of his past life or any idea how to survive in the violent, dangerous world in which he's trapped. Despite his best efforts, he's about to find himself in the middle of a conflict that threatens to sweep away everything, and everyone he's been fighting so hard to protect.

Frozen Prospects

The invitation to join the secretive Guadel should have been the fulfillment of dreams Va'del didn't even realize he had. When his sponsors are killed in an ambush a short time later, he instead finds his probationary status revoked, and becomes a pawn between various factions inside the Guadel ruling body.

Jain's never known any life but that of a Guadel in training. She'd thought herself reconciled to the idea of a loveless marriage for the good of her people, but meeting Va'del changes everything. Their growing attraction flies against hundreds of years of precedent, but as wide-spread attacks threaten their world, the Guadel have no choice but to use even Jain and Va'del in their fight for survival.

CHET

By Larry Murray

Meet Charles Tucker, he has spent nearly 30 years living in denial, trying desperately to hide from his past and the events that shattered his heart beyond any possibility of healing. He can't let anyone close, for doing so would open him up to being hurt again, and there's no way he could survive another wounding.

Meet the Saunders family, new to the neighborhood and teetering on the verge of bankruptcy. Mark, the father, talks a good story but is that all he is? His plan could hold the key to reversing his family's financial misfortunes, or it could wipe out everyone involved.

Meet Chet, a battered old '64 Chevy pickup that was there on the night Charles' life imploded. For nearly three decades, he has been locked away in an old barn, safely out of sight if not completely out of mind. For 29 years Charles has blamed the old pickup for the destruction of his life, now he's about to find that the vehicle that destroyed his life might be the key to his healing and a journey of unexpected miracles.

www.ingramcontent.com/pod-product-compliance
Lightning Source LLC
Chambersburg PA
CBHW020643030726
47498CB00002B/338